CAN'T DREAM WITHOUT YOU

FROM THE DARK CHRONICLES

ALSO BY TANYA REIMER

GHOSTS ON THE PRAIRIES
A Sacred Land Story

CAN'T DREAM WITHOUT YOU

FROM THE DARK CHRONICLES

TANYA REIMER

Elsewhen Press

In memory of my dad and every dream he had.

THE LEGEND OF WHISPERERS

–Taken from the last Notebook of James 2085

Long ago, creatures belonged to two groups: those with magic and those without. Those with magic were fascinated by those without. They intervened in the non-magic world to teach. One group in particular integrated themselves into this non-magic world: the Whisperers.

Whisperers were immortal. They called themselves a conscience for mortals and they took upon themselves the task of guiding mortals along their intriguing journey.

Purposely, Whisperers led their parties astray to study the results. God grew tired of the abuse and offered them a chance to live as mortals. Each immortal was split in two and forced to pair up with mortals. He offered their magic to demons because they were to learn hands-on how to live without magic, to die, and to love. God promised that if Whisperers found their other half and were content with what they'd learnt, He'd allow them to return to the heavens as the immortals they once were.

Time passed. Powerless and confused they were forced to try new things. Some earned back their magic from demons while others discovered how to save memories from past lives or stumbled into secret worlds known as realms. Always, they guided and taught. Sometimes, magic seeped into their teachings.

I am such a creature and we are no longer limited to whispering to humans. We find ourselves fascinated with animals, elements, even dreams.

Slowly, we discovered new powers and found each other. By regrouping into families with leaders, counsellors, and rules, we were able to leave behind Notebooks containing our family secrets about these enchantment whispers.

We each have our place, our calling. A Storm Whisperer whispers to nature. A Light Whisperer guides the light that is someone's spirit. A Love Whisperer, or cupid, influences their emotions. A Dark Whisperer encourages good people to do bad things. And so on…

In these families, we grow powerful and have vowed to never whisper alone. As we pass from life to life, reincarnating, pairing up with human souls, demonic souls, or even with each other, we evolve. This change is seen in our soul as a greyish colour. The transition could take one breath or thousands of lives.

As Grey Whisperers, our ultimate goal is to reach enlightenment and return to the heavens as true Whisperers. Now, we remember why we are here and in the remembering comes an understanding. We master magic. We travel to other realms. We understand concepts others don't and we enjoy teaching and learning.

Some have found their soulmates. A few have even paired up and call themselves whispering gods.

Despite this, we struggle with a new sensation; **we feel more mortal than Whisperer**. We love the feeling of wind on our skin and waking up with aches. We love the touch of our soulmates and the deepness of our emotions. This makes us hesitate to return to the heavens. This fills us with a dread at how powerful we can be. And we must accept the truth: we are unworthy of whispering to mortals.

Many have gone to another realm to study. They call it Utopia, but it's a place where they deepen their studies and worship false gods in hopes that they will one day be worthy.

I am James, some call me Hero, but I am unworthy of that title. I cannot bear to watch this struggle anymore and will live my immortality at one with the world. I will come back if one Grey Whisperer shall prove worthy to end the terror. Until then, I am petrified that hope is lost.

—James

I am James, some call me Hero, but I am unworthy of that title. I cannot bear to watch this struggle anymore and will live my immortality at one with the world. I will come back if one Grey Whisperer shall prove worthy to end the terror. Until then, I am petrified that hope is lost.

AL

Saskatchewan, 2025, after the War of 2019—

Al couldn't kill his son. That was a problem. A big blasted problem.

It was Steven's sixth birthday today. Compared to Al, who was going on two hundred years, that sounded young, but as Al watched his son play he knew he'd already left the boy alive for too long.

Al pretended not to notice the branches move on their own. Steven ran, so happy, chasing nothing, talking to nothing, laughing with nothing. It amazed him how a child could be so unaffected by the hell going on in the world. The war was over, but the world was in bad shape because of it. Whisperers gathered in Utopia to save it, forming a group called *The Get Naked and Muddy Revolution*. Al wasn't welcome among them, but he watched their actions closely in case they came for his son. They'd need a Dream Whisperer like him. He might be only six, but his whispers were powerful; probably the most potent Al had seen to date.

They would have no idea about the magic he was about to master.

Al knew.

That was no imaginary friend chasing after Steven so playfully, but he doubted it was a Whisperer from Utopia either, no; it was a demon. Al used to be able to see demons, but since he displeased Satan, he lost that ability. For the whispering god running Hell, Satan wasn't very understanding of the hell Al lived as an immortal.

Al took out the tattoo making tools and prepared for the ritual that would hopefully keep his young son from earning the ancient power that raised the dead.

Even dead, his wife would be furious with him for doing what he had planned for their son, but Al had no choice. He was determined to keep that magic away from someone as powerful as Steven. If he was just a Dream Whisperer all would be fine, but demons didn't come out to play with simple Dream Whisperers. They were attracted to power.

They were drawn to those who could whisper to them and use the magic they kept. Whoever hid the magic to take the life of an immortal would also be drawn to Steven. Al just had to keep him alive long enough for her to show up, and above all, he had to keep the boy from making more immortals.

A fear washed over Al. What if his son made another immortal? As the last of the immortals, it was Al's duty to end this.

Desperate, he told himself this simple ritual would protect them. As an immortal, time was usually on his side, but with Steven, time ran too fast for him to think.

He flicked open the ancient Notebook and read the details of the ritual he planned to perform on Steven. Hoping he wouldn't scare the child, he planned to put a light twist on it, like a game.

Al always had a backup plan. If this didn't work, he'd give Steven's magic to another, take the power by force.

It will work, he promised himself as he read the familiar script for the last time. After the ritual he'd burn the Notebook so no one would know what the boy was destined to do.

<u>Signs that a Whisperer will summon the power that raises the dead and creates an immortal:</u>

Note that this magic is a soulmate combo. It takes both a male and a female to harness it each life cycle. They will find each other.

The male in the soulmate pair will summon the magic that raises the dead making an immortal. The female will summon the ability to kill this immortal. They must be used in this order and can be used only once.

As children they will leave their bodies while their souls travel to other realms. They will whisper to the light in their souls. They will see demons.

One of them will see souls. Immortal souls are dark-grey, and unlike Grey Whisperers one soul-seer described them as rock-like grey and not see-through.

<u>Solution</u>: Destroy the male before he earns the ability and foolishly creates more immortals. Summon the female's powers to free one immortal. Do this each life until all the immortals are gone.

Destroy. It sounded easy, but Al couldn't kill his son. He just couldn't.

STEVE

Later that night—

Dad shut the Notebook of legends and Steve sneaked under the covers before his dad called lights out.

"Thanks, Dad. That was the *bestest* birthday story ever," Steve lied, not wanting to hurt his dad's feelings when he tried so hard, but Mom's stories had been much better. He'd liked her stories about Cupid Hero the best. He missed the way she'd kiss his forehead at night and would promise him that one day he'd be a hero, too. The one thing he wanted more than anything was to be a hero.

His dad rubbed Steve's wrist tenderly. "You happy with your new magic?"

"Yup."

Steve thought about the story… all the fighting, the swords, the Dream Whisperer, and the guy who whispered to his own soul when he was afraid of the dark. It made a neat light so he could see. He liked that guy and couldn't wait to try out that whisper. He wanted to be a hero like him and save those who died. Steve studied his new tattoo, proud. "When I can bring people back from the dead with my whispers, I'll bring Mom back so you won't be so sad and she can read me stories again."

"That would be selfish of you. Didn't you understand this story at all? Your mother is happy in Afterlight. Why would you trap her to the Mortal Realm when it was time for her to die? Besides, it's not how the power works. You only have a three-day window."

"What's Afterlight?"

"It's a place like the Mortal Realm where we live. Only we live there without these bodies. It's important that we die and make a new home there. Very important. Do you understand the different realms? Have you travelled to them?"

Mom had said that was a secret, so instead Steve asked, "Why would you want to die?"

"By living on different realms we learn the things we need to become whispering gods. You must never lose sight of that goal. We were once these immortal guides but we were sent to live as mortals to learn how to whisper to them properly. One day, we'll return to the heavens as these whispering consciences and be gods again."

Steve didn't care about those stories. He really wanted to know why Mom had left. "Why doesn't Mom want to live with us anymore?"

Dad sighed. Steve pushed closer to the wall. He knew it annoyed his dad when he asked too many questions. Yet Dad took on his teaching stance as if everything was extra important today. Steve waited with his back to the wall, paying close attention to what his dad said. He wasn't prepared for the question Dad whispered, *"What's bothering you, son?"* The whisper was just a breath but it seared into him, burning him to answer. His dad didn't usually use whispering magic on him. Steve would have to answer or the burning would intensify.

Steve shifted on the bed, feeling vulnerable. "I don't want you to die, Dad," he confessed, his hand gripping his pillow.

Dad took a deep breath. "It's an important part of life, son. Can you trust I know this or do you need it explained?"

Steve bit his bottom lip. "I understand," he lied.

"If you meet someone with the ability to restore life like the boy in the story I just read, you tell me. We must find and destroy that magic. And if any Whisperers come from Utopia for you, tell me." The determination in how he stood frightened Steve.

"But *I* want the magic to restore life."

"Yup, to destroy it. Right? We don't let Whisperers walk around raising the dead, interrupting the life cycles. This is dark magic."

Steve had never met another Whisperer. The idea terrified yet thrilled him. Would he tell his dad if he met someone with the ability to restore life? He wasn't sure. It didn't sound like bad magic to him. "Are there many Whisperers with this power?"

"No. It's ancient magic Satan allows once per life cycle. The problem with this story is that the boy is stupid. He doesn't know what he did. Always understand your power before you use it. Always know who can undo the mistakes you make."

Steve gripped his pillow. A hero didn't make mistakes. "Did you ever make a mistake?"

His dad's dark eyes pierced into him and his jaw tensed. "Yes. I won't make another. Now stop asking annoying questions and sleep."

Steve closed his mouth tight. He didn't want to upset his dad. Still... "Dad?"

Dad lightly touched his shoulder as he tucked him in again.

"I can whisper so you can dream about her." Mom used to whisper to the butterflies for him so Steve could dream about being a hero. He missed the butterflies carrying him off to Dreamland.

His dad ran a hand over Steve's hair. "No. Save your whispers for those who need it. I see her enough in my dreams, and it doesn't help. It reminds me that I'm a monster. I made a mistake and have to fix it." He looked sad.

"Could I be a hero, Dad?"

"I suppose." Dad stared for a long time as if hoping to see something heroic in him. "You only have to save one soul to be a hero, Steven. Only one. Make it count."

Maybe he could save his dad from the ugly pain hurting him. "Maybe you need a cupid to help you smile again. I could find Cupid Hero for you."

"Maybe your mother read you too many of those Hero stories. I have to fix my mistakes, myself. Never rely on others to do what you can do."

"But I can help you."

Dad smirked. "Fact that you kept those powers I summoned for you this long is a bloody miracle. They belong to others, but they should help you learn to master the more serious magic you have."

Steve nodded, trying to look like he was responsible.

"You're like your mother, and I count my lucky powers. No one should bother you. Now sleep."

Steve examined the neat tattoo housing his new magic. "You mean I don't get to keep this ability that lets me whisper to my soul?" It was the only one he liked. Whispering to the wind sounded stupid.

Dad sighed. "When did that one show up?"

Steve shrugged. "Today." Maybe he shouldn't have told him.

"We'll see. If someone more powerful summons it, you'll lose it. You didn't earn squat. I called it for you, for fun." He rubbed his finger along his slacks and Steve knew he lied, magic scared him. Mom had told Steve not to talk about his magic with his dad because he didn't always understand how special Steve was.

"Then I'll use it for good and make the whispering gods proud."

"Sure, son. You do that. One of us should make them proud." Dad blew out the light and left for his own room.

Darkness settled on Steve like a scary blanket. He hated the dark. "*Soul, light.*" He used the same whisper from the story his dad had read him and his soul lit up the room. Neat. Steve snuggled in, a lonely ache inside him. He missed his mom. He missed his old town and his friends. This place was empty. Maybe he could whisper to the butterflies and have them whisk him to Dreamland so he could whisper for her.

He really really wanted to but... he was petrified.

"Mischief?" Mischief wasn't afraid of anything.

The black slick demon materialized at the foot of his bed. He looked like a catfish out of water, and his long whiskers curled upright into one of his weird smiles when he showed Steve the red balloon he'd brought him.

"You brought me a gift?"

"*Yes. It will show you who you are.*" His yellow eyes lit up and the black in them made a slender slit.

"Cool."

"*Remember, little one, the monster is not the balloon, nor the one who carries it. It is not the reflection you see, nor the one who protects it. The monster is nothing but air exploded because these things weaken and no one is prepared to contain it. The hero must be the balloon or the world will suffer what was held within.*" He bowed as usual when he told Steve something weird. "*Happy new year, little one.*"

Steve chuckled at his strange friend. "We say 'Happy Birthday' on the Mortal Realm."

"*Birth day? How bizarre. Why would we celebrate that? You were not born today. I was there the day you were born.*

Hell rejoiced at your arrival." He twirled a whisker. "*It wasn't long ago, but it was not today. I have witnessed many days between your birth and this one.*"

"Today, six years ago."

"*Oh. I see. You choose to live in the past. Perhaps my gift is of no value, seeing that it will show you the future, your destiny.*"

"No leave it. I want to see."

"*I doubt you will see much, it is more a feeling than a seeing, really.*" Mischief made his way to the chair in front of his desk. Each step sounded as if he splashed in water, yet his feet were dry. He tied the balloon to the chair working awkwardly with his long fingers.

"Mischief, Dad says we must die. Do you know why?"

"*To live.*"

"We have to die to live?"

"*Your soul is trapped in this tiny body. If you let it go, you can live with me in Hell. Imagine the havoc we could make.*" His whiskers smiled.

"Can you whisk me there?"

"*Of course, but you cannot stay for long or your body will die and Satan will be disappointed in me, as would your father, and I am not sure which is the worse of the two these days.*"

"Do you visit other realms? Like Dreamland or Afterlight or Utopia or Oblivion?"

"*No. I stick to places I am safe. Dreamland is dangerous. Afterlight is for souls. Utopia is for Whisperers. Oblivion is for the lost. I am demonic and enjoy the comforts of Hell.*"

"I can whisper you to Dreamland. You'd be safe with me."

"*How?*"

Steve shrugged. "The butterflies fly me. I could whisper them to take you, too." He was afraid to try it alone and hoped his friend would agree.

"*I will pass. Butterflies give me willy-gibbies.*"

"Really?" Steve laughed. "You? You're so brave."

"*Does your father know you do this?*"

Steve shook his head. "Mom said it was my safe place."

Mischief cocked his head. "*Do you whisper there already?*"

"Once I whispered for ice cream because it's delicious and it tasted better than the ice cream here."

"*Steve...*"

"Okay so maybe I whispered more than once. Mostly, I peek in the doors that line the hallway. Behind each one is a story told with pictures. The butterflies tell me where to peek," he confessed to his best friend. "Sometimes, if a doorknob appears I go in and whisper fun things."

Mischief played with his bottom whisker while he paced, making squishy steps. "*Dreamland is the realm between worlds. Dream Whisperers access things from any realm there. They whisper to anyone via those doors. They are portals to mortal minds. Beware, this is havoc you should not start.*"

"Why does that scare you?"

"*Once, a Dark Dream Whisperer summoned me there and I had to go. Without free will, I did as he whispered. It was not good. I displeased Satan.*" He shivered, making his hands shake it off wildly. "*Satan says we are not safe on that realm until a whispering god is found worthy to protect it. And so we wait for you to become worthy, little one.*"

Mischief blew Steve a kiss and his soul-light blew out. Steve could still see his yellow eyes in the dark.

"Mischief, why do you wait for me? Am I evil?"

"*You are special to Satan. It is you who he wishes to bless with the power to protect the dream realms so his demons can be safe on them. This makes you good. A future whispering god. One day, you will be ready for this task. Perhaps sooner than he thinks. You are smart. Such a good boy.*"

Heavy silence hung over them until his eyes winked out.

Steve thought about the Notebooks Dad had read to him; they said Satan, God of Night, was bad and Archangel, God of Light, was good. Why did he have to be from the dark side? No heroes ever came from the dark side.

He sent his soul-light inside the balloon and it lit up the room with a magical reddish glow. He didn't feel evil. He felt just right. He decided there was no good and bad, there *was just right*, and that was what he would be.

He watched the balloon sway. As sleep overcame him, a

butterfly danced in the red of the balloon skin. Twirling. Twirling, twirling, twirling. Suddenly, hundreds of butterflies gathered and swarmed toward him. Each one was *just right*.

POP!

The balloon exploded, shooting him out of bed and scattering the butterflies.

Dad rushed into the room. "What was that?"

"A monster scared the *just right* butterflies." Steve's eyes were huge.

His dad tossed the blankets and peered under the bed. "Where did it go?"

"Everywhere. It broke out."

Dad picked up the balloon skin. "Who was here?"

Steve stared at his dad, terrified. "You are the only one I see."

"Son, how can I protect you if you're so stupid you can't see the enemy when he's right in your room? Back to bed."

Dad whispered as he paced the room, protecting it from Whisperers, from demons, from butterflies, from monsters, even from Mom. Then he pulled up a chair and sat to watch Steve sleep.

JULIA

Ten years later, in Saskatchewan—

They crowded around the old picnic table while Julia opened her last birthday gift, the one from her grandma. Slowly, she pulled it out of the delicate white box, letting the silver chain glimmer in the sun for everyone to see.

"What do the symbols in each wing mean?" Julia asked her family as she dangled the butterfly pendant. It twirled in front of her, the sun making it sparkle. Each wing was made of a different pattern of swirls. So familiar, entrancing, yet she'd never seen anything like it.

"It's rumoured that it's a gift from the god of light," Grandma explained. "When you wear it, your dreams will come true." Her grandma had a silly smirk, deepening her dimple. "I found it on the hill by your place, the day the war ended, and saved it to give to you. Figured it was probably time to see it on you."

"Actually," James corrected her. He was only thirteen, but her brother knew strange things. He pushed aside a wild brown curl that fell lazily in front of his eye. "It means she has the magic to make dreams come true." He snatched it from Julia, as if knowing weird stuff gave him the right to put his grubby fingers on her things. "This wing means power, this one truth, having the ability to put this into dreams is symbolized in the middle." He pointed to the strange eye at the core of the pendant, then he shot up to put it around Julia's neck. "Now, the other side has a sideways loop, which means spirit or life, and the one above is for other worlds. So if I put them together, I'd say it's a symbol for Dream Whisperer."

"Now you're just making things up."

"Am not."

Julia fixed her long wavy hair, dropping it over the chain. "What does that mean?" They stood eye to eye by the picnic table.

James stared straight ahead and his hands came together in a triangle as he always did when he searched for facts in that weirdo brain of his. "I have no idea. It's just what it symbolises."

Well, she liked it. The warmth and love around her was consuming, and they all laughed with her. It was such a beautiful day, and really, this was the perfect birthday. Her family was together; they were just missing Uncle Jackson, but he'd been distant since Aunt Elma's death. They'd seen such hard times since the war, but it was all she knew. The world before the war was just rumours, then the world during the war became nightmares no one talked about. Now, they were caught in a new world where everyone waited for something, some type of hero to save them.

Still, these were the moments she looked forward to. One day, she'd share this necklace with her own grand-daughter. Life was perfect. The sun warmed them and no one thought about the troubles in the world as they cleared the wrapping paper. It was one happy moment she wanted to make last.

But it was short lived. A red truck pulled into the yard while they were eating the cake Ma had made. Pa jumped to his feet and Julia actually stepped in front of James as she reached for the blade James had given her for her birthday.

Of course, she dropped the knife quickly when Uncle Jackson hopped out of the strange, old truck, his cowboy hat tilted over his eyes.

"He knows better than to swing by when the phones are down," Pa grumbled. The phones were down more than they were working, but Julia didn't bother pointing out the obvious to her father.

"Hey, did I hear someone was of driving age?" Uncle Jackson had a weird smile plastered on his face as he peered over the door to the red truck. "Come on."

Julia rushed to Uncle Jackson, excited. "I can drive this beast?" Would he let her take it to the city? She was dying to see the city. There were rumours that the power was up again and they had lights lining the streets like stars. Slowly, the world came back to life.

Uncle Jackson took off his cowboy hat and flashed a toothy grin. "Heck, this beauty is yours, baby girl. Jump in."

He was giving her this old pickup!?

"Bring her home in an hour," Pa called behind her, waving

to his brother.

"Two," Uncle Jackson called back.

"She has chores to do."

"On her birthday?" Uncle Jackson gagged and hopped in the driver's side of the truck, tossing in his hat. "Wow, he sure is wound tight, eh?"

She slipped in the truck, taking the passenger side, and slamming the heavy door.

"May I come?" James asked but the locks clicked down.

Uncle Jackson mumbled, "We don't need the know-it-all tagging along."

Julia glanced at him surprised, he usually loved to have James around. He'd said it stimulated the brain to talk to a genius.

The truck fired up, purring like a beast.

Julia looked at James, who waited with a broken heart. *Next time*, she mouthed and he broke into a huge grin and ran off excited.

"Thought I could drive," Julia complained, enjoying the oily smells of her new truck.

"Let's go someplace safe first." He glanced over while backing up, his dark eyes piercing into her as he consciously ignored James who waved after them. "Buckle up."

Julia frowned, uneasy. She was sure her uncle's eyes had been green like James'. It was something James had told her he was very proud of.

She slid toward the door as the truck bounced down the driveway. Uncle Jackson gripped the steering wheel. Where was his wedding band? Since Aunt Elma died, he wore that thing faithfully, yet there wasn't even a tan line on his rough farm hands.

STEVE

Later that night—

While Al was in a trance on his knees, facing the forest, Steve stepped up to the girl his dad had tied to the ritual plank.

She pleaded for Al to let her go, and Steve planned to do exactly that.

Her jeans were old, but she wore a beautiful burgundy tank top, showing off her neck. Entranced, Steve touched the pendant around her neck. His fingers tingled as they grazed the symbol for Dream Whisperer. Where had Dad found this girl?

She stopped her frantic yelling as Steve untied the ropes running along her shoulders.

She smelt like... purple flowers. The name of them eluded him, but the fragrance made him so... loopy. What was it he'd wanted to do? His hands fell from the knots to her shoulder. Her skin was warm. Touching her erupted this urge inside him to protect her.

"You're safe with me." His whisper created a strange light under his fingers that spread over the girl.

She glowed?

What had he done to make her glow? Or was it something his dad was doing? Was she dead? Maybe it was his words. *Oh crap.* Panic overpowered him. Steve knew better than to talk during a ritual. No words. It was such a simple blasted rule and he'd broken it without thinking. What was wrong with him? Why did he feel so... dreamy?

He knew everything spoken during a ritual was intensified and might summon magic. Why did he say anything? He shook his head to clear it, but the glow around her brightened.

The silence settled on Steve like a morbid curse.

Was she dead? Had he killed her?

Frantic, he rushed to remove the bag from her head, but Al's hand snapped on Steve's wrist. His piercing dark eyes spoke volumes—he wanted to know what Steve had done to the girl.

How would he explain the glowing to his dad? The silence?

Steve pushed his dad's hand aside, eager to untie her. Get her to safety. Enough of this.

Al whispered for fire, creating a flame in his palm that was to remind Steve of his place. Last time he'd touched things during a ritual he'd suffered burns. Steve shoved his guilty hands in his pockets and took a step back, curving his lips inward so as not to speak, even though there were a few things he wanted to say to his father.

He met Al's dark eyes, hate seething between them.

Screw it. How much worse could things get?

"*Wind*." Steve called on nature to blow out the flames. Wind rushed over them in an even swoop, putting out the fire meant to discipline him.

Al smacked him on the back of the head. Then he checked her wrist for a pulse. The beautiful light around her snapped brown and pulled away from Al, crowding against Steve. She let out a soft whimper as if his dad's touch burnt her delicate olive skin.

Steve felt her fear with her and it stirred a panic in him. "*Don't touch her!*" The ritual amplified the desire behind Steve's words and a knife lifted off the ritual table. It snapped toward his father, catching in his shoulder.

Al dropped to his knees.

With a deep breath, his dad eased the knife out, whispering to the wound, making the blood bubble, but Steve ignored his actions, focused on the greyish light that exploded around Al. Steve watched it closely, feeling like he was in a dream or... more like a nightmare. Why couldn't he keep his mouth shut?

A brown cloud danced in the greyish light around Al, but a few swirls of black tainted it around the knife wound. What was this strange light around the girl and Al? It was a part of them, connected to their bodies. Could it be...? Was it their souls? Why could Steve suddenly see souls? What good was that?

His lips tightened while he debated if he should tell Al about the power. Would he call him a pansy?

Steve glanced at the girl. Even though she was secured to the plank, when her fingers moved, the glowing light searched for him, making Steve forget all about his useless powers.

Steve clasped his hand around hers. Squeezed firmly. The light from her soul melted into his hand, making Steve gasp as it encountered his own soul, shocking life into the depth of his being. *Julia.* Her name was Julia and she wasn't afraid of him, but for him.

He closed his eyes, no longer aware of where their bodies were. *"Butterflies, Dreamland,"* he whispered for the butterflies to whisk their souls off to the one place Al was forbidden.

Eyes open, he relaxed, enjoying the sweet rush of the familiar corridor of Dreamland. The butterflies took off in their magical way, scattering along the corridor as if it were time for him to work.

His soul was completely at one with hers in this magical realm. He was still Steve, yet he felt everything she did. Her hopes, her love—she loved her brother so deeply she would actually kill to keep him safe. Wow. How could one person have so much love in them? Was that normal? Steve doubted he could kill anyone. Ever. Dying to protect someone, now that sounded easier.

Best of all were her dreams. Each was his.

Images passed before him. He reached, almost touching the things she wanted from life: family, laughter, children, a cottage built of stone with a puppy running out front, city lights.

She wanted such simple things from life that he smiled and studied their linked hands as they struggled to be real in the dream world. Hers was around his. He felt alive, full of passion. *Just right.*

She wasn't afraid of him. Peace flashed through them in a sleepy breeze. He relaxed, becoming one with her.

He planned to stay with her forever but a jarring pain brought him back to the Mortal Realm—the horrible world he wanted to escape.

He opened his eyes and glanced at his real hand. It was on fire, gripping hers. Al dug the tip of his knife between their linked hands, and flames surrounded his blade as he tried to sever the link Steve had created.

Steve was dazed as he grounded himself in this world. Shifting from Dreamland was like waking from a deep sleep he never wanted to end. How long was he one with her in Dreamland?

Al's soul flashed bright red as angry flames ate away at it. Their eyes met and Steve knew he'd pay but he didn't let her hand go, despite the burning.

"Dammit, Steven, it's over, you have to let her hand go. Something went wrong. I can't undo the binding ritual, and now that she has your powers, you shouldn't be one with her."

It was over? Then why did Steve feel like it was just starting?

STEVE

Still later that night—

Steve rubbed his free hand on his T-shirt. His skin itched where the *Get Naked and Muddy* slogan rubbed. They were some radical group talking about how people could change the world for the better now that the war wiped out phones, television, and well... everything cool. Steve wasn't sure why, but their ideas intrigued him. They weren't bad ideas but they weren't good either. They were... *just right*. Really, getting back to nature was a just right idea. They'd lived this long without technology, did they really need it?

"I thought I asked you to toss that T-shirt," Al said as he worked on Steve's tattoo. The ritual was almost over. "I hate those bloody back-to-nature freaks. They think they know everything. So annoying."

Steve stared off into the cluster of trees. "Now my clothes annoy you? Piss off. I wear what I want. I like it, and not all their ideas are stupid, some of them make sense in a just-right sort of way that I can appreciate."

From the woods, a butterfly fluttered toward them. The sun streamed through the trees as it set, yet the glow against the butterfly's powdery orange wings was nothing compared to its soul. It mesmerized Steve as it innocently landed on the old wooden table to his right.

Steve watched the butterfly, as still as possible, while Al worked.

"What a mess. I'm not sure how many powers were sucked into your soul," Al said, "but give them time. They should return to the tattoo I'm making. It won't only contain them, but poison them so no one can steal them away from you. Namely, her. Keep her away from these powers. Stay away from hers."

Poison? Al's words jumbled in his brain. It was hard to focus knowing Julia was in the back of the truck. Knowing she didn't think him a monster. Knowing the things she knew.

"And her?"

"She's fine. We have her magic. It's over. Need more lotion for those burns on your hand?" Al offered him some, but already the burns were gone. Al was an incredibly powerful Body Whisperer. Too bad he didn't put those skills to good use and heal others. "Does your hand hurt or can you handle this needle?"

Steve took the needle with ease, but his thoughts were with Julia when he dropped it on the tray beside the others. He wanted to explain this to her. "Al—"

Al glanced toward the truck. His soul flashed brown, as Julia's had when she'd been afraid. "I hate it when you call me Al. Makes me think I disappoint you."

"Things like this don't put you on my hero list, *Dad*. I mean, damn. You kidnapped a girl. What's wrong with you?"

"Save it. You think I enjoy doing this shit? You have no fucking clue the hell I go through for you." Al didn't glance up, but the needle dug in deeper than needed, reminding Steve who was boss.

Steve shifted on the hard stump, uncomfortable in the woods he normally found homey. The butterfly circled the area and landed on his new jeans. Al's hand came up to swat it.

Whomp! Steve snagged Al's wrist before he could kill the butterfly.

Their eyes met, wrists between them as they spoke without words, letting their eyes do the lying to each other.

"You know, there was a time when you thought butterflies were monsters and you would have begged me to squash it."

Al's soul was calm as he studied Steve, giving Steve courage he normally wouldn't have while facing off with his crazy old man.

"Butterflies never scared me, they remind me of Mom. At least take the bag off the girl's head," Steve pleaded. "It's not needed. She's quiet." He wanted to add, *since I held her hand*, but he didn't want to remind this stickler-to-the-rules that he hadn't paid for breaking them during a sacred ritual.

Still, determined to do something for the girl whose life they'd ruined, Steve added, "It'll be dark soon. What's she gonna see? She's scared. Let me explain that she's going home. That she's safe."

The butterfly flew off and Steve let Al's wrist go.

Squinting, his dad tossed the needle aside and snagged the butterfly mid-flight. His dark eyes seared into Steve as if wishing for any other son. "Since when do you care if some bitch is scared?" He squished the butterfly in his fist. "Don't sit here and pretend you're noble. You did something that messed us up. What did you do to her?"

The dreamy light from the butterfly's soul melted away. That wasn't good.

Steve shot up, his fists clenched. He stepped back when Al's soul turned crimson red.

"Make it a swing that counts, pansy. You'll get one and you'll be dead, sixteenth birthday or not—dead. The girl will get it, too."

With a deep breath, Steve sat on the stump. Why was his instinct to punch when he could whisper? No wonder his dad called him a pansy. He needed to stand up to him, think for himself, prove he refused to be the monster Al wanted him to become.

Steve examined his hands, his fears swirling in him again. It wasn't Al's fault Steve was evil. He might dream of being normal, but there was nothing good inside him. It was too late for him. That was clear. He'd merged his soul with pure goodness, and Steve knew he was nothing like that. Al was right, he stole her soul to Dreamland. Who did that?

A damaged butterfly wing blew against his *Get Naked and Muddy* T-shirt and Steve brushed it off. He couldn't even protect the light in a butterfly from this monster's grasp. Why was he afraid? He glanced up at his dad and returned his eyes to his freshly tattooed wrist. The biohazard symbol. Would this symbol make his whispers toxic? It didn't matter. He didn't need to whisper anyway.

"You got something to say to me, pansy?" Al was on the defensive.

Steve shook his head. "No, sir." He could think about standing up to him, but Steve knew better than to question Al. He could summon demons with whispers or make Steve kill Julia with one word if he chose. Magic like that frightened Steve to the core of his soul and he understood why Al was afraid of his power. He was a monster and Steve would be one, too.

What scared Steve the most, was that this ritual hadn't felt wrong. How evil was he now?

The girl called out, "Steve? Did he hurt you? Are you okay?"

She knew his name? It was the first thing she'd said to him and it made him glance toward her. Her soul was bright in the back of the truck, searching for him. She was worried about him?

His gut twisted. Didn't she know he was evil? Hadn't she felt it?

On his feet, he called back, "Are you?"

Dad dropped the tools and smoked him one in the gut. The red in Dad's soul faded to brown. Steve bent over to catch his breath as he stared at his bare feet, at the missing toe, wishing he could be normal and not this freak who would never please the only person in his life.

"I tolerated you holding her hand 'cause it kept her quiet, but I will not stand here and listen to you chat it up with her. She's dead to us."

"She's very much alive to me." Steve's voice was soft, but Al raised an eyebrow, curious.

"You haven't even seen her face."

No, but he'd felt her dreams and anyone who loved their family that deeply and who only wanted a happy moment from life was worth fighting for.

"Where is Uncle Jackson?" she asked, even at a distance her panic rang loud in the air.

"Dead," Al snapped, wiping his hands on his new ritual clothes. He always bought new clothes before a ritual, but this getup was the craziest. He looked like a cowboy—boots and all. "Now shut up or I hit him again." His soul was solid grey. Like a rock wall. It made Steve square his shoulders and face him, despite the pain throbbing in his gut.

"You killed her uncle? Why? What did her uncle have to do with anything?"

Dad was tight against him, his voice low so she couldn't hear. "Nothing you need to know about."

"Fine, but I asked you to remove the bag."

"It's there so you can't see her, pansy." He whacked Steve

on the back of the head, then returned to cleaning the needles. Steve wasn't allowed to touch the ritual tools unless asked. He watched while his dad continued to tie into him, his soul solid grey. "You must never see her until you die and your souls reunite in Afterlight."

"Why would our souls unite after we die?" Steve was confused.

"I told you, I couldn't undo the binding ritual."

"How bad is that? I mean... I don't know what that means."

"You needed a soulmate for this ritual to work, but you don't have one. So I linked your soul to hers."

"What the hell does that mean?" Steve rubbed at his chest as if he might be able to unlink them with that action.

"Means she can't use her horrible magic on you, and she will suck you to Afterlight with her when she dies."

They would be one in their afterlives? Steve didn't understand, but he was sure it meant something not good. Al never made him do anything good.

"Her family is a Forgotten One." Al laughed, but as each of his dry chuckles fell, his soul went from grey to fearful brown. "She spends her days helping people. Ha."

"As a Chosen One, shouldn't we teach Forgotten Ones? Train them how to use their whispering magic?"

Al's soul flashed an angry red. "No, those back to nature freaks from Utopia can worry about that shit." He waved toward Steve's T-shirt as if it was to blame for the things that happened on other spiritual realms like Utopia. Utopia was a myth. A world worthy Whisperers accessed. It was rumoured to contain more Notebooks and treasures than any other spiritual realm, but when he was younger, Steve had spent days whispering himself there; the butterflies could only fly him to Dreamland, and Mischief could only whisk him to Hell.

"You don't have to understand the things I do for you, son, but you have to trust me and stay away from her, she's rotten."

Steve sighed. Of course, she would be now. His nasty soul was tied to hers. Poor girl didn't have a hope. She didn't even know he was evil.

"Is that what happened to Mom? Did you make her soul

turn nasty and cloudy?"

Gosh, he missed her. Steve looked a lot like her with blue eyes and blond hair. *Bet her soul was shiny and happy before Dad got her in his grip.*

His T-shirt was itchy against his skin. Maybe he would toss it when they got home.

"How the fuck would I know what your mother's soul was like?" Al's lip went up in the right corner to highlight his annoyance with Steve. "I don't see souls, only the worthy do. Leave your mother out of this. She was..." His lip vanished he folded it so tight. "Not your business."

"You mean there are Whisperers who see souls? Seems like a stupid power."

His dad took on a teaching stance and his soul returned to solid grey. "No such thing as stupid magic. You think Hero was embarrassed to announce he was a Love Whisperer? Fuck boy, Hero had an entire realm full of knowledge yet it was the simple ability to help soulmates find each other that made him worthy. Those Whisperers ended the War of 2019. Every power counts."

"Hero was more than a cupid." Steve had searched the Notebooks in the house for the stories Mom had read to him, but they were gone.

"You'd better learn to respect magic. It's not a joke."

"Whatever. Not like we'd earn crap like that anyway," Steve lied.

"No, not us," Al agreed. "That's power reserved for Whisperers who found their whispering soul's other half and are destined to become whispering gods at any breath. Apparently, they use this magic to whisper to other Whisperers. Set a few of the unworthy ones straight."

Steve didn't correct him. It was strange that Al didn't know Steve was blessed with this ability. Usually, Al was on top of these things. Steve glanced at the old red truck again and overwhelming panic filled him. The only reason for Dad not to pay him attention was because whatever went wrong during the ritual had him freaked out.

"It would be fun, though. I mean, if you could see souls, son, you'd know everyone's deep dark secrets. You'd know how worthy a Whisperer was at a glance."

"How?"

"Apparently, a light soul means they whisper helpful things, a gloomy soul means they spread evil, but a grey one," he smirked, "well... they guide Whisperers. It means they will soon be a whispering conscience, a god."

"So are Grey Whisperers good or bad?"

"Neither, they just are. They stop thinking in terms of good and evil and accept that everything is perfectly balanced. A grey soul is the last step in a soul's evolution. A Grey Whisperer has two goals: find their soulmate to share what they learnt, and guide Whisperers so they can teach the world as the gods do."

"You know a lot about them." Should he tell his dad that his soul was grey and his theory was probably wrong? He meant to, but the next words out of his mouth were selfish, "I merged with her good soul during the ritual. I didn't mean to, but will my dark soul taint her light soul?"

Dad shrugged. "I suppose. I don't know how it works, but I doubt the opposite is true. Never known a glass of water not to swirl muddy when I add dirt."

He was probably right yet Steve needed to believe her light could shine in his shadowy soul like the moon at night.

Steve had no idea how he'd save her, but a slithering determination crept up on him. He could fix this. He'd undo the binding ritual and walk away. He'd be normal and forget about magic and whispering and the hell Al brought to his life.

As if sensing his panic, his old man stopped cleaning the tools and rubbed his clean-shaven head and chin. "It wasn't by chance I picked her, son. The ritual called for two Whisperers born the same day, same year. Since guys like us don't get soulmates, I had to bind your souls and pretend." He handed Steve a sacred Notebook. It was falling apart. Where did Al find these Notebooks?

"Page ten."

Steve could hardly see in the dim light but he opened it anyway, then slammed it shut—a Notebook about how to cheat to become an immortal whispering conscience—a god. "Ah crap. You stole this power from gods?" This explained why Steve could see souls. Great. Just great.

"You can't steal magic from whispering gods, they transfer them to the worthy. Seems Satan has his eyes on you."

"I'm worthy of evil magic?" Steve was shocked. Why would he be worthy of powers wielded by gods, any god?

Dad's soul flashed brown. "There's nothing evil about magic, it just is. Those stories in those Notebooks put the gods on sides, but they just are. Satan only cares about his demons, he'll whisper whatever it takes to protect them. Might look evil to some, but to them, he's a god. If he gives you magic, you can make it good, evil, or you can just make it what it is; magic. Besides, we both know I ain't worthy of squat. You, my boy, did fine. You're innocent enough to help me pull this off."

"Pull what off?"

"That girl, she don't need those abilities, so here I am, as powerful as a god. Well, if I figure out how to use them."

He stole her magic? Oh no.

"Ah... That would be a *half*-god, or goddess, since you took her magic." Steve stepped toward him, meeting his eyes. "I shared half those godly abilities you stole." The strongest was for sending a soul to Afterlight. The word he needed to whisper was dying to escape his lips. If he used it, would he kill someone? The idea embarrassed him and he pushed the power down to the bottom of his magic.

Dad dropped the ink he had in his hand and his grin grew so big his eyebrows shot up excited. "I know. Do you feel them settling into your tattoo?" He reached for Steve's wrist. "Show me what you got. I'll show you what I got."

"Piss off." Steve pulled away, keeping the Notebook out of his reach so he could read it later. He didn't need Al bragging about how corrupt his son was. Couldn't he see these horrible powers annoyed him?

Steve stormed toward the truck, but his dad reached for Steve's shoulder and pulled him back. "Come on. Show me what you were blessed with."

Steve watched the truck. "My soul was one with hers during that ritual. One. I was still me, but as our souls touched, I learnt what it would be like to live without magic as she does. To have a mother, a brother, even an uncle who loves me. I learnt innocence so pure that butterflies rest on me and don't carry me away to other worlds. I have the ability to make my dreams real. My dreams are hers. It was one moment, Dad, but in that one moment, I was the man I dream of being and I will do anything and everything to live that dream again."

"Shake it off. That's the binding whisper having this effect on you. You're not a man. You're a Whisperer. It makes me gag to hear you talk like this."

"I don't want to. I want to feel this connection to her. It makes me... just right."

Al frowned, deciphering what that meant. "Here's the problem I have with that, son. Your souls linked. If she dies, so do you. When she comes back to live again, so will you. You're linked for eternity unless I find a way to fix this. I can, I just need time."

Dammit. And there it was: the loophole the genius forgot to mention. Steve frowned, taking two deep breaths. "It's a small price to pay."

"Makes me believe you might cooperate just the same."

"What is it you want from me?"

"Well, we both earned new magic during the ritual, but the ones I got should be yours. They're cool, but I'll need you to activate them for me."

Steve shook his head. "No, this new power is mine. If you can't activate her abilities, you aren't worthy." Steve moved toward her, but Al yanked him back, his fingers sharp in Steve's shoulder. He was probably lucky that was all the prick used.

She was quiet, listening. Her soul pulsated in the back of the truck, calling out to him with its bright light that was already greying, polluted by his own. *Julia.* So familiar, as if he'd dreamed of her a thousand times. Julia.

Steve shoved Al's hand off his shoulder, frustrated that he let this man ruin his life. He hated whispering. He hated Al. He hated his life.

"She's quiet," Steve said. It was over. They'd let her go and he'd whisper so she'd forget about him and the horror she'd seen. She'd be free. He was the one who had to remember.

Already, he missed her and she was feet away.

"You prefer it when she screams?" Dad's bushy eyebrows went up, pleased.

Steve watched the truck while he thought about what he asked, because no, he enjoyed these moments of silence when her soul talked to his. "Dad, wouldn't it be better if... if you know... a girl wouldn't scream and would beg you to touch her silently with her body, her soul reaching out for you?"

"Begging's good." Dad slapped him on the back of the head. Not as hard as usual. He even smirked, as if for a moment he was proud of Steve. Maybe in his weird way he was.

"Is it possible for a dream like her to want a monster like me?" This is what he'd felt while they were one. She *needed* him and he *had to* satisfy that need.

Why did she have this effect on him?

"Don't tell me you ain't getting any. Fuck. Want me to bring her back? She make you horny? That why you whispered to the blade? Why not say so? I would have left if I had known her screams turned you on."

Steve's shoulders slouched forward. Too bad. Steve had hoped he could invite her into his arms. He contemplated his fingers and remembered how warm her hand had been in his.

Steve glanced at the truck again, wishing he could melt away with her as one soul. Forget these mortal bodies, these problems. Whisper peaceful dreams to the world forever.

"Let's go. On the way you need to come up with a whisper so she forgets you soul raped her. I want to hear it before you use it on her."

Raped? Steve hadn't touched her more than the hand. Hell no. Soul raped? His stomach twisted and he slouched beside his dad. Now he was a rapist? Was this how she would see it? Would she think he stole her soul? He hadn't. She'd come to him willingly. Hadn't she? He could see her soul. It was beautiful, complete. Well... if he ignored the grey swirls starting to pollute it.

She was silent, but he knew she was fine. Still... he'd touched her without asking. Invaded her soul. He was scum. Steve wanted to vomit. He kept it down because he knew Al would shove his face in it and he hated smelling like puke.

He was sure Al had a big night planned for him after they let the girl go. "We done?" he asked anyway.

"Almost. We'll dump the bitch off in the woods."

"What if I want to steal her home with me?"

"Ha. Funny." Al glanced at him. "Wait. Are you fucking serious?" He frowned. "I can't believe how you screwed this one up. Listen, I'll help you fix this, but you have to do exactly what I say."

Steve nodded, not sure if there was anything to fix.

"Lead her to the highway. I'll blindfold you so you can't see her. Use your other senses to fight her off."

"And if I can't?"

"Then I whisper to her. Whatever the fuck I want."

Steve couldn't have that.

"Don't look at me like I'm the asshole, Steven. You need to break the physical hold she has on you. I don't like how you put living as a mortal above your whispering duties. I'll turn you into a Whisperer yet. You need to resist her—cold. No giving in. A whisper binds you, nothing more. She's not your soulmate."

"What if she is?"

"She's not. Trust me, you're not that worthy. She just happens to have powers that complement yours, that's all. Take her in those woods, fuck her, then spit on her, like the bitch she is. Then you'll be free to whisper with me." He headed to the truck with the bag of ritual stuff over his shoulder.

"May I sit with her? She's afraid."

"Get in the truck, pansy. I got more shit to show ya."

JULIA

Even later that night—

Blindfolded, Julia shot up when she heard strange grunts. *Was that shape-shifting monster beating the terrified boy to death?* "Stop it. Stop it!" she yelled, moving toward them to no avail. Her arms were tied tight and her legs bound around the knees and ankles. She was glad she was in her work jeans because the metal from the truck was cold. She felt it against her arms and through her clothes. She wiggled along the chilly dirty box of the truck, desperately trying to get to him as he gasped for air.

"Oh? A brave one, eh? Come here." The binds loosened and clammy hands yanked her out of the oily-smelling pickup. As he tore the bag off Julia's head, the monster pretending to be her uncle whispered along her ear, sending chills down her entire body, *"Run, girly, run."*

She had this incredible urge to run, yet she glanced around. It was dark, with only the moon for light, and it half hid behind clouds. Trees surrounded them. In the distance, bright yellow eyes shimmered. Everything was scary. Where was the boy? Steve. His name screamed at her like a beacon of safety. She would never forget it. She had no idea how he'd gone with her into her dreams, but it was... *magical.*

"Don't whisper to her," Steve mumbled from the shadows, along the side of the pickup as he struggled for air.

"Are you hurt?" she asked, taking a step toward him.

"How?" He coughed and groaned, recovering from the hits he'd taken moments ago. "How did you refuse his whisper?"

"Run or I kill him," the monster whispered.

Panic gripped Julia and of course she ran into the shadows. She fled as fast as her legs could carry her. Right into the cluster of trees. Woods. Full speed without glancing his way, without checking to see if the freak followed, or where the boy was, she ran into the dismal woods.

His laugher followed her into the darkness. Crisp, haunting laughter she would never forget.

Julia had no idea what was happening, but she'd witnessed

things today that would forever change her. Never again would she trust a man. Everyone was to be feared, avoided. That man, that sicko, had transformed into Uncle Jackson. Where was Uncle Jackson? Why didn't she bring the knife James gave her for her birthday? She needed to keep a knife handy at all times.

How long had he lived as her uncle? Goosebumps rose on her arms at the idea. She wasn't safe anywhere. She needed a big dog to protect her from sickos. Yeah, if she ever got out of this, she'd get a dog, a big mean dog that could tell the difference between Uncle Jackson and a maniac.

Now she'd be lost in woods.

Julia pushed into the bushes as fast as she could. Raised on the prairies, she didn't know the first thing about being in a forest. Where was she? She doubted this was still Saskatchewan, yet they hadn't driven for long... unless she'd passed out? Her hands touched leaves as she ran, but she couldn't identify anything.

Dying in the woods was better than letting that monster hurt the boy. Would he let him go, too? What had that maniac done to them? She felt violated, yet no one had touched her. She kept telling herself this, yet someone had been inside her.

She ran.

It was just a dream.

It didn't make sense.

She'd watched a man magically transform from Uncle Jackson into a bald stranger; really, anything made sense. Anything was possible.

Nothing made sense.

What of the boy? Why was Steve afraid? It occurred to her, that maybe she should go back for him. He was like her—scared, trapped by the monster, too. She wanted to return to him. Leaving Steve behind didn't sit well with her, yet her legs pushed forward as if the whisper controlled them. When she'd get out of these woods, she'd make her way home and ask James and Pa what to do.

Julia ran. She might be brave, but she was smart enough to know when to run. She dodged branches, picked herself up when she fell.

Someone was behind her. Someone making bigger steps. She glanced over her shoulder. Someone closed in.

She picked up the pace, focused on her breath. She needed to keep it even, but she panicked. *Focus.* A branch caught her arm. She wiped the blood on her jeans then tripped over a stump. Like a wild animal, on all fours she pushed on, panting. *Run, Julia.* She needed water. *Don't let the fear in. Just run. Breathe.*

"Julia. Stop. You're hurt. I... stop." It was the boy.

The force pushing her forward ended abruptly and she collapsed beside a tree, clutching it. She would stop for him. Just for a moment. What if he needed her? Maybe they could sneak away. She wanted to know how he was involved in this. Had he been kidnapped, too?

He kept his distance, staying to the shadows like a frightened creature. Was he afraid of her? What did that monster do to make this boy so terrified? She forgot her own qualms for a moment and stood to sneak a better look. It was dark but even through the dense trees, the moonlight found him perfectly.

Was he blindfolded? How strange. She took a few uncertain steps toward him, eager to help. He nursed his side, clearly hurt. She went even quicker, but he slipped back several metres, putting distance between them. Even blindfolded, he was quick and manoeuvred around the trees without effort.

She stopped moving when he clutched his side again. Something was wrapped around his left arm, like a bandage.

"I won't come near you, but you're hurt. What did he do to you? Stop so I can help you."

"You want to help me? Stay away from me." He panted. "Your energy is too much. I... I just want to attack you." He smirked, and it was as if light emanated from him, pouring out to her. She was drawn to it. "That came out wrong. I didn't mean to scare you. I meant, attack as in kiss you nicely, gently, if you'd let me."

She wasn't afraid, but before she could say so, he blurted out, "Lilacs!"

"What?"

"You smell like lilacs. I couldn't remember the name of

them earlier. I felt weird." He spit out blood. "Oh, it hurts to breathe. I think he broke my rib." He poked at it and groaned. "Prick."

"I was scared," she admitted.

"Please don't be afraid of me."

She wasn't. He was in trouble. "Who is that monster who took us?"

"Monster? Al is my dad. He's nuts, and he's using magic that could destroy the world, but I can counter it, so I stay. It's the only way to undo his whispers. He's letting you go so he ain't that bad, right? I'll escort you safely out of these woods, but you have to trust me. I can't look at you. I can't touch you. I'm too weak, Julia. I'll attack you. Stay as far from me as possible. Please." He smelt like pine trees, like the trees around them, only more so, intense. She sneaked up beside him as he spoke, drawn to his strange scent.

"Already you're too close. Please, Julia, for the love of my dreams, back up."

She wanted to push up against his chest and get lost in the fragrance. Rub his scent all over her. She'd never in her life thought about sniffing someone, and this was not the time to think such things, yet it was her entire focus.

"Back up, Julia." His voice shook. "Your lilac aroma is killing me." He had his head against the tree, clutching it. Focusing on it, holding the tree like a lifeline. "He thinks I can fight this bond we have, but I can't. I don't want to."

"What bond?" She knew exactly what he meant. She wanted to run to him and smash herself into his chest, his... soul.

"Here, fix wherever you're bleeding." He peeled off his T-shirt and tossed it at her.

She examined it in the dim light while he adjusted the blindfold. *Get Naked and Muddy.* It was the slogan for the Green Revolution, a radical group encouraging everyone to go green and get back to nature. *Naked and Muddy*, as God intended. James read everything they sent out. He said they were to blame for the power outages, the cell phones dying, the Internet dying... yet he was fascinated with their beliefs because they were also the ones to blame when the phones or the radios came back. Who were these people?

"How do you know I'm bleeding?"

"I just do. When you think hard, I hear these thoughts pulsate in my brain like a beacon. Just now, you were thinking about James and getting naked and muddy. Is he your boyfriend?"

"My brother. He has a T-shirt like yours." Then, with a swallow that sneaked back up her dry throat, she glanced at him. His bare shoulder caught the moonlight like magic, and a tattoo on it intrigued her, called out to her—the symbol from her pendant. "Your tattoo..."

"What about it?"

"What does it mean?"

"Which one?"

"On your shoulder, the butterfly." She wanted to trace it and stepped in closer. She was inches from his skin.

He faced her, his blindfold still in place, but his lips were suddenly near hers. "You're too close." His grip tightened around the tree. "I can't be trusted, I'm evil."

She glanced at his chest, his bare skin. "I... I shouldn't trust men, strangers, anyone, yet you... you don't fall in that category, regardless of what you say, I know you're not evil, you're..." She smelt him again. "Magical."

"Julia, focus. The fragrance is driving me mad. That's powerful. Back up some more. Because now there's a desire between us for skin contact. Are you thinking that? Should we sit and talk? Take a break? Or do you want me to walk you to the highway? Now all I want is to touch your bare thighs. Lick them slowly." He rested his head against the tree. "This will be tough. It's some double connection. I wonder if he knew this? I hate him. Hate what he expects me to do. I wish I knew how to destroy him. Has to be a way." He let out a long breath. "The tattoo isn't a butterfly. It's a symbol for Dream Whisperer, which is what I study to be. Mine is dark because Dad has high hopes for me, wants me nasty like him."

"What's a Whisperer?"

"An idiot with magic that turns whispers into powerful enchantment spells to make you do things his way."

She gripped the T-shirt, listening intently.

"Supposedly, every Whisperer has a unique ability to

whisper to their calling. The more powerful the Whisperer, the more things their whispers affect. My specialty is whispering on the dream realm, but I whisper to the energy around things or people, and if I'm freaked out enough, I even whisper to the wind. I'm figuring it out. Today, I received power to send a soul to Afterlight. Only one Whisperer I want to use that on." He sounded guilty. "But I won't."

"Afterlight?"

"You know, the spiritual realm God made for souls waiting to spend time on the Mortal Realm."

"You mean you can kill someone with words?"

He nodded. Moths were drawn to the strange light coming from him.

"Wow. How do you know what you can do if you never used the power?"

"I sense my magic. It's like recipe books I store and take out when I need, only it's in my wrist."

"Oh. So you're crazy."

His happy chuckles scared a couple of the moths off.

"Do you whisper often?" She had so many questions.

"I don't make people do things they don't want to, it feels like dark magic."

"You can remove free will?"

"I try not to. A good Whisperer taps into what people believe and enhances it. I mean, if you wanted to... say... go out with me but were nervous, I'd give you confidence with a few well-placed whispers."

"My brother says you do whatever you want in life. You make your own choices and magic can't change that."

He rubbed his chin. "Is that how you fought Al's whisper? Your desire was stronger than his?"

She thought about this. "I don't know. I wanted to help you and running wasn't helping." She liked this guy. She wished he'd let her edge in closer. Her eyes swept over him. His jeans fit nicely.

She smelt the T-shirt in her hands—pine trees.

"Julia?"

"Huh?"

"What are you doing? It's killing me. I'm wild with the

need to sniff you again."

She examined the shirt in her hands. "I... I smelt your shirt." Her face warmed. "Sorry. My thoughts wandered... The pine aroma is nice. What's wrong with us? I feel so... loopy."

"Ah hell. I won't survive this, will I? Listen, Julia, it's magic. Dark magic. We can't fight it, but we can use it to our advantage. So focus on getting out of these woods, not on me."

"Dark magic?" Deep down she always believed in magic, but this was the first time she'd ever felt it. Smelt it. It was thrilling. "I didn't know you could smell magic."

"Ha! Funny. I like you."

"Want me to peel off my shirt so you can get a whiff of me? We could kick back and enjoy life. Get off on the smells. Be nasty and dark."

"Hell yeah." He laughed. "You're my kind of girl. Actually." He smirked. "What I want is to inhale your soul into mine, inch by inch while I kiss every part of your body, but I can't or Dad wins. So wipe the blood, toss my shirt, and let me walk you home." He looked much better. "You believe me, right? We can do this. I'm stronger knowing you believe me. We're united. You'll help me fight Al, right? We won't let him win, no matter what."

"Of course, I feel the magic. This isn't normal at all, but I doubt it's dark. No one smells this much pine tree. Why the blindfold?"

"I have to use my other senses to fight you off. It's easier not to use all your senses at once when you need to fight magic this powerful."

"How can you walk around blindfolded?" she asked.

"I use magic to guide me."

"Doesn't sound dangerous."

"I guess it's not. Wanna see me whisper? It's not like Al's nasty shit, my powers are... fun." He put out the palm of his hand and whispered, *"Soul, light."* A swirl of light erupted from inside him and twirled between them.

It danced in front of Julia.

"Neat. You created light out of thin air." Maybe it wasn't the moon highlighting him but a light shining from in the trees.

"Not air. That's a piece of my soul. I whispered to it with a rare power, or so Dad tells me. I'm not sure how much he knows about whispering, but he's the only Whisperer I know so I learn what I can. He studies dark Notebooks. Do you whisper? Think we're soulmates?"

Julia was surprised. Was she a Whisperer? His soulmate? She didn't want to be someone's soulmate. She'd never in her life used magic, yet it would explain the weird bond they shared, and she needed to explain it.

"Do you... do you like being a Whisperer?" she asked.

"No. I feel rotten inside when I whisper. It's wrong." The boy took bold, quick steps, unafraid, through the gloomy forest. Julia followed.

They walked for about twenty minutes. While they walked, he talked, she listened, "Julia, I've been thinking about what you said about trusting me. You have a good soul, but many strangers don't. I can whisper to you, and it will help you be wary of strangers. It's in your nature to trust them. You really are a good person, aren't you? No wonder Dad is afraid of you."

Al was afraid of her? "This will help me how?"

"You'll put up walls. Lifelong friends, people you've known forever, even those can turn on you, but at least those you'll see coming."

"I thought you didn't like whispering," she said.

"I don't, but I will to keep you safe. Subtle things Dad won't think of. I like to stay ahead of him. Now, strangers are harder to trust, harder to see when they've been whispered to, dark whispers I mean."

"Dark whispers? Do you do this to others? Have you actually hurt people? These whispers you want to make on me, are they unholy?"

"I... Julia, don't be afraid of me. If I turn on you, we have a strong enough connection that you'll know. No matter what happens, no matter where you end up, I'll always protect you. Trust that. This connection between us is annoyingly strong." He rubbed his forehead, frustrated.

She wished she could see his face, admire his eyes. "How will I know it's you?"

He rubbed his fingertips. "You'll know."

"Then whisper to me."

"You aren't afraid of much, are you?"

"My brother says the great thing about fear is that it gets your adrenalin going. The secret is to tap into it. Worry about the consequences later."

"Your brother sounds like a smart guy."

"James is something else," Julia agreed, wishing he were with her.

When they made it into the open, they were almost hand in hand. Her fingers grazed his. The things he whispered made sense. She shouldn't trust strangers. She needed to learn the traits of those she loved.

"You found the highway. Come with me," she pleaded. She didn't want him to go back to that freak. She didn't understand what was happening, or what type of magic they were caught in, but she believed it was something powerful. "Come with me." She grabbed his hand without thinking and tingles rushed through her.

He gasped and rolled her into his arms, a hand around her waist and one lost in her long hair. His lips were on hers before she could catch her breath. Their bodies moved to the grass, and already he worked her clothes off. They weren't moving fast enough. She needed him and rolled on top of him to undo his belt. That dreamy feeling was back and she couldn't wait to sink deeper into it.

His dad interrupted them, "Well... well... well... So close yet that don't save the world, now does it? My turn." He yanked her by her hair.

Steve reached for her a moment too late, a knife came hurling at his shoulder, trapping him to the ground.

STEVE

The knife dug deep in Steve's shoulder but he actually experienced more pain from their souls ripping apart than from the blade pinning him to the ground. So this was payback for the knife he'd sent flying at his dad earlier—a shoulder for a shoulder.

Steve gripped the blindfold in his hands but couldn't move, waiting for the pain to ease up. He stared at the moon overhead and prayed to the whispering gods to give him a bloody break. "*Pain, transfer to the soil,*" Steve whispered to minimize the ache as he pulled the blade out. What had Al whispered to create the bubbling blood that healed him? "*Heal,*" he tried, and his shoulder throbbed as it mended itself. He wiped the blood from his dirty fingers on his jeans.

The pain was intense. He didn't breathe, waiting for a break in it.

Worse, his gut clenched from the guilt of using magic. *Why? Shouldn't he self-heal?* His insides screamed that this type of magic was for helping others, not himself.

Julia's screams fired him up and he scrambled to his feet only to be knocked back by a shadow demon.

Dang. Al was whispering to demons again.

As Steve wiggled out of the grasp of the shadow demon, he saw Al dragging Julia to the truck. Then the demon shoved Steve's head in the dirt.

"Mischief, damn it, I need a hand with this lunatic." The stupid demon was so strong he couldn't slip out of its grip.

Mischief slithered from the trees, ripped the monster off him, and tossed him aside.

"Leave her alone," Steve shouted to Al.

Mischief was on all fours growling from the depth of his stomach at the fear demon.

"*Get lost.*" The whisper poured out of Steve.

The demon vanished.

Al was in the truck, pulling out. *Dang.*

Steve rubbed his biohazard tattoo wishing he could erase the damn thing. "Don't you have anyone else to harass?" he yelled after Al. The ability to move a soul from a body to

Afterlight throbbed in his wrist. A familiar sensation that usually happened when he needed to whisper to the magic coursing there. It was hard to refuse that pulsating. It would be easy. It would break the link between Al and his body. One easy whisper. Easy but wrong. Steve rubbed his tattoo afraid of the magic throbbing in it. He was a monster. So powerful he scared off a shadow demon with a whisper.

Loneliness settled on him once the truck was out of sight. He'd have to jog home, and they were hours from the stupid old house they lived in. Steve kicked the grass, frustrated, and something sparkled in the dark. Mischief picked it up before Steve could and it dangled in his shiny long fingers.

Steve snagged it from him. It was her necklace. His heart sped up. A link. If he could whisper to his soul, why not to one he was linked to? Dad would never know. He could find her. And then what?

Steve grinned.

"*Oh no.*" Mischief grumbled. "*I know that look. We will disappoint Al even more.*"

STEVE

A year later—

Al had returned Julia to her world and left Steve alone.

Steve's hunt for Julia had been long but he was excited. Dreamland was a fun loophole where they were safe. Steve plopped on the bed and slid his hand under his pillow. His fingers fumbled with the newspaper clipping Mischief had brought him. It was about Julia. Another link. It told about an award she'd won for her volunteer work in the community. Eyes closed, he focused on her, waiting for the butterflies to take him to her. The trip was quick and they dropped him in front of the door to her dreams and crowded on it so he couldn't see through the window. Instinctively, he reached for the doorknob but there was none.

"Doorknobs only appear when the dreamer asks for help. We have to wait for that sacred moment," someone to his left said. "First day as a Dream Whisperer or what?"

Steve jumped and faced him, thinking about how Mischief was worried Dark Whisperers would come here. The butterflies scattered.

He'd never met anyone on this side of the doors before and Steve took a step back.

This guy was relaxed as he leaned against the door to James' room, his hand out where the doorknob should be. He'd be waiting a long time 'cause that wasn't the real door. Only one way to get into James' dreams and that was through Julia's.

The stranger was tall and skinny, his face scarred by acne. When he saw Steve he bowed his head and dropped to his knees. "Forgive me, my Lord. I didn't see your soul with all the butterflies around you. I am yours to serve in this life, as Slumber." His words rushed out as if he'd studied them but hadn't believed he'd need to say them. "I seek the counsel of the wise Hero. I've been approached to join a group of Whisperers from Utopia to fight for the *Get Naked and Muddy Revolution*, but my brother says to avoid such groups. I need guidance." He waited as if Steve could offer such guidance. When he said nothing, Slumber continued, "If you could grant me access to this room, I'll return to the mortal corridor." He stayed on his knees not looking up. "I must speak to Hero at once."

Steve glanced around. Was he talking to him? "Hero is a legend my mother told me about when I was a boy. Behind that door is a mortal. James only lets his sister and me in. Guy's a paranoid bugger. What's wrong with you? You drunk? Get up."

"Drugs, my Lord. I need guidance." He stayed on his knees, not looking at Steve.

"You a Whisperer? Get up, talk to me." Steve was excited. Another Whisperer.

"Yes, one of your Dream Whisperers. I admit, I suck lately, but... guide me to be worthy."

Steve looked down the endless corridor of doors. If he took the door above his head, he'd find another corridor like this one. It was infinity. "I guess I could use a guy like you helping me since I kind of have my own troubles these days. There are just so many doors. I found one last night that lets me summon souls to me with a whisper, which was pretty cool, 'cause it might save me time."

"What?" Slumber glanced up, shocked. When he winced, his buckteeth came over his bottom lip. "You mean you've reincarnated? Oh shit. Who protects Dreamland if we're both living on the Mortal Realm?"

Steve shrugged and leaned against the door to Julia's dreams so he was closer to her. "Not much happens here anyway. You're like the first soul I ever met on this side of the doors."

Slumber sighed and got to his feet. "I guess I don't come here often. So you don't remember me? When I come to Dreamland, I remember all my time here, since we were first given life. You are destined to protect this realm and I'm destined to protect the one that joins to it known as Inspiration. Every room in Dreamland links to Inspiration. If I ever find my soulmate we'll whisper in Inspiration as an immortal god. For now, I have to be content just whispering to a few souls a day."

They stood in silence, both leaning against their doors,

waiting. Finally, Slumber asked, "Think guys like us get soulmates?"

"My dad says no."

"Yeah, he's probably right. So if you see Hero, ask him what's wrong with me. I feel broken inside. I don't think I should go to Utopia feeling like this."

"You talk of heroes but my dad says you only have to save one to be a hero. And James says that when we're lost and confused it helps to remember that someone loves us enough to die with us. We might not know them yet, but they exist 'cause every soul has a mate, even if we never meet. This is all the inspiration a hero needs."

He nodded as if Steve was a genius. "I will do my best. Find one soul to help and one to love. I can do that. So, will I see ya around?"

"I usually only hang out here," Steve confessed.

"On the Whisperer floor? Well, stay out of the black doors and pay attention to what happens behind the grey ones." Rainbows shot out from under James' door. "Shit." He jumped back. "Did you see that?"

"Yeah, that's James at work. The idiot practices shooting rainbows in his sleep. It's funny."

"Nothing funny about Cupid Hero at work. I think he might have gotten me with that. How do I look?" He stood in front of Steve, humble and ready to be knocked off his feet by a strong wind.

"Ready to take on the world," Steve lied and Slumber smiled. Not a silly shy smile, but a full grin as if all his worries were over. He flashed out, leaving behind a pinkish grey light that slowly vanished.

Steve looked at the newspaper clipping in his hand about Julia. He didn't have to wait for a doorknob to appear. If he used this link, he could walk into her room and wait for her there, or go see James. Still, he didn't dare use it. What if Slumber was one of Al's spies?

Instead, he sat on the floor, stressed, listening to her cry on the other side of the door. Why was she so sad today? He glanced up at the doorknob when it appeared, letting him know she needed him but he didn't dare touch it. Finally, he called the butterflies to take him home. He didn't want to risk going in and that Dream Whisperer following him.

Back in his room he studied the clipping with his gut twisting. He missed her. Julia. Nights when he didn't see her were tough.

"Proud of yourself?" Al asked while he pawed through Steve's drawers.

"Hell, Dad." Steve shot out of bed and slid the clipping under the covers. "What are you doing in my room? I thought you were out whispering or ruining lives or whatever you do."

Al leaned against the dresser, kicking the clothes Steve had tossed on the floor. He knew better. Al hated anything out of place. He'd been so eager to slip off to Dreamland that he hadn't been thinking straight.

"What I've been doing is making heart attacks. I whispered his heart to stop beating so it looks like natural causes, if you can call me that."

Who?! Steve gripped the covers as if they could absorb the pain he was about to experience. "You can do that?" Steve studied his old man.

"Can now." The prick was getting more and more dangerous. He'd shaved his head, which meant he'd done another ritual. Who knew what he summoned this time. Where did he learn these things? Were there more Notebooks he studied? Steve planned to search his room for them. Burn them.

He studied his good old dad, but it made his stomach turn if their eyes met. Still, Dad was well dressed and he'd cleaned up. He always dressed his best before he summoned anything—magic or demons—it was a weird habit. Even Al's soul was neater, with the swirling clouds clustered together.

"So... who?"

"Her old man."

Nooooo! his insides screamed but he kept his face uninterested. No wonder she was crying and James was flinging rainbows around. "Whose old man? I don't know who you're talking about." Steve's voice was steady and firm. He'd deal with the pain of this loss when he was alone.

Guilt gripped him—this was his fault.

"Sure you don't." Sarcasm dripped down Al's voice. "Your

bitch." Al paused, waiting for Steve to blow up at him. Not today. Steve felt the loss deep in his soul. He was too numb to move. "The woman you drool over. I told you to stay away from her. Steve. Wake up. You have to sever this link. It was a tool for a fucking ritual. What's wrong with you? Don't you understand that this is for your own good? You have to learn to stay away from her, forget her. Can't be that hard."

"No idea what you rant about."

"Play dumb, I kill the brother, see if you survive that emotional blizzard. Tell me why you did it. Why you went behind my back and found her? Why do you tolerate me torturing her? What's your limit?" He actually seemed curious.

"I don't care if you kill them all," Steve lied. "My soul aches for her. I need her to function. I want her and I'll get her. If I have to kill you, I will." If he acted like he didn't care about her family, then Al wouldn't bother with them. The truth was Steve did care. He cared about them deeply. The mother, the father, the brother, even the dog. He cared because Julia cared about them. Especially, James, her brother. Steve cared about him as if he were his own brother, his best friend, yet they'd never actually met.

"Get a girlfriend."

"I want her. Only her."

"She doesn't even know you exist, pansy. I'll whisper to her so she forgets you every goddamn day. You'll be nothing but a dream to her."

"She's a whisper I can't refuse. Besides, I haven't been near her, Dad, swear. Clearly. Look at me. I'm a wreck." Yet he had every part of her memorized. Her voice tics, her laughter, her blasted ankles were etched into his mind.

"Yet you saw her."

"Just a dream, Dad. Nothing more." His hands ached to touch her. He wasn't sure if the attraction was to her soul or her body. Maybe it was both. He wanted to be near her. To protect everyone she loved, everyone she helped.

"Let me talk to her, Al. I won't ask for anything else, not ever. I have to help her through this loss."

"Call me Dad. Now dress. I'll show you why you need to sever this bond. You'll see firsthand how her pain weakens you. It's a vicious circle that will make you hate her. End it." He placed a knife on the dresser. "If you can't break this bond, tell me now, because I'll have to kill you and try again in another life. We screwed up. It's over."

"You're sick. If you want me dead, do it already. Stop torturing me."

"Is this what you think I'm doing? I'm trying to save you. I have to kill her but I can't without killing you. She has you obsessed. Unfocused." He sighed. "I'm not out of tricks yet, but..." Al dusted off his hands on his shirt. "We'll try it another way. Dress. We got shit to do. Honestly, son, watching you destroy yourself over her is what's making me sick. As if a gal is worth this much agony." He rubbed his jaw thoughtfully then snooped in Steve's bed for the clipping while Steve dressed.

He pulled it out with a few swear words. "Dammit, pansy. Another one?" Steve moved for it but Al glared at him, his soul red. "You know, Steven. One day, you'll have the gonads to stand up to me."

Stand up to him? He should kill the prick. Steve clenched his fists, controlling the rage so he didn't whisper something that stupid.

Al made a show of spitting on the newspaper. It tore.

Steve wanted to rip it from him, but he had no idea what his dad was capable of and it wasn't just him anymore, he could go after Julia's family now. Steve had to keep them safe, and this meant obedience.

Al ground the clipping into the floor with his foot. "Meet me at the sacred spot in an hour. I can't believe I ended up with a son like you." He sighed. "What I deserve. One weak moment and I have to pay for it for eternity. The whispering gods have a sick sense of humour."

The minute he was out of the room, Steve fell on the clipping like a rabid animal. He smoothed it on the floor. Since Dad took the pendant from him, these clippings were the best contact he had with Julia. Why would his dad do this to him? Didn't he even have the tiniest morsel of dignity in him?

Steve inspected every inch of her wrinkled head and sat on the floor gaping at the image.

It was ruined.

Mischief appeared and sat beside him.

Steve ran his fingers over it in desperation, leaving a trail of black ink behind. It was faint, but the connection was there. Hope.

Steve leaned against the bed. He took in a deep breath, feeling her grief through his link to Dreamland. He knew how much she loved her dad. She called him Papa.

"Why does he do this?" Steve asked Mischief.

"*Because he doesn't want you with her.*"

"I get that. But why?"

"*That is a good question. What would you teach her?*"

Steve thought about this. Al might have her magic, but it was hers. What if Steve taught her how to call on it and use it? What difference would that make?

Steve wiped his stupid overwhelming tears, torn between frantic panic and hate for Al.

Two nights ago, he'd had the best conversation with Julia. A real conversation... in Dreamland, but still. Julia had told him a story about her pa and he whispered it to her now, sending it through the damaged image, hoping their connection was strong enough that he wouldn't need to go to Dreamland right now. "*Remember how your pa built a doghouse, and the dog wouldn't go in it? He actually spent the night in the doghouse with him. Your ma was so lonely, she joined him.*"

Her voice filled his thoughts, "*Must have been crowded in the doghouse because the dog sneaked in their bed.*" Julia. The only woman in his life. Yet she didn't even know he existed.

She thought he was a dream.

Maybe Al was right, maybe he didn't deserve his magic. What had he ever done worthwhile?

Steve studied the ruined paper clipping as if he could repair the damage with his eyes. He had to help her. This was his fault.

He stood and snatched the knife, the force of this decision pushing him forward.

Mischief leapt to his feet.

"I'll bring her to Dreamland. I'll protect her with whispers so she'll remember me. I'll whisper nice things."

That wouldn't be enough.

He had to find her.

If he had an hour to run to the sacred spot, Steve needed to motor. It was a long hike through the deserted village, through the tunnels snaking around the lake, then through the woods.

No. Screw him.

Steve grabbed a clean shirt.

"Mischief, I'm not coming back."

His days whispering with Al were over.

JAMES

Four years later—

James was eighteen today and he was training with Steve in their cottage. It was a place they'd built together. The cottage linked the dream realm with the mortal one.

He'd never met Steve in real life but he was by far his best friend. They met every night in this cottage of dreams, in this place where no one bothered them while they trained. Well. Except Jules.

James pulled the blade away from Steve's neck, proud of his skills with the sword. He swung it around a bit more, making a trail of rainbow light. He loved this place. He knew Steve called it a dream, but it felt so real and he felt at home.

Normally, James wouldn't mind Jules hanging with his friends, but Steve got so blasted stupid around her it was annoying. Usually, James just left when she showed and went to read the Notebooks Steve had collected over the years.

Every day he looked forward to visiting this place, 'cause everyday was a new adventure.

Steve's muscles glistened from the sweat of their workout and he lay on the carpet as if James had killed him.

"Steve. You suck. Whisper. When I get your neck under my blade, whisper. Get a drink, we're doing it again." James shook out his muscles.

Steve whispered up a couple beers and handed one up to James from where he sat on the floor. "How will using a sword help me protect Julia from my dad?"

"Your weapon is not the sword, moron." James groaned. Would he ever get through to this guy? "I give you a gun, a sword, anything, and you think this is your weapon? Words. Use your words. These weapons are to help your parties focus. Like with the doorknobs that let you in these rooms. They only appear when you're allowed in, well, holding a gun on someone gives you that in, and your whisper will be more effective." James paced around him acting angry, but he loved talking with Steve about magic and whispering.

"Julia's memories were gone this morning," Steve

reminded him. "We might not be able to see Al, but he's here someplace. He has a plan."

"We have a better one. I think it's the eagle erasing her memories. I told Bobby to shoot the damn thing this morning and he freaked. Didn't know the guy had a thing for birds." James sat on the ground by Steve, nursing his beer. Everything tasted so much better in the cottage.

"Bobby was at your house this morning? Why you letting Julia hang around that cop?" Steve asked, his jaw tight. He didn't like Bobby from day one.

Not that James blamed him. The guy was shifty. "'Cause we can't always be around to watch her, and he don't mind. Only Jules really doesn't like him." James rubbed his head. Truth was, he didn't like Bobby either and he had no idea why he even let the prick hang around him. Yet... he felt this strange *urge* to be nice to him.

"Good. You think he's a good cop? You don't buy his act, do you?"

"Nope."

"You know, a guy like you would make a good cop." Steve was relaxed again.

"Last thing I want to be. I can't tell you what I want to be, though." James lay back, his arms under his head. "But it involves whispering like you, only better."

Rainbows danced on the ceiling of their training room.

"No need to tell me. I see it in your soul and it's nothing to be embarrassed about, James. In fact, it was Al who once told me that it wasn't with brains or muscle that a hero saved the world, but with love."

"I'm sure your bonehead pa said something that great."

"I might have tweaked it up, but that was the general idea, sure. He's not all bad, James. He just gets bad ideas." Steve closed his eyes. "Sometimes, I think he can't really help it, it's almost like there's just a nasty inside us we can't fight."

"You seem to do fine."

Steve took a deep breath. "I'm a monster, James."

"Maybe but you're a good one."

"How do you know?"

"For starters, you don't whisper to my sister, and he does. Burns me." Despite his words, James smiled, feeling so peaceful inside. There was no anger in the cottage.

"He wants to keep me away from Julia, but even when she forgets me, I don't think she really does."

"Love. I'm doing all this for love." James rested, smiling like a fool. "I figured out what that group is doing."

"The *Get Naked and Muddy* radicals?" Steve sat to listen better. "You still think they're Whisperers?"

"Yup. They're uniting, planning to reset social beliefs but they're missing a couple key Whisperers and are sending out an invite."

"What if they're looking for us?" Steve said dreamily.

"Yeah, what if? I might give them an answer once school's out." His school friends were going off in a few weeks to be mechanics and teachers and all sorts of boring things. But James, he wanted to be a cupid, and there was no better school for that than right here with Steve. The Notebooks had everything he needed to know about whispering. Life was perfect.

"You know how to contact them?"

"I have ideas. So what you wanna train with now? Wolves?"

"I'm going to get Julia. The days she forgets about me, I find her in her dream room all alone staring at butterflies, and I hate that. She's always happier here."

"Your dad annoys me. Where is the prick?"

"Wish I knew. But odds are, he's making my life hell, one whisper at a time."

JULIA

Two weeks later—

Flustered, Julia shut the door and faced her brother. When she saw him leaning patiently against the veranda railing she dropped her keys and the clatter they made when they hit the wooden veranda made her jump. She couldn't believe how grownup James looked today. Eighteen. He was eighteen, she reminded herself. Graduated and old enough to go off to the city. He was determined to become a cop. Seeing him like this made her feel like time was slipping through her fingers. She needed to pull her life together.

"Jules, you coming?" The old wood creaked slightly from James' weight.

Julia would miss that creak. Odd, that such a small thing should make her sad inside. Was a creak that big of a deal? It haunted her as she snapped up the keys and said bye to Max, their St Bernard.

Without James, there would be no more creaks.

That was a big deal. Did she want to stay in a house that didn't creak?

No, Julia, move to the cottage. The cottage. You might forget me, but remember the cottage, and how wonderfully happy we are there. The words whispered in her mind and she saw the cottage of her dreams clearly. Yeah, she wanted to live there, raise kids there, plant a garden, just live a fun life with... there was an image she couldn't grasp and it was this image that kept her from moving forward with her life. Who was haunting her sleep? Why couldn't she let him go?

"Okay, let's go." She couldn't delay this anymore. Tears were close. "James, I can't believe how grownup you look."

"Yeah, yeah, all macho and shit. Get over it Jules and let's go."

Gently, on her tippy toes, she pushed aside one of James' wild curls and forced a smile, but the lump, it wouldn't go down her throat no matter how hard she swallowed.

James glared and picked up his bag while shaking his head, "Jules, cripes, stop looking at me like that. You promised no waterworks. I can't be all in your face forever. I'm eighteen, time to move out and move on. I got shit that needs doing, a life to live. And so do you. You stayed for me, but now, you need to make your own path."

Her entire world was about to crash around her. She liked things the way they were, the way they'd been for so long. This was a good life. Why was he determined to run from it so suddenly? It was as if he forgot who he was.

"And promise you'll be nice to Bobby. He's got a bit of a thing for you. Well, if he was smart, now that I'm outta your face, he should be moving in here getting all in your pants."

She rolled her eyes. Lucky for her, Bobby wasn't that brilliant. "I'm always nice to Officer Bobby, but he's not allowed near the inside of these pants."

"You treat him like he's a stranger with a Taser shoved up his ass."

She grinned at her brother's weird imagery. "He is a stranger, and I wish he used his Taser, then at least he'd give me a jolt once in a while."

"Yeah, I get it. You have livelier relationships with your dreams."

"What does that mean?"

"Nothing." James looked ready to punch something when he climbed in the car. She followed him, fumbling with her purse while she pulled back her hair in a loose pony so she'd be at least half-ready for work.

James tried the radio, something he did every time he was in the car. When he heard voices, he listened for a moment then turned it off. "We'll lose the radio at two today and the phones will come back."

"How do you know that?"

"Why ask *how* I know things if you trust that I'm right?"

She shook her head at her weird brother.

"Listen, Jules, you can't keep living in this box of yours."

"I'm not sure what that means, James." She glanced at his index finger and sighed when it shook wildly. His tic meant he was figuring her out, putting things together from her tells. Who knew what James saw when he studied her. Her brother was a genius with a gift for reading people. The next words out of his mouth would sum up his assessment and she wasn't looking forward to it.

"You'll be alone out here, and I'd like to know you're at least dating. Don't be mad, but I've explained things to Bobby so he understands and doesn't push you away."

So James thought she needed a man. "Great. What did you tell him? You didn't tell him I was kidnapped five years ago, did you? Or about Pa or Ma? Heavens, you didn't tell him about how bad luck follows us with every breath?"

His eyebrows fell together in his deep man-do-I-really-come-off-that-stupid frown. "Told him you were a freak with a phobia of outsiders who is saving herself for some guy haunting her sleep night after night, is all."

She blushed as she climbed in the car. "Oh that should keep his Taser under control."

He chuckled. "It did. He likes freaks. The guy is nuts about you. Blinded by his dick. Give him a chance, will ya?"

She thought about dating a lot these days, but not Bobby. He wasn't magical. "I can't, James. I just can't."

"Is it that stranger thing again?" James shook his head. "A weird phobia but I know it's real to you. Still, he's taking the time to get to know you and to me he's a friend, kind of, so that has to count for something, right?"

"I suppose. I could invite him over for supper with a few of my friends." She did live a boring life. "I would like to see the city lights. They say they're beautiful. Maybe he'd take me and we could visit you."

"Oh, he'd like that. At least try. If you have these walls up, it'll never happen, then you'll be sitting in the house alone forever and I'll be worried, and you don't want me to worry about you. Do you?"

James had a way to win her over and she chuckled. "No, James, I wouldn't want that. I want you to kick some ass." She started the car but didn't move. Just watched the swallows nesting on the old satellite dish off the side of the house. She didn't remember it ever working. Suddenly, a bald eagle landed on the dish.

"That bird is getting annoying," James mumbled.

She wasn't sure why he hated it, but it made her nervous, too, as it glared at her.

"What are you waiting for?" James asked.

Good question. Maybe it was time to move out and find a new nest. God knew she wasn't doing anything but holding on to memories she didn't need. Without James here, this place wouldn't feel like home.

Tears were even closer to the surface despite the laughter from moments ago. "Won't you miss this place?" Why did it feel like she was the one moving out? Moving into the cottage she decorated last night with... A shadow helped her but she couldn't remember his face and this overwhelming panic tore into her. Why couldn't she remember him? He'd made her popcorn. They'd talked about travelling. About going on a balloon ride. He loved the city lights and showed her how they looked by creating an image with his words. *Magical.*

"I'll miss sneaking out," he teased her. "And giving you a hard time."

"You know, Ma would be proud of you." She hated these moments where she wanted Ma here and she wasn't. It wasn't fair.

"Jules, is it weird that I don't remember how she died? I mean, why did I wake up one morning with those memories erased? It's as if someone whispered them away while I slept."

She felt like that a lot. "You mean like how I forgot about the details of the kidnapping?"

They stared ahead, silent.

"Maybe these are memories we don't need," she told him. "It's a blessing."

"Yeah, but what if more memories are missing. I don't like that."

"As long as you know I love you," Julia teased.

He smiled and it made her feel better when that dimple flashed. "*Je t'aime,*" James whispered in French. They were French Canadians born on the prairies. They didn't speak French as much, now that their mother was gone, yet he always expressed his deepest love in French as if it was founded in the core of his soul in the language.

His words sent a warmth right through her and she actually felt the warmth of his love for her. He smirked, pleased with himself and his big decision as she pulled out of their yard.

"Read anything interesting lately?" He always asked this as they drove down the lane. He bet her once there wasn't any fact she could give him that he didn't already know, and so, she collected impossible things to test his knowledge. Of course, she always threw him the facts twisted.

"Yes, there's this pink fairy liquor—"

"You mean green fairy. No such thing as pink fairy liquor," he corrected her without a hesitation. He pulled out his notepad and scribbled something on it. "Here, this is the recipe, but don't be making that shit without me at home. It will seriously mess you up. Plus, it's kind of illegal so don't tell Bobby I gave you that. He's already all up in my face about every breath I take."

She glanced at the recipe of herbs he handed her.

"You didn't drink it, did you?"

"I do not have time in this life to get this messed up." He studied the recipe. "That is weird, eh? How do I know these things? Something in me searches my brain, and *voilà*, the info about it is there, ready for me to share."

"You said *this life* again. As if you lived a thousand lives."

"Feels like I have. Man. I'm old inside. You ever feel that way?"

"No, James. I must be brand new."

He chuckled.

The drive to town was fifteen minutes and when she saw the grain elevators, she relaxed. Officer Bobby was in town today and he'd be by the store to say hi, to see how she'd survived James leaving. It made her feel safe to know he was around, yet at the same time, she dreaded it. It was always the same with him. Argh. He'd probably try to touch her again, and that would be a train wreck. Would she settle for Mr. Disappointment? She sighed, because it always felt like someone... *magical* wanted to sweep her up on an adventure, yet return her home safely every night.

Bobby wouldn't wait forever, and she felt time demanding things of her.

It wasn't her fault. Every time Bobby brushed her skin, she expected something, waited for it. Yet there was nothing thrilling between them. Not a tingle, not a spark, nothing but a warm, soothing friendship. Was that all there'd ever be?

Would it grow into more? A passion? A desire? A want? Something damn it! Shouldn't there be something? Argh. What did she know? Still... she wanted *a dream*.

She wanted more.

"Will you at least move to town? So I know you aren't alone on the farm?" James asked.

"As if. I hate the idea," she lied. It was no longer home. She wanted the cottage in her dreams. "You leaving is all the change I can handle today." Then she decided to tell James about her dreams. "Actually, I dream about a cottage. This small thing, made of stones, you know how I love stone houses. Well anyway, this one is perfectly mine. It has this wrap-around veranda and the inside is simple and cozy. The lake has plenty of room for waterskiing, which sounds fun. It has two floors, with three bedrooms upstairs, one is yours, and I share mine with..."

His green eyes bore into her. "Who?" he snapped.

She ignored his glare.

"That ain't all you dream about. Who is he?"

Her cheeks warmed. "I... I don't remember."

"Hmmm. Sounds nice. I hope you find your dream place. You see yourself with Bobby perhaps?"

She pulled into the fuel station and turned the car off. "Let it go, James. Bobby and I won't happen."

James glanced over, tense. "You mentioned a Steve before." His eyes studied her, stopping on her hand, which was on her stomach. "A driver who comes by twice a week with deliveries."

Her heart picked up at the mention of his name but she could hardly remember what he looked like.

James spoke crisply, "Well, make sure I meet him if you see him moving into that cottage with you. I'll be home next weekend if I find a ride." He climbed out of the car, somewhat gruffly, and she followed.

"You don't have to follow me, Jules. I can wait for the bus alone. I'm not a baby."

No. James never was a baby. Always, he protected her. Julia hugged him about a dozen times and he never fought off one hug. She was lost in his huge arms with no idea when he got so big. All these changes.

"I promised not to cry, and we'll see each other real soon, but..." Tears fell even as she said it. It felt nice to cry.

He wiped her tears. "Oh Jules." He held her again. "Be safe, *comprends?*" The one French word meaning *'understand?'* snapped in her soul and she saw the world for a moment as him, so clear, so real. She understood it all.

Giggles overwhelmed her.

"Now that's better." He laughed with her.

Suddenly, she felt empty and alone, even if she was in his arms. What would she do alone in that big house tonight? More than ever, she wished she could drive into her dreams. She was always happy in them, finding the perfect balance between family and fun.

James was leaving. She should, too. This was it. It was time to start a new life. Yet... there was something missing.

"Jules, get to work. Everyone is watching you and you're making an ass of yourself. I'll be fine and I'll call you the minute I arrive in Regina. The phones will be up by then, you'll see. You sure you'll be okay?" Quietly, he whispered so only she could hear, "*Des questions?*"

He did it again. His French question seared into her. She had thousands, just exploding. She thought about asking him about the untingles between her and Bobby or about the strange magical dreams, but shook her head, wiped her tears, and left him there because one question was never enough. Once James got teaching and explaining things, he'd miss his bus and she'd be late for work.

This was it. "Time to let go." She walked away.

For the first time in her life, she was alone. She paused with her hand on the door to her car. The idea didn't terrify her as much as it should have; it was freeing.

JULIA

Julia was the first to arrive at the grocery store, always was. It was almost a comfort to see the familiar loading dock down the back alley, waiting for her to bring it to life. As she searched her purse for the keys, the freight arrived and pulled up to the loading dock.

She checked her watch. Steve was early today, maybe they'd get a good jump on things for a change. It would be a distraction from missing James.

She waved to the young driver and Steve waved back in his usual casual way. She blushed instantly. She wouldn't mind adding this hottie to her dream.

Truth was, she liked Bobby because he was safe, but seeing Steve just now reminded her that she was alive. That an animal-like beast lived in her, craving freedom. Her breathing increased and she found her eyes hunting for him.

What was wrong with her? Why did Steve make her feel so aware, so... *sexual*?

Like a dream.

Well. She wouldn't mind dreaming about him. Steve. Just Steve. No one else. Why would there be anyone else when she could dream about Steve?

She shook her head. No. Why dream about a total stranger?

His eyes locked on her as he climbed out of the truck, and she felt as if he saw through her clothes, which made her slow her actions. Was she even moving? Julia was uncomfortable with strangers, but... well... he felt familiar. Even though he kept a huge, impossible distance between their bodies, in the past they'd talked closely. It was a blur, but she remembered that much. They'd talked as if they knew each other their entire lives. She could have grown up with him, except he was the opposite of her. He didn't like familiar things, he liked to try new things. He was twenty-one, like her. Born and raised on the prairies, like her. They even shared the same birthday. His dad raised him, and when he was nervous, he rubbed the tattoo on his left wrist as if it gave him courage. It was kind of sexy but she didn't know what the tattoo was and unknown things scared her. Maybe she'd ask him what it meant. Why hadn't she? Frankly, she didn't care. She wanted to rub the tattoo against her bare skin like poison she needed to seep into her naked pores. Something about him made her want to be... *bad.*

Steve was out of the truck. She wasn't moving, lost in these thoughts about him.

"Hi, Julia, guess I'm early today." He took off his ball cap and paused for a moment to capture her beauty. There was no other word for it. That's exactly what he did, worshiped her from afar.

She hadn't moved. "Yeah, you must be making good time." She smiled as their eyes locked. It was like looking away from a cyclone. She knew she should, but she was drawn to the excitement of how he admired her.

He waited, the distance between them familiar, yet everything about him was unknown.

"You got a haircut... I think." She liked his blond hair, how it brushed along his forehead, and curled up a touch, like a tease. Wow. She wanted him to be the one. Him. Hell with Bobby and his boring touches. If James liked him so much, why didn't he date him? Steve was turning her on with a look and he was twenty feet away. Why was he so far?

He beamed, excited that she noticed his new do. She wanted to say more but couldn't find the words.

"Is it too short? I don't look like a goofball do I?"

Never. "It's very nice. The chicks will find it irresistible." Yummy was the word that burst into her mind.

He swallowed, and even at this distance, the action had an effect on her.

"The chicks? As in, you approve, right? You." He spoke the word as if undressing her and she blushed. "Right, Julia? You're the only one I care about. I want it right for when we face my dad. Everything has to be perfect."

His pa?

"Are you asking me out? In your new military haircut?"

He chuckled. "My old man drilled the military in me. Maybe I did go too short. So what are the plans for this weekend? Another gagging date with Mr. Boring or may I have a turn? I don't like you alone. If James is gone, you're coming with me to the cottage. At least invite me over. I'll sit in my truck and make sure no one stops by."

"I..." She hadn't mentioned Bobby to him, had she? Or James leaving. Had she? Everything was fuzzy when Steve was around. She couldn't be sure. "I thought you were on the outs with your pa."

He sucked in air and almost stumbled toward her. "You remember me today, right?" He was over six feet tall and it didn't take Steve long to make the strides so he was right next to her. She dropped her keys nervously. He'd never been this close to her. Never.

"How much do you remember?" His eyes studied her as if seeing her soul. His body called out to hers with each movement. She warmed at the thought, wishing she could move against him in a naked dance.

"I don't know, it feels like a dream," she confessed.

He bent to pick up the keys for her, moving into her space extra slow. "Yes, the dreams. Those are good, remember last night." Their energy mingled and she caught her breath.

So did he.

Time paused and she actually thought about how nice he smelt today. Like pine trees. She believed what he said once about being outdoors a lot, even though she couldn't remember when he'd said it. It felt like a dream, too. Why did he have this effect on her? Things were foggy when he was around.

He had a nice tan.

"*Now, remember me, the real me.*" His whisper seethed into her. But there was too much to remember.

Touching would be better than remembering. She wanted to reach out and smooth her hands all over him.

She realized she was about to touch his chest so she pulled away. She'd never actually run her hands down someone's chest before. What was wrong with her?

He slipped her keys in his shirt pocket, glaring in her eyes, daring her to fish them out. Was this his idea of flirting? On previous deliveries, they'd flirted harmlessly. He was charming after all, but today his presence was intense. She met his blue eyes. Crystal blue. Too blue. She wanted to sink into them forever. This desire was too deep to deal with. She almost needed James to explain it. What would James say if she told him Steve made her heart beat this fast and all they were doing was standing here?

James never left her alone with men. He normally pushed guys like this back right about now, telling them to take a hike. Well, maybe not guys like *this*. She doubted anyone else was like Steve. So innocent yet so... *naughty*.

She blushed.

Bobby never made her blush. Never. Was this normal? Safe? It felt... *magical*. She glanced up and met his blue eyes. Yeah, definitely too blue.

She closed her eyes. She was twenty-one. If she wanted to strip down naked, she could. Maybe she should. She was hot enough. Naked against Steve would be nice. It was exactly what her body screamed.

"Hey, guess what I adopted to keep me company on these long hauls?" He asked the question mischievously but didn't wait for her to answer. No one ever did. "A puppy. I took your advice and found myself a dog, even named her after you."

"Oh?" A dog? It dawned on her that she hadn't answered him about the date to meet his pa. She was so... loopy. She wanted to go on a date with Steve.

She studied the bulge of keys in his pocket and glanced at his truck. Had he brought the puppy today? "I do have to open the store."

He grabbed her hand and a rush, a real live tingle, worked its way from his hand and jolted through her entire body. She caught her breath. It was so unreal. It reminded her of a nightmare she couldn't quite remember.

"The tingle," she mumbled and stepped back, because there was too much of him. How had he done that to her? It was thrilling, yet... *fearsome*. Torn between running and asking him to touch her again, she stared at his lips while a memory fought for freedom. "In the woods... you glowed." She frowned. "Was that a dream?"

"You remember a lot today. James must have whispered." He put a hand along her cheek and gazed in her eyes. "I missed you, but moments like this are worth the wait." His eyes swept over her body hungrily, ready to grab her, but a bald eagle swooped over them, making a pepping sound. Its wings were so close, Julia ducked.

Steve brought her down with him and watched it closely as it soared toward his truck. Its dive ended as if it hit a shield. An explosion of light met it and the majestic bird fell to the ground, shook itself off with another pepping remark, and flew off.

Steve was on his feet, ready to... she had no idea what he was ready to do, but he looked ready to tackle the poor bird.

"That was weird," she said.

He helped her to her feet. "I have to sneak you out of here. We have to get into the truck, it's safe."

She shook her head to clear it, confused. "I always feel like I'm... forgetting things around you. What's wrong?"

Steve faced her, grabbing her arms. "That bird makes you forget me. *Don't forget me. Remember the dreams.* I'm getting through. Not sure how, but don't forget me." His desperation was consuming. She didn't want to forget anything.

Argh. She needed focus.

"Julia." He was near her lips, talking to them. "Do you remember me in the woods?"

She nodded. "How does a bird make me forget?"

"James said the bird comes by your place every so often. Happens to be the same days you forget about me. Sometimes, Julia, I had your memories back, only to find them missing the next night."

"James knows you?"

"He used to. Do you remember Al?"

She shivered, but the name didn't invoke any other memories.

"He kidnapped you five years ago. I walked with you in the woods." He glanced over his shoulder to see if the bird was around. "Something is wrong with James now."

She scanned the skies, but if the eagle was lingering, she couldn't see it.

"Julia, say something."

"I dreamed of you," she confessed, wishing she could remember how or what happened in those dreams.

"Hell, believe me, I was there." He put his hands on her hips and she melted toward him, as close as she could. "We need to get out of here." He waited, eyes closed, daring her to be bold enough to touch him back.

She placed her right palm against his chest. Such a gentle, simple touch. Yet inside, everything changed. A woman exploded to life with need. She wrapped her left hand around his and took in a deep breath unable to let go.

Calmly, pretending nothing happened between them, she followed him as he led her to the front of his truck to visit his puppy or keep her safe. She couldn't remember anymore. Her world was fuzzy, distorted by urges.

"Yeah, I'll go with you to meet your pa, Steve. I'll go anywhere and everywhere with you," she said without thinking. "I'd probably even go to Hell and back with you." Something so unlike her. If James had heard her say it, he would have died of shock.

"Cool, but not something to joke about. That's kind of the problem. I don't want you to come to Hell with me. I know what happens on that realm, and it sucks. Can you focus? You look drunk." He took a deep breath as if his next word might be one he'd regret and he whispered, "*Comprends?*"

Julia stepped away from him as a flood of memories crashed into her. "You were the boy from the woods, the day I was kidnapped. Al..." She took another step away. To think, she'd just about climbed in his truck.

"Julia. I kept you safe."

"No." She almost ran toward the grocery store but froze. The bald eagle was between her and the door. Walking slowly toward her.

JULIA

Steve pulled Julia toward the truck. "In the truck, Julia, the bird can't come near it. Only you and James and I can climb in this truck."

"What?"

"My whispers protect it. Magic. Remember?"

Whispers. Magic.

She stumbled back and Steve caught her. *"Get in the back, it's safe,"* he whispered gently to her neck and goosebumps jumped to meet his words. He offered her a boost up the high step, and his hand ran up her leg, sending shivers along her thigh. For a moment, she forgot about the eagle, the memories, the dog, the store, her brother... it was a distant dream. She wanted him to touch her everywhere. She wanted something real like his touch.

He paused, too, enjoying the tingles with her.

The pepping of the eagle reminded her that the real world existed and this stranger was behind her and she should be at work. What was she doing? This wasn't like her at all. She opened her eyes and glanced around, focusing. Something was wrong. She shoved his hand off her thigh, pausing with it in hers. She felt drugged, entranced.

"Steve, where is the dog?" She searched the truck with her eyes. It was spotless. She doubted a puppy played in here. Her stomach knotted. Something wasn't right. Had he lied to her?

Claustrophobic, she tried to break free.

"Dog? Oh. I didn't bring her today. I'm sorry, I should have. That would have kept you focused. Do you hear me? Or are you entranced? Julia? Focus. Al is coming for you, *comprends?"*

Al. Yes, she remembered the shifter from five years ago who had pretended to be Uncle Jackson. Steve was planted in the doorway. Too intense. Too much Steve, yet not enough. As she got closer, she wanted more, despite the foreboding or maybe because of it. It was as if Steve was safe and everything else was... unsafe. Nothing made sense.

"Steve." She breathed against his chest, tired of this

confusion. She wanted to remember last night's dream in detail. He smelt outdoorsy. Woods. Pine trees. Like an adventure. It was almost hard to focus. She was dizzy. "Let me by. I shouldn't be alone with you."

"Julia, I have to protect you now that James is gone."

James. He'd mentioned James. "You know my brother?"

"Kind of. Get in the back, Julia. We don't have time anymore to build up defences between us. Please. Hurry."

"No, let me pass."

He brought up a gun.

She stared at it in his hand, by his side.

A gun.

Her entire world went blank. *What the hell?* This wasn't the first time she'd seen a gun. Its presence was like a knife holding her down. She didn't dare move as more memories washed into her.

What did he plan to do with the gun?

Kill the bird, the words jolted in her mind as if she'd thought them, but they were his.

The last time she'd seen a gun it had been pointed at her brother, and her mother took the hit... the memory paralysed her. Yet James said to never fear a gun because all it could do was kill you, and really, you were already dead, you just thought you were alive because you were that bloody stupid.

Focus. Steve asked her to focus and now he brought out a gun.

"Steve?"

He might have a gun, but the energy coming from him was thrilling. He put a hand on her shoulder and his touch was so exciting she forgot about the gun and met his eyes.

"I'm sorry, Julia. I know you hate guns. It's not loaded. I... I don't know the first thing about guns. This was James' idea. He said it would help us focus if the connection between us made us loopy, if the eagle showed and erased me from your mind again. Sometimes, I trust him too much. What does he know about this pull between us, eh?" His lips gently brushed hers as he spoke. "I don't want to whisper. Focus for me. Try not to touch me. Your confusion makes me dizzy. Should I whisper? Maybe it would be easier."

She remembered what he said five years ago about

whispering and how it changed free will. How could she not remember the boy from the woods?

"You're scaring me, Steve." She was more afraid of the idea of him whispering to her than anything.

"I doubt that. You don't scare easily. I see confusion in your soul, but not fear."

"You see my soul?"

He nodded. "I'm so entranced by it, I can't keep track of what's real. Please Julia. Please, I'll explain later. You have to trust me. I'd never hurt you." His voice was soft. "I have no other way to fix this, but I will. *Crawl in the sleeper. It's a big bed. I'll keep you safe. Have good dreams, Julia, good dreams about me all over you.* I can't wait to spend time with you in our cottage." His whispers penetrated her until it was all she wanted, all she needed to do was to crawl in the sleeper of his truck and dream. She wanted nothing more than to dream about the two of them in the stone cottage by the lake she didn't know. Entranced, she did as he asked, and when he shut the door, goosebumps overcame her.

STEVE

I did it. Deep breaths. Steve rested his head against the cold door to the sleeper of his cab, sorting through his emotions, identifying mostly fear and guilt. Breathing. Contemplating the locks in his hand.

The eagle didn't make sense to him. It wasn't a demon. Its soul was grey and cloudy like... damn. Al could shift into birds? What the heck? He had no idea Whisperers could shift into anything.

Steve sucked in quick breaths, very afraid. Mostly for Julia. Steve trusted his own arms less than Al's. All he wanted to do was please her over and over again. That wasn't healthy. Wasn't safe. If he wasn't careful, it's what he'd whisper.

He'd focus on protecting her. She was all he had left to protect. He'd lost everyone else.

Would this stupid plan of James' work? At least with her brother she'd been safe.

Steve took in a few more deep breaths. James said, if Al turned him, Steve was to do specific things. None of the things made sense to Steve, but he trusted James when it came to protecting Julia.

Steve snapped the first lock in place before he changed his mind, telling himself he planned this for way too long to get emotional. Yet he was emotional. *Moving was hard around Julia.*

He held the last two locks in his hand. If he didn't lock her in, he'd crawl beside her, and no one would be able to tear him off her. They would die going at it in the back of his truck.

He swallowed as the images consumed him.

He had to take things slow.

Already, his nails dug into the locks. The locks were to keep him out and away from her. How would he ever stop making love to her? She was like a magnet, no, like a tornado who sucked him in. He frowned. Had she thought that earlier or had he? He wasn't sure. He shouldn't have been in her thoughts, it was wrong.

No, it wasn't.

They were one.

Still. This felt like kidnapping. He had no idea if he whispered or not, and he shouldn't whisper to her. He'd been mesmerized with her body, with her soul... The pull of her was extreme.

His focus was off as he snapped lock two in place.

He did it?

Steve stared at it surprised. Heck. If he could do two locks, he could do three.

"Steve?" If his bond with her weren't so strong, he would have never heard her through the padding.

"Julia." His face was against the door instantly. "I'm sorry, Julia."

"I'm scared."

He knew she wasn't afraid of much, yet he believed her. "Me too, girl. Sleep. I'm here. You're safe. I won't hurt you. I'm strong enough." He snapped the last lock in place and the click it made echoed in the cab of the truck, whipping him back to reality. "I'm strong enough," he repeated in case the lie might become true. Well. It was time to face Al. Show Al what Steve learnt these past five years. *Binding a soul to an innocent woman was nothing.*

"*Satan*," he whispered.

"*Now what? I'm busy, you know, wild boy.*" A mysterious swirl materialized in front of him and the air in the cab chilled. Satan always called him wild boy, but Steve had no idea why.

"I have a creep after my girl, need me a demon to vanish him."

"*Protection? Or Stealth?*" Satan was the whispering conscience who protected demons, no matter the cost.

"Both. Brains too, they might have to think on the spot. Pick one who is hard to whisper to because my dad, he's known to whisper to demons."

"*Mischief is always happy to help, ask him.*"

When Steve had shared a pizza and beer with Mischief last week—well, Mischief ate the souls out of fish, but Steve enjoyed the pizza and beer—he'd said Al whispered to him and he'd looked terrified. Steve didn't want to ask his friend to go up against him.

"Anyone else?"

"*I suppose Scat might be bored. Can you whisper in your state, wild boy?*"

"Told you, I don't mess with your demons. They deserve to live happy and free. Most are my only friends, and I don't whisper to friends."

"*Yet you bother me. You think a whispering conscience has time for your Wild problems?*"

"If it's a bother to help me, then forget it. I thought I taught your demons neat ways to protect themselves in Dreamland, but if you don't think so..."

The dark cloud let out a long grumble. "*Tell me his name.*"

"Al Eagle."

"*No.*" A pause. "*Keep my demons away from the earth bound.*"

"Earth bound? Explain."

The cloud vanished. Steve didn't know why he couldn't use demons to fight Al, but he trusted Satan when it came to demons. He wouldn't risk it.

No James. No demons. Al versus Steve. Well. First, he had to bring Julia to safety and unbind her soul from his so if something went wrong when he faced Al, she didn't die with him.

And Bobby. He needed to keep that prick from getting in the way.

The eagle soared over them. With Julia's keys in his hand, Steve rushed to her car so he could hide it. He opened the door and pulled away when the stench of wet dog blasted him. *Wow, Julia. What a mess.* The floor of her car was littered in gravel and crushed leaves, empty soda cans and sub wrappings. Yuck. At first, he climbed in feeling disgusted with her. Then the idea hit him like a wave of freedom... could he be messy like this, too? The thought was thrilling. He glanced around. Al had no more control over his life yet he followed his strict regime. Why? What was wrong with him? Why did he let his father dictate his life? He could steal a cue from Julia and toss garbage around. Steve chuckled at the idea. What a girl. He moved a wrapper aside with his foot to reveal a switchblade. What the heck? He shook the soda can and it too concealed a much larger knife.

Wow Julia. He smirked. *Nice.*

He searched her car and actually found a few more weapons. He knew Al made her life hell, but he didn't know it affected her stability. Guilt rubbed his soul. He was the worst Whisperer in the world. One girl. One blasted girl and he couldn't even protect her.

Steve pulled out, driving her car toward her place while he thought about how perfect things could be for them if Al wasn't around.

Following James' detailed plan, he stopped about a mile out of town. He pulled over by an old house and left a simple note on the seat. She was sure to be missing for days before they'd find the car, and with the note, they'd think she'd jumped in the water and was long gone.

He was a monster.

Still. It made sense. This would keep Bobby busy.

Quickly, Steve jogged to the store. The eagle dived for him a few times, but Steve tossed a few whispers at the wind and a gust took the bird out of the way.

For now, the bird was content watching. A terrifying chill swept over him as he studied the bird's soul while he ran. What if that was Al? He'd have to ask Mischief if shape-shifting magic existed.

"Hi, Steve," the workers greeted him, waiting by the back door of the grocery store.

Steve flashed his winning smile and played his part. "Hey. No one was here when I arrived so I went for breakfast." Lying was easy for him. He hated that.

"Yeah, there isn't anyone here to open the store yet. Tammy went to find a manager. Julia should have arrived by now." No one looked too upset. "Her brother left today. She probably wanted to see him off. She'll be here soon."

Steve glanced around, pretending not to listen, but watching their souls for any sign that something was wrong. No one gave him a second glance. They rarely did anyway, well, except for Julia.

He couldn't wait to slip his hands on her. Tonight. Alone in that big bed, all night. He'd done his homework, and despite what his old man had said, Steve would find a way to make her happy.

JAMES

A semi pulled into the fuel station. Stations were few between Parksville and Regina so James was used to the big rigs stopping here to fuel up with synthetic oils for the journey. Julia drilled it in him to be wary of them. It was instinct to pull his bag closer to his body. Then he relaxed when he realized she wasn't around to freak out. She actually let him go. He was free.

The idea petrified yet excited him. Did she know his rage was out of control? He was too tired to comprehend the full meaning of her final statement. *Time to let go.* Really, it was him who was letting go. He let out a long breath, trusting Bobby to protect her.

His finger shook. Could he do this? Walk away from her? He didn't have much choice. She wasn't safe with him anymore. Not that he trusted Bobby a whole lot, but more than he trusted himself.

James stifled a yawn. He was beyond exhausted. Jules was having nightmares again and he was up half the night fighting off the rage they ignited in him. What did she dream about to trigger such intense fury in him? Well, not what—it was *who*? *Who* did he need to beat the *merde* out of now?

His rage was wild. Stepping back for a spell wouldn't hurt. This prick might come out of the woods and onto the prairies to play. Besides, he needed to do something with this life.

James rubbed his hand over his forehead. When he pulled it away, his index finger twitched. He hated that but he couldn't control it. The habit happened whenever he thought about the *merde* his sister went through and the things he'd done to fix them. Fix them. Hmmm.

For some reason, innocent girls like Jules attracted pinheads. He wasn't sure what gave her nightmares this week, or... *argh.* Why lie to himself about this? Those were clearly hot sex dreams she'd had, and whoever was responsible for them, he wanted to rip in two.

She'd be safe with Bobby because he was about creating an image, and James liked that, but it wasn't Bobby turning her on like a banshee in heat. She wouldn't even look Bobby in his eyes.

Who then? *Who* the hell was it? It pissed him off that she hid this from him. Jules wasn't one to hide things. She knew better. He couldn't protect her if she hid things. She knew what happened the last time she kept secrets, and they had no one left to lose. It was just them. Then again, she wasn't herself lately. She was... his brain searched for the word he wanted—*Wild?* The definition came with the word, only he doubted he'd find a definition like this in any old dictionary.

Druid Wild magic allows demons, mortals, and magical creatures the freedom of being themselves without restriction of society's beliefs—without consequence for their choices.

Victims of Wild magic appear unfocused and uncaring about things they normally were passionate about. They fixate on self-gratification and basic primal urges: hunger, sex, and survival.

The most vulnerable are those who put others above themselves. To access Wild magic, use a whispering ritual. Housing it in a Druid tattoo is ideal as the host can control it. The owner of this magic then spreads it with nothing but a whisper.

This was how she acted and it pissed him off because Jules needed to focus, prepare... he had no idea what for. He didn't like her *Wild*, meant someone had *whispered* to her. Used magic on her.

The driver climbed out of the truck that normally delivered to Jules' store and nodded to James. It was instinct on James' part to evaluate him with one quick sweep. He had a tattoo James recognized instantly as the biohazard symbol. A chill washed over him. Was this the Wild Magic Whisperer?

Why was the idiot grinning at him as if he was happy to see him? He didn't know this guy. James never forgot a name or a face. Yet he knew the symbol. It belonged to the enemy. *The enemy?* What a strange thought, but it was exactly how he felt.

James crossed his arms and stared at the empty highway, as if wishing for the bus to appear would make it materialize. Why was it late?

"Nice day, eh?" The driver of the semi came up to him.

James gave the driver one more swift glance, scanning for simple details to add to his first assessment. His mind clicked the details together. *Steve* was embroidered on his workshirt, which was ironed and well taken care of. This guy grew up under a rigid regime. He'd chalked Steve up as a military guy on first appearance, but now he changed his mind. This look wasn't recent. He grew up with these values. Yeah, Steve was raised under a firm fist. He was in good shape, too. Now that he was closer, James was impressed. He wasn't as well-built as James, but when his shirt tightened, he saw the muscles indicating that he wasn't only a runner, but a hard worker. His tan suggested outdoor work, too. Julia's age.

Why would he think Steve his enemy? 'Cause of a tattoo? Weird, but tattoos often stirred his anger.

James knew all this by looking at him, but a lot of good this talent did him. He sighed. He couldn't believe the bus was late, and focused on that. Maybe he should call Jules to drive him.

"Miss your ride?"

So he was determined to make small talk. Why?

"Hmmm… Looks like the bus is late."

"You headed to the city?" Steve asked.

"Considering the RCMP. Off to check things out. Not planning on coming back."

"Cool. I'm through every week, know the area well, but I'm not sure I've met you." He was staring at James as if he couldn't believe James didn't know him.

"Then why you looking at me like you want to sit and share a beer? I have enough friends, back the hell off."

"You remind me of my best friend, is all. Haven't seen him in about two weeks. It was his birthday. Did you need a ride? I'm heading to Regina. Might hit the library today for research. Did you know a tornado blew through the library in 1913?"

"June 30, 1912. It was a Sunday so most people were at home but the bloody tornado reached winds of over 417 kilometers an hour. It hit more than the library. Twenty-eight people died, but so many lost homes and pets that a part of them never recovered. The library itself had been open for six weeks." James could have kept teaching but Steve stared at him with the biggest, stupidest grin he'd ever seen so he walked away. Why did he do that? How did he even know something like that? He'd never picked up a history book, yet he could see the cyclone coming in the city as if he'd witnessed it himself.

Steve kept pace beside him. "You know dumbass things. I could use the company if you want a ride."

James knew Jules wouldn't approve of him bumming a ride. She was cautious about things like getting in a stranger's vehicle, or going near strangers, or talking to strangers. Then again, she'd talked about a Steve truck driver on several occasions yet for the love of these prairies, he couldn't remember what she'd said about him. He rubbed his forehead, frustrated. His memory was usually infallible.

Still, logic told him Steve delivered to her store and therefore it was easy to assume Jules knew him. It was also fair to say he was probably the Steve with the pinhead pa. That much he remembered, but it was foggy, as if a dream. Still, Steve's pa annoyed him.

"*Julia ever mention me?*" The guy's voice was hardly a whisper yet his question ignited a memory of Jules talking about him. Her eyes lighting up. James thought back to when she touched her stomach lightly in the car. He'd seen her do that before, when she'd mentioned Steve. Not many guys got a reaction that physical.

He could see why. James liked Steve, too. *He was the enemy*, a voice nagged him, like with the memories, he didn't know why he felt this.

What if this was the guy she dreamed about? James took a better look at him. Yeah, might be. He had a rough look to him that might get the girls Wild. If Jules was into him, technically, that made him a friend of his sister so bumming a ride from him was fine.

"You deliver to the store in town? Where my sister works?"

"If your sister is Julia, I asked her out and she said yeah.

Looks like we might have to face my dad this weekend. Should be hell, but she's game."

James took a step to tower over him, ready to pound the guy to dust. "Hmmm."

Steve didn't back up. He grinned. It impressed James when guys stood their ground around him, and he smiled at him even if he shouldn't have. He liked something about Steve. What?

"Then maybe I will take you up on that ride so we get to know each other properly." James glanced at the ticket in his hand. He'd squeezed it in his angry fist. Why did Jules dating set him off? Never failed. So far, zero scumbuckets lived up to his expectations. Still, he had hope for this one. If she agreed to a date, James would at least give him a chance. One.

James took a couple deep breaths and fixed the ticket. He could get his forty bucks back and have extra money… He could use extra cash. God he could use the forty bucks for anything other than bus fare. "Give me a minute."

"I have time. I'm unloading a crate here."

Inside, James went to the counter. "Hey, Jeanne."

The redhead behind the counter smiled. James grew up in Parksville and everyone knew him. "Yeah, James?"

"Do you know the pinhead out there?"

"Steve? Sure. He's been delivering for a while. Why?"

"He offered to give me a ride to the city. Could save me forty bucks. Should I jump on that?"

"The bus is running late today. Might be another hour or even more, James."

"You serious? Why?"

Jeanne shrugged while refunding his ticket. "Dunno."

"Thanks. You're swell. I'll do this."

"Anytime, James. I know how hard it is."

James wasn't sure if she meant living with Jules or leaving home, and he was afraid to ask.

"And Jeanne, if this… Steve." His name was spewed from his mouth. "Wanted to date my sister, what would you say? Is he worthy? Nice enough to date Jules?"

"Our Julia? Of course. Steve's a great guy. Not many left, but James… the choice is up to Julia. Don't you think?"

"Hmmm.... I suppose. In the end it might be, but someone needs to weed out the thistles. *Comprends?*"

She paused for a moment and smiled as if the world made sense. "Of course I understand. Now, you get your butt to the city and best keep your nose out of your sister's love life. You're not cupid, you know."

James didn't see that happening anytime soon but he nodded just the same. "Cupid is..." He wanted to say a stupid myth but he was drowning in facts that made him pause. "He's busy and could use a hand." He rushed out in case Steve changed his mind, but not before pushing aside the new details he knew about Eros, aka Cupid, the Whisperer of love. Wow, the guy had a lot to do.

Steve was shutting the back of his semi. James paused, studying him. Watching how slow he worked, as if entranced.

"So you're into my sister, eh?" James slapped Steve on the back.

"She made me tingly when she grabbed my hand. Told me she'd never let it go again with tingles that wicked."

She touched him!?! James was shocked. Jules was not one to touch people. "She looks you in the eyes?"

"Hell yeah. And said something about going to Hell with me, but I'm not supposed to tell you that part."

"Hmmm. Then why did you?" James clenched his fists again, yet he couldn't bring himself to punch this guy.

"So you don't beat me up. Why else? Look at you, ready to wallop me." Steve got ready to climb in the truck. "We good?"

"I don't know." James could see Jules with Steve, yet the idea angered him. The rage was confusing.

"Why not?" Steve asked.

"I have to think, *comprends?* Let me think."

"Take your time. *Let me know when you're finished thinking and you're ready to live this life.*"

"This life?" James repeated the whisper. A heavy burden was on him. Was there something he was supposed to do in this life? Because really, he didn't want to waste it.

JAMES

"That's a wild scratch on your arm," James said as he settled in to Steve's semi, fishing for details. They hadn't moved yet, Steve was busy with a clipboard.

James relaxed. Jules was safe for a spell and… he glanced at Steve. He might have found the prick giving Jules those Wild dreams. Could Steve protect Jules from…? James scratched his head. Was James the threat? For the love of these prairies, he couldn't remember why Jules was in danger.

Steve glanced up from his work order. "This scratch?" It ran all the way up his arm. "Wrestled me a ferocious kitty. Beast broke into a house while my old man and I were hunting up north. Most dangerous thing I ever did, but I stepped between the kitty and a woman protecting her child."

James paused. Was he serious? "You fought a wildcat? Like a bobcat?"

"Gee, Scat is more like a panther. Who the hell needs protection from a bobcat?"

Scat? James shivered but the name didn't invoke more information than that. "There are two types of men in the world, Steve: those who protect at all cost and those who survive at all costs. You expect me to believe you're the worthier of the two?"

Steve chuckled. "Acted on instinct, nothing worthy about that. Most days, I feel like a monster, not a man."

Yeah. James nodded. If Jules wanted to hook up with Steve, that was cool with him. *Holy truth*, that would be great. Heck with Bobby, this was the one. He had no idea why he was excited about the idea but everything in him wanted to see them together. In fact, he was so excited, he felt all… *sparkly inside?*

Steve's eyes were huge as he stared at James. "You're sparkling. You okay? I mean, you… ah… comfy?" Steve dropped the clipboard in a slot along his seat.

Wow. Steve had a home for everything.

"It's a long haul," Steve reminded him. "Much more comfortable than an unreliable bus, eh? They tell you why it was late?"

"Nope."

"Oh. Weird. What are the reasons a bus could be late? Wanna make bets, see who is closest?" He fired up the truck.

"Flat tire would be the most obvious answer. Of course the most logical would be pick up or delivery being late in one spot delaying the rest over a series of spots, leading to extreme delays later in the day." He shrugged as his mind actually calculated how late each stop would have to be to end up being an hour late. Cripes, his brain was annoying. "But what do I know, right?" He wiped the numbers clean from his mind and stared out the window.

"That's boring. What if the driver was tired of driving and pulled over to read for a spell? Then decided to share the story with those on her bus?" Steve checked his mirrors.

Why wasn't he driving? What were they waiting for?

"Yeah, right." James chuckled, the possibility hadn't figured in the equations because human nature set the odds against it. "What are the chances of that happening?"

"Well. If I'm right, promise not to punch me, no matter what I tell you I did with your sister. Okay? Plus, you have to promise to trust me." He smirked.

James clenched his fists, ready to hit him, then he realized it was a joke. "Oh, you're on. If I'm right and it's a flat tire, I punch you for the heck of it. Deal?"

"Well, that's not fair. How about I punch you for taking the most practical bet?"

James laughed. "*Sacré!* Funny, Steve! I like that. Think your puny muscles could smash me?"

Steve laughed, too. Then he hit the door leading to the back compartment. "You comfy, too?" His hand lingered on the metal door. Steve closed his eyes and his laugher ended. He was... frozen?

James darted his eyes over the scene, trying to grasp what had happened, but he couldn't focus. He was hot. Then like last night, anger exploded in him. "You okay man? Why aren't you moving?" James demanded, leaning forward uneasy, resisting the urge to smoke him.

Last night, when he'd heard Jules talking in her sleep he'd opened the door to her bedroom and felt... exactly like he did now. Angry. Only this time it was Steve sitting in front of him with his eyes closed.

Was Steve dreaming?

Why would it piss him off?

It was... weirdly infuriating.

Steve opened his eyes and stared at James in disbelief. "Huh?" Steve swallowed. "Sorry." Steve took two deep breaths pulling himself together. "Sugar rush or something."

"Something?"

"Just dreaming. It always gives me a head rush." He rubbed his tattoo wildly and glanced at James with panicky eyes as if James might kill him.

"Good thing you weren't driving." James sat back. The new energy had him tense and angry and everything blurred, like last night. And the night before. And the one before that...

He focused on his surroundings, hoping to obliterate this rage. He picked a dog collar off the floor. The tag read Julia. Hmmm. He'd named his dog Julia. "Where is Julia?" James asked showing him the collar he'd picked up.

"In the back."

"Bring her out," James ordered.

"Julia stays in the back where she's safe." Steve gripped the steering wheel yet they hadn't moved.

"You named your dog after your date? Did you name her?"

"My date, no. The dog, yeah." Steve glanced at James and back at the road. "I don't like you this way. You're not yourself. One minute you're sparkly and happy and the next fiery. What the heck is wrong with you? Why are you so weird these days?"

"What's wrong with *moi*? That's my sister's name and it's your dog's name. You're the weird one."

"I know. I asked her out, remember? Julia. The hot girl from the grocery store. Long brown hair, keeps it in a pony. Brown eyes, long lashes, two dozen freckles on her nose. Twenty-four. Exactly." Steve sat back, not driving. He looked ready to get naked and jack-off at the image he'd created.

James frowned. The world fuzzed in as if he was tripping on bad drugs. Same rage as last night swept over him. *Jules was dreaming... only Jules wasn't here.* "That's my sister, calm down and focus on me for a minute. You asked her out before today?"

"I asked her out every week for years. Not that I mean to." His voice was feeble. He closed his eyes and mumbled, "Damn it. I can't focus around her. How can I drive, James? I need help. Help me get this rig moving."

He needed to focus? Well, James needed more facts. "So asking her out is instinct?"

"Yeah." Steve clutched the steering wheel until his knuckles turned white, then he slowly put the truck in motion. "Your sister takes a long time to say yes."

"Most men go through me if they want to actually survive the process. Focus on that."

Steve glanced over, pale. "You're here, aren't you? Despite my better judgement."

What was that supposed to mean? "You asking me for permission to date my sister? After the fact? Is this some sort of get-to-know-my-date's-brother ride along?"

"You're not the problem, James, you're the blasted solution. I'm telling you I'll marry her and I hope to hell you keep a certain someone out of the way for me so I can undo the shit he did to us, first."

James adjusted himself so he could glare at Steve. Maybe he didn't like him. He never met anyone before who he couldn't get a proper read on. Was he the enemy, his friend, or some guy he needed to toss into Oblivion?

With a deep breath, Steve got them moving. He watched the road but it took an awful lot of focus. He pushed the semi to a higher gear, then glanced over.

"You keep a pretty clean truck," James said, making small talk while he categorized this guy.

They picked up speed.

"She's my baby. I live in here. Have to keep her clean. Besides it's not as if I hide weapons in my trash. Nope, no need when the air around me is lethal." He wiped an invisible piece of dust off the dashboard and inspected his fingers as if it might bite him.

What did that mean? Why would he say that? Did he know about Jules' weird obsession about hiding weapons...

everywhere? James studied him, but Steve gave nothing away. Nothing. Everyone had tells. How did Steve hide from him?

"Well, it's clean." There was no other word for it in James' mind. The truck was perfect, not even a grain of sand on the floor. Jules would go nuts in something this clean. She liked things crazy messy.

Then again, this type of cleanliness was a different kind of berserk. Every knob shone and the windows were insect splatter free. "I have to ask, how do you keep the bugs off your windshield? I mean ours is smeared in grasshopper guts and stuff. Actually, I prefer things messy, but I might come to terms with things clean, too." Yeah, James liked Steve for the opposite reasons he liked Jules. This was interesting. It's as if they were... a peanut butter and jelly sandwich not put together.

And there it was, he'd classed him as perfect for Jules.

James had never actually found a guy he thought was perfect for her before. Bobby would do in a pinch to protect her, but deep down, James knew someone like Steve was out there. He never actually thought he'd be sitting in a semi looking at him.

"I'll let you in on a secret—Pledge, and I thought that this morning myself, messy is kind of nice, isn't it? Freeing. Sometimes, you gotta smoosh the sandwich together, right?"

Could Steve read his thoughts or had James said that aloud? James glanced over, sure he hadn't said the sandwich part aloud.

So. Steve was a mind reader. Strange but that didn't surprise him at all, there were all kinds of weird in this world.

Not that it was a big deal if Steve could read minds, James could think in a few other languages. Like with the facts, he knew them. If someone spoke a language around him he didn't know, his brain made sense of things until he knew what they were saying and could answer.

What were they talking about aloud? Oh yeah, his clean truck. "Pledge? You mean the furniture cleaner? We don't keep that around our house. Jules has a phobia of the stuff. She doesn't like chemicals."

"None?" Steve looked surprise by this. He pulled the sleeve

on his left arm down while driving, to hide his biohazard tattoo. "I suppose that makes sense," he said, even though nothing Jules did made sense to anyone except her. "And yes, Pledge, the one and only. Stuff makes the bugs slide right off. I'd bathe in it if I could."

"Hmmm…" Movement in the cab behind them made James turn around. It sounded like whimpering and reminded James of the sounds Jules made in her sleep while dreaming those dreams that annoyed him.

Steve clutched the steering wheel. "I have to pull over. Talk to me. I need sugar. Grab water under the seat." He panted while beads of sweat collected on his forehead as he slowed the truck, but didn't stop.

Sugar? Yeah, whatever dude, James thought. He didn't know what had Steve so fired-up, and he sure as hell couldn't ask.

Served him right for catching a ride with someone dangling over Oblivion.

"Yeah, I could use air myself. Those sounds piss me off." No reason. He wanted to kill someone, and frankly, Steve would do just fine. "You sure you're okay? Because I can kill you."

"Kill me? Oh yeah, the keys." Steve fumbled with keys he pulled from his shirt pocket. "Take these." He tossed James some keys and the anger in him died instantly. "Give these to me when you trust me again. They're the keys to my sleeper. Let me stop so we can discuss things."

Discuss things? James examined the keys, wondering what was wrong with this freak. Why would Steve trust him with his keys? Yet James was much calmer with the keys in his hands. They could be the keys to anything, yet James didn't care. If Steve trusted him with his keys, he couldn't be all-bad. "You're weird."

"Weird I could live with. I'm a monster."

"And giving me these keys helps with that?" James tightened them in his fist, ready to hand them back. Yet he didn't. He wanted to know what was happening.

"I trust you, you trust me."

Once the beast stopped, Steve faced James, clearly ready to talk about whatever had him goofy a moment ago. James didn't want to hear it. He undid his seatbelt, made his way across the cab, and smoked Steve. His head slammed into the window leaving him unconscious.

There. Discussion over. Cripes, that felt nice to hit him. He should have done that earlier.

James had no idea what was going on but he always responded to his anger and if he felt like hitting this pinhead, so be it. Done. Hopefully, Jules would forgive him.

He turned on the radio to calm himself. He needed to hear those voices from that *Get Naked and Muddy Revolutionary* group again, telling him how to fix things. People sharing good stories, good news. He took deep breaths, calming the rage. Anything could trigger a reaction, and once he calmed, well, he'd deal with the consequences. It was easier to talk his way out of trouble than most would think. Besides, he was mad, but Steve was clearly having other issues that wouldn't be so easy to explain.

The radio blared news at him, *"Here's a funny story, Grace; the Greyhound bus that travels the southern part of the province met delays today when the driver pulled over near Nullepart, Saskatchewan and wouldn't continue. She pulled out a Get Naked and Muddy magazine and read, delaying passengers by hours. The driver commented that she needed to share what she'd read with the other passengers."* Grace chuckled, but James turned off the radio.

What the heck was going on? Nullepart was by their place, not far from Parksville. It wasn't a town anymore, just a cemetery with an old abandoned church.

James sat and took several breaths. The sounds from the sleeper stopped. Something was wrong. How could Steve know that?

"Did you hit me?" Steve asked rubbing his jaw.

"Yeah, you freaked me out. Need another one? Or you got your hormones under control? I swear if you so much as touch yourself I am outta here."

Steve rubbed his jaw. "Wow. You respond well to my whispers."

"What does that mean?"

"First off, cut the swearing. You don't have to come off tough or stupid to me, I know who you are. I know how your brain constantly dumps facts on you that you have no idea what to do with. It's information you access from a place known as Knowledge Realm. It's an entire world of facts you built in a previous life and your soul is linked to it. You use the facts from this plane of spiritual existence to help you accomplish great things in this life. You told me once that knowing everything is your goal, because then, when you become an immortal light you will whisk that knowledge onto the world in one final whisper."

That did sound like a good plan. "I don't remember saying that." James was frustrated. If what Steve said was true, then James knew weird things because of past lives, yet why couldn't he remember them?

"I access a realm like you do. Mine is Dreamland and you come to this realm when you sleep and we talk. I teach you what I know about whispering and you teach me what you know about life, girls, fighting, and shit I won't ever have to know. You used to remember the things we talked about, but for the past two weeks when I go to see you, you try to kill me."

"Whispering." James repeated the word and expected to be bombarded by facts, but he got nothing except the information about Eros and Cupids again. "Cupid was a Love Whisperer," he mumbled.

"That's right. A real hero. We train to protect your sister from my dad, and it was going well," Steve told him.

"Why don't I remember this?"

"Good question. You went from wanting to be a cupid to a cop. Said you were moving to Regina. Best guess is that Al whispered to you through someone you trust. Which means he's been watching you for a while and waiting to learn your weaknesses."

"Al? That sounds familiar yet I got nothing. Information wants to come to me but can't. How do I go to it?"

"You didn't investigate in the sleeper, did you?" Steve asked rubbing the back of his head.

"No. Should I?" James studied the keys. The idea hadn't even crossed his mind, but now he wanted to. "I was more concerned about what has you so turned on. For a guy excited about dating my sister, why the heck you getting off with me sitting beside you?"

"She's sending me dreams. Images in my mind. It's a magical connection we share. Because of the cottage we built, I can see her dreams while sitting here. Do you believe in magic, James?"

"Hmmm... 'Fraid I've seen a few things that don't require blind beliefs."

Steve actually looked relieved. "Well. Your fist set me straight. Let's see. I do that again, you hit me and go in. Deal?"

"Nope. You won the bet. I'll give you one free pass where I won't hit you, but I ain't promising it will last. And like hell will I trust you, yet."

"Really? Cool. Any questions about what I told you? Aren't you curious about what a Whisperer is or does? Do you remember the cottage?"

"Wow, you're weird." James dropped the keys in his pocket, because truth was, he wanted a safety zone. Steve was one brick shy of a load, magic or not. "I know how to talk to people, moron. I might not go around calling myself a Whisperer, but I get what I want with words. Like a cupid arrow, I aim and fire."

"Cupids again. You're nuts with that. I told you once before it's called a Love Whisperer and the power is so rare only one Notebook I know about had any reports on it. My mom used to read it to me. It was about a freak who called himself Hero."

"Hero?" Did Steve know Hero? James slid forward as if the next words out of Steve's mouth might change his life.

"Yeah, he's a warrior who was so overly intelligent, I couldn't understand half his teachings, but his stories were funny. I told you some, but you insisted I was missing important details."

James frowned. "Impossible that I forgot Hero." James glanced at Steve. Cripes, he could remember that conversation but Steve was a blur in the memory. "It's not that your stories weren't complete, it's that you didn't understand the teachings." He rubbed his head, no idea what he meant.

"You're remembering. Cool. I've seen you in action, and I

must admit you are smooth, but let me show you how it works with magic. Sit and put on your seatbelt."

James did.

"Now. Take off your seatbelt."

"Why?"

"Do you want to remove it?"

"Not really."

Steve smirked and whispered, "*Remove the seatbelt*." This time his voice was softer and James knew he had to take off his seatbelt. It was urgent, there was no doubt, he had the clip undone before Steve said belt. It was a brilliant idea. It was probably James' idea actually. Steve didn't look smart enough to think something like that up, even though he'd said it.

"You'd better remove yours too," James said. "Clearly it's important."

"Yeah. There you have it. A whisper. It affects your free will, alters your reality, which in my mind, makes it dark magic. There might be a good use for it, but I can't find it. So I don't whisper. I spend my time undoing what my old man does and I spent years protecting Julia and training you."

"So if I don't remember our training does that mean it never happened?"

"James, I don't remember being born, yet here I am. So you gonna help me with this idiot between Julia and me?"

"I highly doubt Officer Bobby is a problem for a guy like you. You should hear my sister moaning for you at night. Trust me, you're the winner here. Scoop her up and back off."

Steve pulled onto the highway but James wasn't doing up his belt, heck no.

JULIA

Where was she? In a bed?

It was dark.

The rocking movement of a vehicle woke her but Julia wanted to return to her dreams. To the warmth of his arms. She'd read somewhere that if you held someone long enough your heart beat as one. She wondered if it was true for dreams too, because it sure felt like he was dreaming with her.

Julia felt great, so refreshed. That was the best sleep. She sat up and stretched with plenty of sitting room, but no legroom. This must be a bed or… The truck. She was in the back of Steve's truck.

She made out the outline of the door and banged on it, the last trace of the dream floated off her fists. Where was the handle? Julia touched each wall. They surrounded her. Smooth. It was a giant bed. She ruffled the bed, and found a blanket and a couple pillows. Nothing else. Yet they were so inviting.

Things weren't blurry anymore.

Why was Al after her again? Was she safe in here? It felt safe. She grabbed a pillow and smelt it. Steve's fragrance seared through her and Julia pressed her ear to the door. Two muffled voices echoed on the other side.

Was that James? Was she dreaming?

It was James! "James!" she yelled. *Why was James here?* The idea was bizarre. No, no, Steve said he knew James. Why didn't James tell her he knew Steve? They were supposed to tell each other everything.

Everything.

Yet how could she tell him anything? Her memories were like dreams.

Yet were they?

Her voice was dry and it echoed in the small compartment. The voices on the other side didn't change their tone. She banged several more times.

Her ears rang, but she didn't seem to make any progress. "I want to know what's going on," she yelled, banging.

Julia couldn't believe Steve would harm her.

Steve.

His touch lingered with her. Like in her dream. Was that a dream?

Were the dreams real? *Oh my God!* What if the dreams were real?

Sitting alone in the back of the semi, anything felt possible.

Steve said he had to protect her. From Al.

She banged on the door for Steve to let her out. Enough of this, they needed to talk.

JAMES

James glanced at the sleeper in Steve's truck. Sealed tight. "Cripes man, how big's your dog? You hiding a bunch of rabid wolves?" His body tensed, ready for action but James wasn't fastening his seatbelt. Not a chance in hell. He said he wouldn't punch Steve, he didn't say anything about tearing him to pieces.

"James, what made you jump to the conclusion that my dog is back there?" Steve wondered.

James replayed the conversation in his mind. He had no idea, but probable solutions pointed to it being a dog. He glanced at the collar he'd tossed on the floor. It had a price tag on it.

His finger twitched wildly. Many improbable solutions nagged him. Really. Why not put the collar on the dog? He had a place for everything so why leave the collar lying around?

"She's panicking," Steve said. "We'll pull over at the next stop and I'll calm Julia down. Okay?"

James frowned as the improbable solutions gained favour. "Julia is a stupid name for a grown man to name his dog. Change it."

"You always this bossy? You realize you're a kid, right?"

James glanced over. He didn't feel like a kid. "You realize you're a bloody pinhead who asked my sister out and is dangling over Oblivion? *Comprends?*"

"*Ah oui, je comprends, mon ami.*"

James smiled. "*Sacré*. The pinhead knows French. Well anyway, I can be as bossy as I want if I'm right. As I was saying, now that you asked my sister out you need a better name for your dog. She'll think you're an idiot. You know, I'm excellent at handling dogs. I wouldn't mind having a look at her. Jules talks to dogs, kind of like you explained: whispering, or whatever."

"No, that ain't gonna happen until I know what's wrong with you." Steve laughed, and the sound was crisp and dry and it actually made James shift uneasy in his seat. "Julia and I need to talk alone. She's afraid and your anger isn't in check."

Hmmm. James didn't like his tone. The way Steve said the name of his dog was the same way it caught when he'd said his sister's name. James wasn't so sure there was a dog back there.

The banging grew louder. James turned to steal a better look at the door. He almost shouted, *What the hell, buddy? You have three padlocks on this door*? Luckily, his instincts took over and he silently gave Steve a questioning look, but Steve watched the road. Something strange was happening and James had to accept these improbable things as real.

So what was he accepting exactly?

No one kept a dog padlocked in the sleeper of their truck then gave a hitchhiker the key unless they were losing it and Steve seemed relatively sane.

Steve mumbled to himself now, whispering stuff, rubbing his tattoo, invoking his magic.

Okay, maybe sane was a stretch. Steve was dangling over Oblivion. Only way to describe it. He could be either the enemy or the friend.

"I like your tattoo. Wanna see mine?" James rolled up the sleeve on his T-shirt to show off the eye on his upper shoulder. He rubbed it too, invoking his own type of magic, but his was real—fear. "It means these muscles are watching you." James tensed them. The air in the cab was heavy, as if James might rip Steve apart for no reason. Steve was clearly strong, but not like James.

"It would take a maniac on a death wish to even think about going near you or your sister. It's what I like about you. It's why I trained you so well. You took good care of Julia for me, and I appreciate that. Now we clearly have a problem. Someone compromised you. You can't even see the truth about what I'm keeping in my cab. Since when don't you believe in improbable things?"

Steve was right, James felt a block in his thought process. "Hmmm." What exactly was bothering him? "You talk about my sister like she's yours. I don't like that."

"She is. If this is what is clouding your judgement, get over it."

"She's *my* sister. Mine." James stressed the mine.

"She's my soulmate, and cupid says that trumps a grumpy brother," Steve tossed back, as if they'd held this conversation before and Steve was used to winning it.

He was right, cupid did say that. Only James didn't know why or when. James rolled his sleeve down and settled back in the seat. He hadn't put on his seatbelt. He didn't want to. In fact, he might never wear it again.

"Yet the warning needed to be made clear for a few pinheads that she's my sister and now I might need to make it for you. I'm not sure how clear this needs to get and I'm not sure why I'm making it. If she looked you in the eyes and took your hand, she made the choice, but if you're nutso, I'm setting ground rules anyway, hell with it." His grip slipped on his anger. Steve might tumble into Oblivion quickly.

Steve chuckled. "Damn, you're cool. You should see your soul. Incredible. You're reaching out to spiritual realms and accessing information while you sit here and calmly yell at me, sparkling like some cupid-freak."

"Sparkling? Realms? Like magical planes?"

"Of course. Is this how you find the answers you need? Stop thinking about tossing me into Oblivion, that isn't a realm that can contain me."

James panicked inside. He needed information he couldn't access. "Why not? What do you know about Oblivion?"

"Spiritual realm not many escape. It's where Satan sends the guys who use his demons inappropriately for a time out."

Wow. James sat back. "Yet you can't be contained there? Why not?"

"I whisper to my soul, send it back to the Mortal Realm." He shrugged. "Nothing special, I have powers that can't contain my soul." Steve smirked. "Plus, I made friends with Satan. It wasn't hard, he shares my sense of humour."

James tossed him on the friend side, because when he said things like that, he wanted to learn a lot more about Steve. "So why did you need your tattoo?"

"My old man gave me this tattoo. Does knowing that help? It's used to contain the magic I was blessed with on my sixteenth birthday, from the soulmate bonding whisper Al performed on Julia and me. Stupidest ritual ever, but I did earn neat magic and so did Julia. Al took hers away."

James watched him closely, studying him. "You're the guy who led her out of the woods." It wasn't a question. Things were coming together.

"Yeah, my old man got his hands on her. It was his birthday gift to me. Nice guy eh? Magical prick."

"Bonding ceremonies?" Information pounded in his brain and James placed his hands in the familiar triangle he always made while filtering information he didn't understand. "Many lives ago, whispering gods were known as a conscience. They were supposed to guide mortals between right and wrong but often led them astray. Since they weren't guiding properly, God sent them to live on the Mortal Realm to learn what it was they were doing wrong. They gave up their powers to demons. But most importantly, they split their souls in two so they could speed up the learning process." James felt the knowledge pouring out of him. "When these souls reunite, they earn powers back, they share what they learnt in past lives, and if their learning is done, they are allowed to blend as one, returning to the heavens to guide as a conscience again. However, when they died, I mean, if they didn't return to the heavens as this supreme-being-conscience thing and passed on like a mortal, they risked losing or never finding their soulmate again. So a bonding ceremony was created to link their souls which allows them to find each other in their next lives or in afterlives. It is powerful and can only be done between two Whisperers born the same day, same year, who are true soulmates."

"Holy hell. Where did that come from? You sure?"

James studied his shaking index finger. "I know that to be fact." James pulled on the seatbelt he wasn't wearing. He thought about this. Logic told him that seatbelts saved lives, that there would be a fine if he was caught without one, that at the speed they were driving he should have it on.

So why didn't he have it on?

Where did this urge inside him come from to not wear the seatbelt? He knew he should. Steve had told him not to and so he'd listened.

He fastened the seatbelt because he didn't have to listen to Steve or his stupid magical whispers. He was smart enough to live his own life without others telling him what he should and shouldn't do.

"What are you doing?" Steve swerved. "Are you putting your seatbelt on? That's hardly been ten minutes. It's been eight, if that." He looked torn between some type of weird elation and tears.

"So? I realized it was a stupid idea and it was yours. You made me think it was mine and I don't like that. You're a maniac and I need my seatbelt on. Keep us on the road, *comprends?*"

The banging resumed.

"I need to pull over. You fought off a whisper in effect. You read a script right out of sacred Notebooks. What are you?"

"See that town up ahead. Get us there."

Finally, they pulled over. This time at a rundown fuel station. James scanned the area. The town was north of the fuel station. There was only one car by the building. The place was clean. He sighed. He wouldn't get much help here.

"You mind giving me a few moments alone with her?" Steve asked. "And, man. I'm proud of you for fighting off a whisper that fast. I mean it was a simple whisper, but wow. We can try a harder one later, if you want." Steve climbed out of the semi.

"Yeah, sure." James got out, too. "Whatever. I need to use the can. Are you sure I can't help? I do know a lot about dogs. My sister is nuts about them."

"Again with the dog. Really? You're accessing memories from past lives but can't grasp what's going on here? What's up with that?" Steve shook his head. "You trying not to see the truth because it scares you or what? Fight the whisper holding you back, James. Focus."

James' index finger shook and he pushed his hand in his pocket. No, he saw the truth, trouble was, if he said it aloud he was officially taking sides and he wasn't sure yet if Steve was good news or bad.

"Give me a few minutes, okay?" Steve asked.

"Yeah. Come get me, I guess, unless you want me to catch another ride or something. The bus must come here too, right? Then again it's hours late." James let his eyes rest on Steve for a moment. "Steve, I don't play games." James evaluated him from the tip of his toes to the top of his head and walked away.

"Come on. You're mad about the bus? It was a joke. Don't be like that. How else was I gonna get you alone so I could talk to you about your sister? I need you, James, even compromised, you're the guy I trust when it comes to Julia's safety. Where's your sense of humour? Besides, I can't be trusted alone with her. You know that. I need you there to punch me when I go nuts."

"Ever hear of coming over for lunch?" James said over his shoulder.

"Your dog tried to go home with me last time I was by."

James froze. When was this pinhead by their place? He turned around and Steve stared at him. The panic was back in his eyes, as if he was afraid of himself. James could kind of relate to that. He did scare himself, too, when the anger took over.

"You see. It's time you pay attention. Isn't it?" Steve said. "Now go inside, and do whatever it is you do, and come back. I was serious when I said someone was hunting your sister. I got to her first. Doesn't mean she's any safer with me. It means I let you come along because she's safe with you, *comprends?*" Steve mocked James' French. "I need the keys. If I ain't out in ten minutes be prepared to shoot me with the gun I'm sure you have on you somewhere."

James held the keys in his fist as things clicked in his mind. He didn't like the images he created, and many of them involved realities, worlds, and possibilities that shouldn't and couldn't exist.

Magic did exist. Other realms were a possibility.

He returned the keys to his pocket. "Use your spare set. These are mine." He walked toward the store, thinking. Yeah, he'd seen *merde* he didn't need to think about and if Steve was involved in it, he wasn't happy about that. Damn right he'd protect Jules from him, but first he needed a safety net. He needed Bobby.

JULIA

The door opened and light overwhelmed Julia. As her eyes absorbed the shadows found in the light, her nose caught his outdoor fragrance—Steve. She closed her eyes, torn between the comfort of pine scent and the new fear it created in her. What if he whispered to her again?

"Julia." Steve spoke in a quick breath. He crawled on the bunk beside her. Tense.

He'd left the door open, but diving for it meant brushing against him and she wasn't sure she could. She sat against the wall and studied him. His eyebrows knitted in. His breaths deepened, full of anxiety.

"Did you see Al?" she asked.

The muscles in his upper arm tighten. "No. He clearly turned your brother. Pisses me off. James was our best bet. Now it's just us, but I don't trust myself around you." He sat opposite her.

"What's the plan? You can't keep me in here."

"Depends on James. If he responds to my whispers I'll leave you with him. If he doesn't, I have to drop you off and he'll find you."

"Find me?" She planned to run the first chance she got.

He sighed as if reading her mind while his hand crept up her leg. His arm was strong and she watched it, wondering what it would feel like to rub the tension out of that muscle.

"The most important thing is to undo the bond Al did on our sixteenth birthdays. Then we might be able to sit without these weird thoughts crossing our minds. Will you please stop ogling my muscles?" Steve wouldn't look at her, but her foot rubbed against his arm as if out of her control and his hand sneaked up her pant cuff and removed her sock.

"This bond is what causes the connection we share?" she asked as he massaged her foot.

"Yeah." He slouched and his hand gripped her ankle firmly.

"And if I don't want to undo it?"

He pulled her closer. "Gosh. My dreams are finally real." He took a deep breath and nuzzled into her hair as he clutched her against his chest. "I need to kiss you."

Her hands were exploring under his shirt. His skin was so warm and firm. She spoke to his chest, "You know, it looks like you kidnapped me. Bobby will be hunting you."

He groaned. "I am so sick of you talking about that loser." He tilted her head so their lips brushed when he spoke. "You know I didn't kidnap you, right? You understand that we need barriers between us, right? Al will do a lot worse to you now that James is out of the way."

She reached up and touched his lips wondering what he would taste like.

"Kidnapping is hardly a crime to do to someone who is one with your soul." His words softened her. He was right.

"I don't think Bobby will understand things the way we do."

His jaw tightened. "All that matters is what you know. I don't give two shits what that dweeb thinks."

"I suppose, after my last dream I might be open to kidnapping by you," she teased.

He shared his crooked half-smile. "Always with the jokes at the most inappropriate moments." He shook his head and let their lips meet. His touch sent waves of want through her and her body heaved up for him to devour.

His breaths increased as he tasted her deeply, his tongue exploring hers, his hands trapping her head to his lips. He pulled away sternly and stared at her, panting.

She couldn't breathe without him.

"Why were you making that noise anyway?" he demanded, as if changing the subject could form a wall between them. "You can't do that to me, your brother is ready to kill me. I feel like a maniac." His hands held her firmly so she was forced to look at his lips. "You have no idea how hard this is for me." His steady hand shook as he tried to pull it off her.

"I wanted to hear what you guys were saying," she muttered, her lips and throat so dry from yelling that her voice croaked. Free from his grip she pushed him into the wall and kissed him savagely.

He groaned, sinking with her into the blankets and pillows. She ripped open his shirt and he flipped her over so he was on top. He peeled his shirt off for her, then stared at her neck.

Her lips. His hands daringly sneaked under her shirt. She knew he wanted to stop but she was such a monster she reached for the button on his jeans.

"Julia?" He hovered over her, not moving. "Do you think I'm a..." He let go of her shirt and picked up his. "Where's James when I need him? Damn it." He shook his head. "Sounds like you need water. It's in that far corner. See the latch? Help yourself. Turn the light on."

He pushed a button and the light came on overhead. If she'd felt inches higher, she would have found it.

Was he leaving her? She sat up, pulled her shirt down, and put distance between them.

He was engrossed with her lips. Intently studying them while on his knees with his shirt dangling in his hand.

"Steve, what were you about to ask me? Do I think you're a what?"

STEVE

A monster, he thought the word but couldn't voice it. He'd heard her think it. He shouldn't have been in her mind but the word jumped out at him. Monster. Monster. All his life he wanted to be a hero yet here he was; a monster who couldn't be trusted to even talk to her.

"I'm sorry." Steve couldn't get out everything he wanted to say fast enough, and he felt claustrophobic in the sleeper. "Julia, for five years I wanted to say sorry. I'm sorry this happened and I want to fix this. Let me unbind your soul from mine so we stop attacking each other. Please," he pleaded to her hair as her soul snuggled against his. He had no idea how she ended up in his arms again but he clung to her. He repeated his apology as his hands explored her. Something he couldn't control, even though he knew he should.

"This will be okay, Julia, promise. Stay in here, safe. I can't drive with your soul near mine. I can't focus with you awake and this close. Your emotions are connected to mine so please behave. Can you get off me?" No way could he let her go. His hands slid down her back and in her pants. He gripped her ass. My God. She felt so good in his hands.

Her tongue swirled on his chest, tasting him. Her soul vibrated with a strange dancing rainbow he'd never seen before and he was at its mercy. "I can't control this monster who I am... James will be back..."

There was nothing sweet and innocent about her soul. Those rainbows twirled in a violent orgasmic dance. He felt naughtier than heck knowing she flashed that soul for him.

He was so spellbound by the rainbow, he forgot to watch her face and when she looked up at him, her tears caught him off guard.

Why was she crying?

Steve swept his hand over her soul, hoping to sense what these excited colours meant.

Confusion.

He pushed his hand deeper in her soul, finding the connection along her belly, by her hips. She moaned as if he were inside her. Her head fell in the palm of his hand. He was in control of her. He could do anything he wanted.

Steve closed his eyes and tried to feel what she felt in the depth of her soul.

So much love for everyone, but in it was a shadow he was probably feeding. Desire. Hate. Want.

This is why she was confused. He was a monster hurting her soul.

Steve bowed his head and held her hands in his. One of them had to be strong.

"I shouldn't ask for forgiveness, Julia, but I am sorry. I should have killed my dad that day. I live with that pain. I'm a coward. I want you to let me fix this so you can be free."

"Will I have these... I mean when we touch will we... us... will we be the same?"

"I have no idea. We should be talking. Not touching."

She had the top of her head against his chest while she played with the button on his pants.

"Talking? What would we talk about?" Victoriously, she pulled away when the button on his jeans opened. "Getting naked and muddy?" That was the slogan for the group who controlled the communications. When she said it, his palms grew itchy. Like he should be listening to them. Doing what they said.

"We have lots to talk about. For one thing that group who controls the communications is a threat."

"They do good things." Her hand rested lightly against his chest, shooting tingles through his entire torso. She pulled away and came in again, as if torn between how wrong this attraction was and how *real* it was.

"One dark whisper in their system and it's over."

Before he could stop her, she slid her hands in his pants.

He groaned against her, feeling fire course through his entire body and out his throat. Gosh, Julia. He pulled her hands out of his pants and held them against his chest. Their eyes locked. "Please, you have to stay away from me, Julia. I don't want to hurt you. This... it can't be right."

Dreadful, painful tears that just about killed him met his soft plea.

He backed out of the sleeper with a deep ache inside.

BOBBY

Bobby felt slightly out of his element. Julia was reliable, if she was missing she was more than likely dead. He didn't like the way everyone in this shithole town avoided his eyes. Someone knew something, but no one talked. It was moments like this where it was clear he didn't fit in with this tight town of morons who grew up together. He hated the dump.

Already, their actions confused him. The stores weren't open for business and didn't look like they were planning to open either. Entire place shut down, as if Julia were some queen. He was sure they wouldn't be closing shit if he went missing.

The town folk gathered on Main Street waiting for Constable Bobby Smith to tell them what to do so they could criticize his plan to shit and do their own thing. Bloody hicks. He swore they shared a brain. Today the bloody banker used it.

Still, he organized a search party with a crew who studied the pavement and mumbled things he pretended not to hear but filed away for when knocking heads together was allowed.

"Julia is important to me," he reminded them, which got more mumbling. "To us," he corrected himself, but he felt their trust in him slipping. Dammit. He needed James to get them fired-up. He had no idea how to talk to these hicks.

"Someone find me James." Bobby wanted him here before he found out his sister was missing and took the law in his own hands. "If someone took Julia, we'll bring them down nice and easy, no blood bath. I don't want anyone shot on my watch." He had an image to uphold and the fact that he had to remind people of that aloud told him how nutso this crew was.

"If you don't want a blood bath," the banker shouted. "Then you'd better lock James up, because my bets are that whoever placed a hand on his sister is already worm food."

"Find James, Julia won't be far," Bobby agreed. The boy would have theories. He'd be able to put these idiots to work.

James was a fricking genius. No. Genius was an understatement. Bobby was sure they gave out awards to geniuses who James would put to shame. Best part was, he acted like a moron so no one knew the clicking happening in that brain of his. But Bobby did. Bobby knew how to use guys like James and he sure didn't need James going after Julia and mucking up everything he worked so hard to build for himself in this town.

Someone else added, "Ah, not that you'd ever know. James will waltz up to you and say, 'What? We waz shopping.'" They laughed, but Bobby didn't join in.

The crowd was fired-up now. Saying his name made them eager to help and already they paired off, ready to work.

Of course, James was more than the illusion he portrayed to these saps. He spoke for Julia when she paused or took too long to search for a word. Others wouldn't notice but Bobby was trained to notice such things. He liked how James protected his sister. It was nuts and he respected it. Not that James gave him much choice. He thought back to a conversation not long ago.

"James, are you all up in my face for a reason?"

"Of course, do I look like a guy who hangs with lost causes for fun, moron? I want to talk to you about my sister." He'd worn a *Get Naked and Muddy* T-shirt and for some reason, it had made Bobby uncomfortable to have him in his home.

"Listen, James. I heard the rumours about how you beat up guys who date your sister, and that won't fly with me. If I want to ask her out, I will. This is between her and me. Your eager muscles can sit this one out. Capish?"

James had sat back. "Hmmm. Actually. You might do. I see a type of survival instinct in you, and frankly, that attitude is dead on for a gal like Jules. She's innocent so keep your pecker in your pants unless you're in it for the long haul. If you don't think she's worth it, I'm outta here." James shot up to go, but Bobby was quick to grab his arm.

"James, tell me what has you worried."

"Nightmares. I want to find someone to hold her while she sleeps. I have to move on with my life, man. I can't be here forever. She needs a husband, and you and your guns will do in a pinch."

He wanted her married. Made sense. Marriage he could do. That would add to his image real nice-like. "What's giving her nightmares?"

"Heck if I know. Been going on since forever. They've changed, which is why I'm here." He paused. "She trusts me. So you'll come to our place as my friend, and we'll hang out every day as best pals and you'll eat supper at our place until she meets your eyes. You know, until she likes you and you ain't some stranger hanging over Oblivion. Make her happy, she'll make others happy. Everyone wins. *Comprends?*"

"I have no idea what that means, but what I heard is that you trust me, and I find that interesting."

"Well, don't." James shoved his shaking hand in his pocket and said casually, "I was walking down the street thinking you are the biggest phoney I ever laid eyes on and it hits me, like a whisper to my very essence: you're about presentation. Means you have big messy secrets I'll be able to hold over your head if you so much as think about breathing on her the wrong way. You're clearly pretending to be the good guy, and pretending is the realest thing I got."

"Officer Bobby," someone interrupted his memories and Bobby cringed. He'd planned on being professional around this town and having these mindless twits call him Constable Smith, but Julia picked Bobby for a name and it stuck. People of all ages, all over town called him Bobby, or worse, Officer Bobby.

At first, he was upset, but Julia wasn't saying it to tease or make fun of him. She'd said, "Robert? Now that's not your name. Bobby fits you much better. Officer Bobby. It's who you are. You're a nice guy, and Bobby fits you."

She'd called him a nice guy.

Julia. He missed her already and she'd only been missing for two hours. He considered the losers waiting for their marching orders. "Okay, I've traced the roads she usually travels. She's not there. Jeanne at the fuel bar said she dropped her brother off this morning to catch the bus, so she made it to town. Now somewhere between the fuel bar and work she plum vanished. I want everyone asked if they saw anything unusual and I want anything out of the ordinary brought to my attention. Especially..." He cleared his throat.

"Any bald eagles circling town. Now, spread out in pairs. I'll be at the store, searching. Plus, dammit, where is James?"

The groups took off in the directions he pointed each one.

What if she was dead? Did murders happen in small towns? Had Mr. Eagle come for her? He'd told Bobby his job was almost done, but for the life of him, he had no idea what he'd even done. His job was simple: keep other assholes away from Julia, namely some prick who Mr. Eagle called Steven. But there was no Steven. Not a one.

Bobby's gut clenched so tight he couldn't breathe right. If one of them came back and told him she was dead what would he do?

He was close to failing at the simplest job Mr. Eagle had ever given him.

Yet that wasn't what made the vomit creep up the back of his throat. How would he face these people again? Face James? Disappointing James was worse than disappointing Mr. Eagle.

No one would ever be the same without Julia. She was the heart and soul of the community. Everyone loved her. She organized the daycare committee, and got the ball rolling on the hospital fundraiser, and by the looks on the faces of the people as they searched the streets for her, she'd touched each of their lives in a way he couldn't even imagine. Who didn't she help, day or night? She was Julia. Her heart was open to everyone. Except him. Why? Why didn't she warm up to him?

He took a deep breath. This town was under his skin. How had this happened?

What was he doing?

It was her. Julia. She was magical and she made the boring old people in this town magical, too.

He thought about their last date. Was that even a date? In his mind it was. In hers, it was probably more a stranger invading her home and James being difficult. Bobby had gone over to her place, pretending he belonged. Like he was family, but the stupid dog didn't help. Why did the dog hate him? That was the worst. James said it wasn't his fault; St. Bernards were moody. It was still weird and, really, it's hard to win someone over when the dumbass St. Bernard tears the chocolates and flowers to pieces before you even get to the door. Plus, he wanted to be professional, and he hardly knew her, and...

He sighed.

Why did he even care?

He just did.

Last night, when she'd passed the butter their fingers had grazed and like usual, he paused waiting for the tingles to pass through them. He'd waited for her to look at him 'cause James said he couldn't make a move until she met his eyes, but if he didn't kiss her soon he'd shoot someone.

"Julia, where are you?" he whispered desperately to the street.

"Yes. Where is the bitch you're supposed to keep an eye on?"

He was here. Bobby spun around. Mr. Eagle hadn't spoken with him since James had the bright idea to move out. Would he get an earful for that, too? For some reason, Mr. Eagle found James fascinating. Was always asking questions about him, telling Bobby what to say to him.

Bobby took a deep breath and stepped toward the bald man. He leaned against the store, waiting for Bobby. When he was feet away, Mr. Eagle rolled up his plaid sleeves slowly. He had an odd tattoo on his left wrist. "Miss me?"

"I did what you asked."

"I don't remember asking you to let some pansy steal her. Good thing I walk around in disguise, covering for your sorry ass." He shook his head and folded his arms over his chest. "You didn't notice Steven and he was right there, right under your goddamn nose. If that boy helps her summon her magic I will kill you. I worked too blasted hard to keep it away from him."

Bobby swallowed the lump in his throat, but acted as if he knew what this guy meant. "I'll find her, and I'll marry her," he reassured him. "He won't go near her."

"Marriage? Is this what has you avoiding my calls?" Mr. Eagle smiled. "My. Haven't you been busy thinking for yourself? I don't remember whispering that." He tilted his head to study Bobby. "What the hell is wrong with you pansies?"

"You suggested I build a perfect image and keep her safe. This takes time."

"I said keep her away from Steven. All I care about."

"Whatever. I won her over. I did. Now I'll marry her. James says it's the best way to protect her." He loved being around her. He didn't think she minded him either, even if he wasn't the best-looking guy. Lately, they were seeing each other daily. James made sure of that.

"James. I see. Since when do you listen to that brat?"

"James knows—"

"I don't give a fucking whisper what that asswipe knows. If he knew anything, he wouldn't be riding with my stupid stubborn son, he'd be standing here, smacking sense into you for me. Christ. While you sit and moan to me about marriage, some pansy has his paws all over her, his tongue in her mouth. Think James can help you with that or you listening to me again?" His dark eyes penetrated right into Bobby who backed up, uncomfortable. Mr. Eagle laughed. "You think she'll fuck a pathetic wretch like you without my help? Hahaha."

Bobby's senses were alert as he stepped away from the laughter as if it were a serpent coiling out to snag him. "Tell me what to do. How can I fix this? How do I get her back?"

Mr. Eagle showed him his wrist. The tattoo on it made Bobby dizzy. "*Shoot to kill*. I'm done with him. He's lost to me." His voice was hardly a whisper, but Bobby rubbed his hand over his gun.

Of course, he'd shoot to kill. No one took his girl. He didn't need some idiot reminding him of that.

Someone down the street yelled out James' name.

Bobby paused, slipping his hand off his gun. James said Julia didn't believe in violence. He couldn't shoot to kill. Yet the urge in him was fierce. He had to protect her.

For the first time since he met Mr. Eagle, he wasn't sure he was right.

Bobby needed James. James would know what to do. Where was he?

JAMES

James worked fast in case Steve left the truck. He'd searched the area for a hard hook-up into the telephone lines but there were none around.

He went back in the convenience store and picked up the phone on the counter. It was dead. He hung up the useless phone. Too many problems, too little time.

"No answer?" the young attendant behind the counter asked. He adjusted his hat and rubbed a finger along his nose.

"Phone isn't working. It's day nine. For some reason I thought I might catch a break. Do you have a radio?"

"No. What do you mean it's day nine?"

James leaned on the counter. "The pattern. You know, it's Morse code brought to a whole new level, and the message gets repeated over and over again. Clear as bloody mud. I just don't know what it means. Sometimes, I feel like I should know but I can't grasp it."

The young attendant leaned closer to him as if James was telling him something he didn't know. "You telling me the days we lose the phones are part of a pattern to signal someone? That's genius. How did you figure that out?"

James could see the cycle like a message written on a paper in front of him. "Not a big secret. I thought everyone knew this."

"You kidding, man? No one even knows Morse code."

"Really? Well, it's simple." He pulled a pen off the counter to create a visual for the boy. "Four days without the radio is the letter H. A good day where everything works means it's time for a new letter, two days in a row means a new word."

He admired James, mesmerized, so James kept teaching the obvious.

"One day without the radio is the letter E. One day with no radio sandwiched between a day where the telephones won't work is an R. Each combo makes a different letter. The pattern is Morse code," James repeated.

"Wow. How long does the cycle take?"

James finished the cycle for him, and slid the paper across the counter.

. . . .   .   . ‾ .   ‾ ‾ ‾   /   ‾ . ‾ .   . ‾   . ‾ . .   . ‾ . .   /   ‾ ‾   .

"Takes 45 days to complete."

"Cool. What does it say?"

"Hero call me."

"What does that mean?"

"I haven't a clue, but I assume once the hero makes the call it will end and we'll be able to return to our lives."

"You think it's the crew from the Green Revolution sending this out?"

"Of course."

"So why would the *Get Naked and Muddy* weirdoes need a hero to make a call?"

James rubbed his head. Too many problems. "Does the bus pass through here?" James asked.

"Nope, swings up to Highway One."

Hmmm. James felt like a pawn in a game only he was dumb enough to set up.

He studied the truck from the window. Steve rested against it, no smile. James watched him closely. Every movement was a tell. He'd fought with someone he cared about. He was angry with himself. Steve rubbed his tattoo. No. Not anger, it was disappointment etched in his actions.

Hmmm.

James stood back and thought about this. Why would Steve be disappointed? James actually felt sorry for him. How could he not? Something about Steve screamed, damn-my-life-sucks-and-it's-about-to-get-worse. Some guys didn't get the girls or the breaks. Steve was one of those guys. James wanted to help him in the worst way, even if he wanted to hate him. It was confusing, yet... these wishes were real, and something inside him screamed that he knew Steve well.

He'd never forgotten a face, a name, a date, or a time. Yet something nagged at him.

James could always see the possibilities of every situation. It was called interpreting. He'd studied it when he was fourteen.

The problems before him were simple:

- Either Steve did have a big dog in the back of the truck, or he held his sister. He knew which possibility he wanted to be true, and pretended was true, but he also knew which was more than likely right.

- Problem was—and this translated as a big bloody problem—either Jules was Steve's soulmate and bonding with her turned him into something that scared him to the point he put padlocks on the door or they weren't soulmates and this bond was killing him, and so he wanted to haul her someplace secret to kill her.

- Either some guy was after his sister or there wasn't anyone after her and Steve wanted him chasing ducks.

His finger shook.

It didn't matter what he believed, the truth stared him in the face, and he'd better learn to believe it in an awful hurry.

Maybe his nerves were making him imagine things. *It could be a dog, right?* he asked himself.

He knew it wasn't.

No one locked a dog with three padlocks. That was stupid. What would you lock with one padlock? Nothing. It didn't make sense. Why give him the keys? Why fall in a trance? Was he from a cult? Was that why he rubbed his tattoo?

He thought of how he'd said her name.

I am a Dream Whisperer.

Her dreams...

Magic.

If he accepted magic, not just magic, but whispering magic, the other facts made sense. James was a good judge of character, and Steve didn't give him a bad vibe. He might be nutso, but he wasn't a threat. He needed his help, and James was curious. Plus, he'd seen Jules while she dreamed, and how turned on she'd been. It wasn't a leap to say she could be turning Steve on if their souls were linked. Not a leap at all. That wasn't normal dreaming, he knew that much.

All fingers pointed to the stupid improbable things. How could improbable things be the ones that made sense? In what type of twisted universe had he landed?

James wanted to see inside the sleeper. That was it. Now that he'd made the decision, there was no other option.

But Bobby first. The words screamed in his mind like a whisper he couldn't ignore. He didn't like the idea of that phoney being in on this, but he needed a back-up. He wouldn't risk Jules' life if he were wrong about this. He sure as heck didn't need Bobby coming in here, storming the place with his gun drawn and his testosterone spiking.

James grabbed the pen and paper off the counter, and a business card. He scribbled and folded the paper in half and slid it across the counter to the attendant who eyed him curiously.

"Here. Take this. I have your card. My name is James. Phones will be up in roughly two hours. I'll call you then."

"And if you don't call in two hours?" He checked his watch.

"Then read the message and make a phone call to an Officer Bobby. The number you need is on that paper. Tell him what I wrote and that my sister is in trouble."

"What?" The guy chuckled. "This is a joke, right?"

"I'm having a somewhat bizarre and confusing day, and I'm not sure what's happening, so no."

The attendant glanced out the window. "You in trouble?"

"Do I look like a guy who's in trouble?"

"Well, not really. You kind of look like a guy who dishes out trouble though."

James raised an eyebrow. "You asking for trouble or will you help my sister?"

The attendant swallowed. "I don't see your sister."

"You ever find yourself pissed at someone?"

"Yeah, I guess."

"Can you see that rage?"

"No."

"Yet you know it's real, right, without having seen it?"

"Yeah, I guess, I feel it. What I feel is real."

"Sometimes, we don't have to see things to believe they exist. If I tell you I have a sister, believe that."

He chuckled. "I guess. When you put it like that, it's not hard to believe."

"What is that asshole doing?"

The attendant glanced out the window with James. "Looks to me like he's dumping sugar packs in his water, ain't no law against that. Oh wait, that's Steve, he's cool."

Everyone knew this guy. Everyone liked Steve. James thought about that. The pimply kid waved to Steve who smiled meekly.

"Tell me about him."

"He normally doesn't give rides. Hitchers mess up his truck. He doesn't like that. Once, he told me I had potential and it was the weirdest thing, ya know, but after he left, I had this urge to better myself. Signed up for night classes. I'm earning myself a massage therapy degree." He smirked. "You know him?"

"Yeah, he's dating my sister."

James grabbed his bag but before he headed for the door he leaned over the counter and whispered, *"Tu vas faire l'appel,"* he told him to make the call in French. "It's probably nothing, but I'd feel safer if I knew someone would call in two hours. All you gotta do, nothing more, one phone call. No one even needs to know it was you."

"Yeah sure, what the hell. You brightened my day. You'll call, right? You won't forget? I don't want to get Steve in trouble."

James showed him the card and tucked it in his pocket. "More like help Steve. If I don't call, Bobby better be there to stop me from ripping him to pieces."

He walked out to meet Steve, but before he opened the door the attendant said, "You be careful, I don't want to have to open this, but in two hours, I will. And... Well, thanks for teaching me those cool things."

"Thank you for wanting to learn them." James nodded to him and stood face to face with Steve who opened the door at the same time.

"All's good in the world of canines again?" James asked.

"Stop it, James. Stop pretending you don't know what's up. It's driving me nuts. Did Al whisper to you? Are you doing things you don't want to do because they're brilliant ideas? Like with the seatbelt?"

James felt like this a lot lately. It was annoying.

Like Bobby, Steve wasn't afraid to look James in the eyes.

He liked that. Made them equals. Meant Steve wouldn't cower when push came to shove. And it would. It always did.

The tension between them was thrilling. There was a secret, and James had it figured out. He'd open that sleeper and rip his sister out.

"She can come out," Steve said casually, keeping their eyes locked. The tension deflated instantly.

James hadn't expected him to admit it. So... if he wasn't keeping her by force... *sacré,* what was going on?

"Now that I see you studying me with those calculating eyes again, she can come out. You have to keep her off me while I'm driving." He blushed. "Drives me nuts when she gets in my space."

"Hmmm." James hated it when he said things like that, which was weird. He should be happy his sister had a soulmate. He knew he should, but he wasn't at all. Stupid rage was out of his control.

James followed Steve to the truck, confused. He couldn't remember the last time someone confused him. He thought he had it figured out and wham, the rage was back.

They were down the highway again in no time, and James was no closer to figuring things out. The sleeper was still locked. With three padlocks.

"Three locks. A dog named after my sister." James kicked back casually, relaxed. "You said you'd let her out yet didn't. What exactly am I supposed to think here?"

"What? You have keys, numbnuts, use them." Steve stared at him blankly. "You on drugs or something? I don't want none of that in here."

James continued to stare ahead. "Do I look like I'm on drugs, moron? *Sacré.* What are you doing with my sister in your sleeper?"

"I graduated from pinhead to moron, did I?" Steve's jaw tightened. "When you mumble in French I get nervous. If your finger stops twitching I'll have to ask you to leave."

James' finger twitched wildly, and James caught Steve glancing at it before his eyes returned to the road. "How do you know about my habits?"

"You're my best friend."

Despite himself and the anger from a moment ago, James

smirked. Steve said something like that last time they talked and... James frowned. The images vanished as quickly as they sneaked in his mind. They were at a cottage talking. Did he know Steve? "Yeah, well, I know a few things about you, too. Want me to hold your second set of keys, in case you go nuts when my sister dreams about getting with you again? Because that's magic I don't know how to contain. You got a name for that?"

Steve gripped the steering wheel. "Normally, it's your basic dream whispering but it's extra potent because we're connected by a soul whisper."

"Where are you from?"

"What's with the third degree? You remember something about me, James? Someone erased me from your mind about two weeks before your graduation, just after your birthday, actually."

About the time Bobby started talking marriage.

Something was wrong. A nagging ate at him. James replayed the last sentence in his head, what was wrong with that sentence? Something made him terribly uncomfortable.

"What is it, James? You look like you're gonna puke."

There it was again. Another sentence he didn't like. "How do you know my name? I made a point not to tell you."

Steve shrugged. "That's what's bothering you? Seriously? What am I gonna do with you? Let's see. How about, we pretend Julia told me. I slept with her in a dream last night, but normally, in our dreams, we talk about you."

"Does she remember her dreams?"

"I whispered to her so she does. Especially last night, because damn." Steve's grin grew. "But sometimes, this bald eagle shows up at your place, and those days she doesn't remember much about me."

"Did my sister climb in this truck on her own or did you force her?"

"No idea. I might have whispered. I was entranced. I tend to get... loopy around her."

"Two wrong ends on a magnet?"

"More like two right ends." He glanced at James. "I'm sorry if that angers you, but it's the truth, and so we need barriers. Locks. Keys her brother must hold, but James, I opened the lock with words, that's how weak I am."

Weak? He opened locks with words and he thought himself weak? James considered his word choice. He was weak because he wanted to stay away from her but couldn't? Wow. He liked this pinhead more and more. "Would you hurt her?"

"Like I said, she's not necessarily safe with me. All I want to do is slam my soul into hers. Plain and simple. I have no idea what her real world is like. I imagine her being like me, living in a world where everyone tolerates her and calls her freak."

"No one thinks you're a freak, man. So far, everyone I asked about you says you're this superhero they want to drool all over because you leave them feeling great about themselves."

"What do I know? I live in Dreamland with her. Built my house between realms so we could experience both and hide from Al. Nothing there matters but her silently begging me to hold her."

"I suggest you shut up or I undo this seatbelt and you'll find your head misplaced up your asshole *et puis un—*"

"Yeah, well, forget the French. I get it. Thing is, Al is hunting her because he wants to prove to me that I'm a screw up. He'll do things to her that won't be nice."

"Like what?"

"He could rip out her soul, bring her to another realm and feed her to a hungry demon for all I know."

"So tell me what this prick looks like."

"He's bald, dark eyes, lets off a scary vibe, and at no time, should you trust him. *Comprends?* He knew you were leaving today which makes me think he whispered to you. Makes me nervous. How did he whisper to you?"

"Why would I believe you over any other pinhead?"

"Al's the one who killed your mom, your dad, your uncle, even your last damn dog. You know this, deep down, you know this, James."

"I can't believe we're running away from an asswipe named Al."

"You don't run from anything and I'm done running. We're laying a trap. A trap you helped me set in our sleep. Now, take a deep breath, because you're awake, this is real, and if we make one mistake it's Julia's life on the line and neither of us can live with a mistake like that."

"So what's the plan?"

"That's not how it works, James. I can't tell you. You're compromised, and your plan—the plan you made—accounts for this. You have to fly by the seat of your pants. That's what you wanted."

Sounded about right. "So I told you I'd trust you blind?"

"You said you'd trust that things existed that you can't see. Like... rage."

"*Merde.*" He put his hand in his pocket so Steve couldn't see his finger twitching. Only he'd be dumb enough to make a plan he wouldn't tell himself about. It did explain a few things.

STEVE

Steve glanced at James as he brought them on the open road. James' soul was relaxed and calm, expanding out, absorbing the energy from the world around him as he pretended to hate life.

The only physical thing giving away what his soul did was his index finger. It twitched on his lap.

James wore a plain black T-shirt and jeans, but the shirt was tight against his muscles and the sleeves rolled up a touch as if they were dying to escape and beat him to Oblivion.

Damn, he was intimidating. Did James have any idea that he looked like a bear to the rest of the world? Hell, Steve almost felt sorry for Al. Almost. James had a spirit that grabbed and sensed ideas as if they were objects he could manipulate. He sucked in everything Steve told him about whispering. Good or bad, he wanted to know it all. Not once did he judge Steve. Never did he look at him as if he were a monster, not even when he accepted the truth about his sister being in the sleeper.

Steve drove in silence, weighing the pros and cons of his situation. The big question was how deep had Al got? What was the trigger? The one thing that would make James snap? Was there a way to win James back to his side? Really, they were a few hours in and James hadn't killed him yet and if James was compromised, well... Steve should be dead.

He glanced at James again and smiled. "Just remember, James, I share a link with Julia's soul. If you kill me, she dies."

"I figured that much out on my own, and by my calculations, it means if Al kills her, you die. Don't pretend to be all noble on me. What I see is a dick hoping to survive. You kidnapped her so Al couldn't kill you via her."

That would be how James would see it. Maybe he was right. Maybe this was about self-survival. Steve couldn't tell, he was too close to the problem.

"So where do I drop you off when we get to the city?" Steve asked, watching James' soul for any indication that

James might kill him.

"We're still playing that card?" James eyed him carefully.

"I have no choice. I don't know what Al whispered to you and what will make you kill me. If you can fight it, we can do this the easy way."

James' eyebrow went up and he smirked, but his soul flashed out in an angry flare that slapped Steve and snapped back. It left Steve with a shiver.

"Then I have a ride waiting for me at the bus station, but she's working today and won't be there until later." James glanced uneasy at the tiny door behind him. "What about Jules?"

"Pretend there is no her for a moment, just us. She's safe. This is working. Let's talk, see if we can do this the easy way."

"I can do that. You like driving this thing?" His soul expanded, taking in the entire truck in one brief sweep.

Steve smiled, there was no one in the world like James. His soul was the most interesting thing he'd ever seen. He appreciated how James worked. If he didn't get information one way, he fished around for another way in. Wow. The boy was relentless.

"Yeah. It keeps me where I need to be. Close to Julia. Close to Al. Close to you."

"Hmmm… You sleep with her in real life? Because if that's the case, I have to say I'm surprised she hid this from me." He sniffed, as if he could smell the sex on Steve. His soul erupted in flames.

Steve was suddenly very happy James hadn't caught him with his paws on Julia.

"Right there, what did you think with the sniff that pissed you off?" Steve sat tense.

"None of your bloody business."

"It was the trigger, the one thing that will make you kill me."

James nodded. "Yeah, it might."

"What might? Me sleeping with Julia? Is this what Al whispered to you, for you to kill me if I go near Julia, because James, we have a big problem if you can't fight the whisper." Steve pulled out his cloth from his shirt pocket and wiped a smudge on his dash. Then he narrowed his eyes to glare at James. He knew the quickest way to calm James was to stand up to him. "You make this smudge on my dash?"

"I don't know. I asked you a question and I expect an answer. You sleep with her for real, *Merdo*?"

Merdo? That wasn't even a word. Great, he was losing control.

His soul grew hot, as it turned from dancing flames to a raging fire.

"I guess. No. Yes. I don't know. Dreams are real life to me, James. Feels real to me. I sleep in a place that borders on Dreamland and the Mortal Realm, and in my bed at night, her soul comes to me, beautiful and happy. That feels real. This feels like a dream."

The flames were making him nervous so he brought James' attention back to his hands. Steve had to give him something, make him look at them. "Try not to touch anything, I think your hands are sticky."

The fire in his soul died when James brought his hands up to check. "Sorry. I was digging around for a hard hook-up but all the wires were cut."

A pounding started from in the sleeper. Boom. Boom-boom. Boom. Boom-boom. Then it started over again. James' soul exploded, almost knocking Steve off the road.

Steve pulled onto the gravel shoulder.

Not a car in sight.

JAMES

Steve geared down, which made James glance over. James had no idea what to think about Steve. On one hand, if Jules wanted to date him, he was trustworthy; she was an excellent judge of character. On the other hand, he was taking this fool's word on all this. He needed one fact. One.

The seatbelt tightened against him. Was that how he'd undone the seatbelt whisper? By finding a fact?

It all felt like a horrible dream.

Dreams... Something almost came back to him. So close yet he couldn't put his finger on what.

Steve said, "Well, I'll let Julia out. Julia and I will be in the same tiny area. Breathing the same air. Touching. How does this idea sit with you?"

James tightened his jaw. "I can't allow that."

"And why not?"

"No idea. Makes me want to kill you."

"I see that. Is it like the seatbelt? You know better yet can't control the urge to do it?"

His anger grew, his fists tightened.

"Get out, James. You're a danger to Julia. Your rage is out of control. You warned me this might happen, but until this moment, until I saw your soul go nuclear, I never in my life thought you were a threat to her."

"I'd never hurt my sister." Yet this was exactly what had him worried. Why was he lying to Steve?

"You kill me, she dies. I can't stress that enough, and you look like you're thinking up ways to pull me into your soul and incinerate me, so scram."

"What?" Had James heard correctly, he'd leave him here?

"Either you get out nicely or I help you." Steve rested a Taurus 1911 across his lap. A beautiful gun. James' favourite. The silver caught the light and made it shine in the sun. James wanted to pick it up and hold it. *What a waste on a pinhead*, he thought.

"Only reason to own a pistol like that is because you wanna pretend you're intimidating. Wanna know what kind of gun a guy who is intimidating carries?" James clicked open his knife.

"For Pete's sake. You told me the gun would make you focus, see me clearly."

"Oh I see you, pinhead."

"Will you get out? You suggested the gun, James. Now, consider yourself lucky I even stopped. You're a threat to Julia. Al won't allow us together and he got his dirty paws on you to stop us. So get out. I don't want to see you again until you're thinking on your own. Fight it. Whatever you did to overcome the seatbelt whisper, do the same thing."

"That was logic. Facts."

"Facts?" Steve frowned. "Fact is, I am with Julia. Me. She's linked to my soul because of Al and I want to undo the link so she can live a normal life. So I can live a normal life. Al says the only way to do this is to ignore her, to fight it, but I want to break the link with magic, because it's impossible for me to stay away from her. She's ruining my life or I'm ruining hers, who knows."

James swallowed hard. "Wow. That is not a fact, that is you telling me improbable shit. I'm so flipping confused. One minute I think you need my help, and the next you're tossing me out in the middle of bloody nowhere."

"Here's another fact for you, James. This isn't anywhere. Look around carefully. Very carefully. Everywhere counts—you taught me that. Pay attention to the world, it talks to you—you taught me that. You think anyone else figured out the Morse code shit with the radios? You are the only freak on the bloody planet who gets it, which means the message is for you, yet you're so blind you won't accept this possibility. I need to let Julia out in the next few minutes, but I can't do that if you plan to kill me, ultimately killing her, so instead, I am asking you to step out of this vehicle. Right here, in the middle of a nowhere that counts. Find her. Keep her safe."

"Why let her out here?"

"Exactly the question you need to ask yourself. Why for the love of these whispers would I let Julia out and leave you alive to find her? And just so you know, I will have to tie her up, she was thinking about running off and I don't want her running to Al. So you better damn well get to her quickly." Steve banged the steering wheel. "Damn it, James. Get out. I can't believe he got to you like this."

James surveyed the prairies slowly, not a house in sight, not a car, not a living creature. They were in the middle of nowhere. Yet he knew exactly what Steve meant. "I'm being tracked. How?"

"I have no idea how Al whispers. He gets to people without me knowing and I don't see how. Best I figure is that he compromises people they know and trust, but how? I got thinking today that maybe he was the eagle."

"So I watch which way you go and snag Jules when you drop her off?"

Steve handed James a brochure. "Do some sightseeing. Check out the bed and breakfast not far down the next turn off. Spend the night there."

James opened it. In marker he read:

Go north, stay at the stone cottage.

"Hmmm. How do I know you won't shoot me in the back when I turn around?"

"Same question to you, James."

"Ha. Ha. Ha."

James pointed to the gun on Steve's lap with his knife. "You plan to use that thing on this Al?"

"Shooting him won't work. I've seen him heal a bullet wound with whispers. If you don't bolt, I'll use it on you, because no one but you dies if I shoot you. And you won't self-heal." Steve was relaxed. It made James nervous. "What are you waiting for? Get out."

James threw himself at Steve, grabbing for the gun on his lap.

Steve slid back as he whispered for speed and smashed the gun into James' jaw. James didn't even see him move. Light exploded in his mind and his teeth shifted. No time to feel them, he targeted the keys in the ignition, focusing on one thing until the dizziness ended. He yanked them from the slot as Steve pulled back on his hair. James wouldn't go down easy. If his sister was in that sleeper, he was staying.

Magic—he felt it, every time Steve moved. As if he controlled the air around him with those weird whispers.

This time, Steve whispered for strength and threw a punch that hit James square in the jaw. He flew back and sprawled on the seat, shocked. No one had ever knocked him over.

James shook it off and dived for Steve again, this time with his blade. Steve stopped him with the barrel of the gun. "Calm down, James. Just go. I hate whispering, and you're pissing me off."

"No. Let me stay with her. I won't make a fuss. I can control it."

"Prove it. Watch me grab her around the waist."

James smoked him one. Dammit. He felt like killing him for talking about it.

Steve rubbed his jaw. "So much for your promise not to punch me."

James knew he should apologize but hitting him was the best thing he had planned for Steve.

"It won't work this way, and you know it. The thought of us together makes you want to kill me. Al wins. You have no choice. Get out. The three of us can't be in the same room together. I have things to do so I need you protecting her."

Steve was a blur, moving around as James lashed out, not sure where he was aiming. James caught his cheek with the blade.

"Damn it, James, you cut me."

"Good."

"Not good."

The gun was directly in his face. James stopped moving and contemplated the barrel. One small movement of a finger and his life would be over. It was odd, but that thought brought a smile to his lips. Really, he was already dead. His body just didn't know it.

"I'm not asking you to leave anymore." Steve was firm.

James' hands moved on their own, coming around Steve's neck, ignoring the gun in his face.

"For Pete's sake, boy. What is wrong with you? We're on the same side. Will you leave?"

Steve stopped pointing the gun at him long enough to turn it around and use it like a hammer to knock him on the back of the head. James moved out of the way, but Steve was quick.

It was the last thing James remembered before butterflies carried him off. Stupid butterflies. Why was he always dreaming about them? That was not funny, Steve. Not cool.

JULIA

Julia pressed her ear against the door of the sleeper to pick up on the fine shuffling sounds. They'd definitely stopped moving. Had James heard her? Could they hear her? Of course they could if she heard them.

She slumped against the door, waiting... listening. It sounded like they were fighting. Then the silence expanded to forever. Her cheek throbbed but she had no idea why.

Finally, the door moved. It popped open but Steve didn't come in. When the truck moved forward Julia climbed out.

"Oh, you're coming out?" Steve said, as if she'd napped. "Keep your distance from me. I'm driving and I get lightheaded around you. We're almost there."

He was worried about *her* attacking him?

They picked up speed and she slumped in the seat. There was a fresh drop of blood on one of the gears. She talked but her throat was dry. Words weren't forming. Finally, she managed a feeble, "James?"

"James will meet up with you later. He can't be in the same room as both of us, only one at a time. One of Al's jokes. Sorry, but until I figure out how to undo that curse we'll work around it. Can we sit like this for a few minutes without getting naked?"

Now that he said it, naked was all she wanted. Desperately. Her clothes were restricting and tight. His looked unnecessary.

"You sound dry. *Have some water.*" He pointed to the bottle of water rolling on the floor between them. She snagged it, eagerly.

It was open but she wouldn't need much to wet her lips. It felt wonderful to get moisture in her mouth and she finished it in a moment.

"Now don't get mad, but I need you to get comfortable because that water will make you sleepy."

She dropped the bottle. "What?"

"Sorry, but I need you to sleep without dreams for a bit so I can focus."

She closed her eyes in disgust. Tears flowed in anger. How

could she be so stupid? Of course he'd poison the water. She hated him.

Without thinking, she charged him. "You sick bastard," she said as she strangled him.

The moment their skin brushed, his desires swirled with hers. She understood how deeply he cared for her.

"I'm following a plan," he mumbled, tilting his head toward her.

She forgot about hating him as her hands slipped from around his neck to ripping his clothes off. He smelt incredible. How could she be upset with anyone who smelt like this? Closer, she sniffed his neck, lost in the pine fragrance.

"I'm driving," he mumbled. "Hell, Julia. Let me pull over first." He swerved, losing control of the big rig for a moment. It was enough to bring them all over the road. Thrown across the cab, Julia glanced at her hands. The blood on them wasn't hers.

Steve bled along his cheek from a deep scratch. She touched her sore cheek. It was in the same spot.

"Are you hurt?" she wondered, and it occurred to her that she cared if he was hurt. The blood on the gears was his, and there was enough that she should clean him up. She smelt her fingertips. Pine trees. How could blood smell like pine trees?

Magic.

No other reason.

"Julia?" He huffed as he got things under control. He hadn't panicked the entire time.

"I can't tell which are my emotions and which are yours," she said. "I feel mixed up."

"What were you thinking? You'll pass out at any minute, but come here." He had his seatbelt off and moved to pick her off the floor. "I missed you. Did I ever miss you."

She'd ripped his shirt. He peeled it off again and she understood why. Her clothes felt heavy on her. "Join me in the sleeper, skin against skin until you pass out."

Julia knew she should leave. She reached for the door handle but couldn't pull it. "I should leave, Steve."

He nodded. "You should. You're not any safer with me. Peel your shirt off and come anyway. Sucks when you lose control, doesn't it? But Julia, who cares?"

"James is where?"

"Your brother is down the road. He'll blow my head off when he finds us." He winked at her. "James isn't far, promise."

Steve was far enough from her that she felt her own passions and she wanted him to step closer so she could experience his.

Julia looked out the window. No vehicles or houses. No one to help her.

Julia looked back toward Steve, meeting his soft blue eyes. She forgot where they were, who they were.

A dream.

Steve's arms came around her and the need exploded deep inside her like a craving she'd never fulfill. Like five years ago.

His other hand came in her hair and before he could pull her to him, she went to him. She met his lips, and it blew a wild fire in her. He half pushed, half carried her to the sleeper.

She fell under him. "Steve," she breathed as he explored her neck with his kisses, and he worked off her pants. "Steve, I'm tired." Yet she wanted him to keep going.

"Oh hell, I forgot." He came back to her lips. "Damn it." He breathed with her. "I'll stay with you until you fall asleep. When you wake, you'll be alone or with James, but our place was built between realms so Al can't find you. Stay there, wait for James."

"How will he know where to find me?"

"He helped me build it. Trust us. Okay? Check out your new home and wait for me." He licked her neck. "Remember what you did to me last night?"

She shivered so deep it echoed inside her stomach. What was wrong with her?

"What's wrong, Julia?"

Wrong? She felt herself falling for him. She wanted to say, thank you for snagging her before Al did. Surely, he wouldn't be offering her water. Words were too heavy on her tongue.

Al was a monster. She shook, as memories returned of the

bag over her head from five years ago and how he'd breathed on her neck and rubbed against her. She hadn't wanted that monster near her.

Steve was the opposite.

Steve backed up, scrutinizing her as if he wanted to redo everything. "Julia, I..."

Her eyes were heavy with sleep but he looked at her with teary eyes that broke her heart.

"I'm sorry. I'm a monster." He slouched.

She reached for his hand. "Steve," she said but he stared at her hand touching his, then he left without another word. But she'd seen the tears.

Drained, she couldn't call after him.

BOBBY

Bobby was desperate for a miracle. He'd called the town's only clergyman, a bloody priest, Father something-or-another, to listen while he bounced ideas off him. He was a smart man. Apart from James he was the most level-headed guy around. Bobby needed to hear himself think. Besides, if talking to the town priest wasn't good for his image, really, nothing was.

They were standing in the back alley behind the store where Julia worked. "So if she made it this far, why not open the door? Why?" Bobby wondered aloud. They faced the staff door to the grocery store. Not a bloody sign anywhere that Julia was in trouble.

"How do you know she made it here?" Father was taking this seriously. He'd even come out in his collar, which impressed Bobby a bit. He didn't know what that meant, but Julia would, and she'd like that. She'd said she liked this guy, even though he was a stranger. Why like him and not Bobby? Bobby tried hard to win her over. He planned to ask her what more he could do.

If he found her.

When he found her.

Oh, he'd find her. He'd kill the creep who took her from under his nose. No. Keeping his image clean was important. He had no idea what he'd do. He was torn. What would Julia want him to do? He needed James. The solution rested with the boy. Things made sense when James was around.

Bobby continued to explain what he knew, "Lily said she waved to her as she pulled up to the curb in her car. Lily was taking her dog for a walk. She said she saw her get out and that's all she noticed."

"Okay, did she make it to the door or climb back in her car and drive away?"

Bobby liked people who were at their best when they had a problem to solve.

The tall, bald guy with dark eyes approached them and stood to listen. He had his sleeves rolled up and showed off his tattooed arms.

"Can we help you, Mr. Eagle?" Bobby asked. *What was this guy's problem?*

"*Ignore me.*" The man's voice was a whisper and the two men paid him no attention after that. Not sure why, but Bobby didn't care if he stayed to listen. In fact, it was a good idea; he might be able to help. They could use all the help they could get—this was Julia after all.

"The security code was never entered this morning," Bobby told them. "It's a neat gadget that records the last time a number was punched in and if it was correct. The last number was during closing last night. Means she drove away again, right?"

"Maybe she forgot the keys and went home. How well did you guys check the ditches? That's a good stretch to her place."

"I did a quick tour and didn't notice anything odd. No signs of a car going off road." Bobby stared at the open field at the end of the back alley. He'd double check himself. It was a good idea. "Truck driver pulled up right after Lily turned the corner and he said he never saw anything."

"It wouldn't hurt to do another tour of the area and see if you find anything. Drive to her house. Maybe she went home. Maybe she was sidetracked. People don't vanish."

"I know, Father. This is personal. I care about Julia. I've thought about marrying this woman. I'm not thinking straight. Thanks for hearing me out."

"You sound smitten."

Bobby sighed. "It's hard to tell with her. She doesn't let you near her, but the air around her is sweeter. I look forward to the moments I spend with her like they're rare treats. Now that she's missing there's this panic inside me that I'm about to die, physically die if I don't find her."

Father placed a hand on Bobby's shoulder, and the bald man got in closer to watch the action, as if curious. "Take deep breaths. One at a time and focus on each breath. We'll find her but you must have a clear head, and James needs to know what is going on. I should talk to him."

"No one can find him. He was waiting for the bus, but the bus didn't show. Something about the driver stopping to read. I'm guessing he hitched a ride with a trucker but no one's talking. I'll have to slam heads together."

"Want me to threaten time in Hell?"

Mr. Eagle chuckled. "I like you." He pointed to the priest. "We'll have a chat later."

Bobby ignored him, as his earlier whisper instructed. "Maybe later. James will be in Regina soon, and checking in if we ever get our phones back. I'll talk to Betty at the café. The other employees said the driver of the freight truck was eating when they pulled up, maybe he said something."

"Mind if I come?" the priest asked.

"The more ears and eyes I have on this the better, I feel flustered."

"I owe Julia," Father said. "She helped me out a few times."

"With what?" Bobby was instantly curious. What was Julia up to that had Mr. Eagle obsessed with her?

"I can't tell you that, Constable Smith. Let's say Julia has a wonderful way with words and sometimes, in my line of work, a woman's touch is needed."

Bobby liked that. He liked that a lot. His girl helped people undercover. That would help his image.

They walked the back alley and down Main Street. The café was two buildings down from the grocery store, but everything was within walking distance in this crap hole of a town.

Betty was busy making coffee for the wanna-be heroes—on the house.

"Any luck, Officer Bobby?" She looked worried.

"I was wondering if you remember what time it was when the truck driver came in for breakfast this morning. Maybe he noticed something, said something in the moment."

"What truck driver?" She poured them each a cup of coffee and slid it over. The man in the plaid shirt took his without a word, but Father was grateful.

"The one who came to the grocery store this morning. He told the staff at the store that he was waiting for someone to unlock the door and he ducked over here to grab a bite."

"Nope. Never saw him."

Of course she didn't. This was a freaking nightmare.

"This morning I saw Julia drive by while I turned the open

sign. She went around the corner like usual and that was it. My first customer was an hour later when Mitch came to tell me our sweet Julia was missing. It was her who helped me when I first found out I had cancer. Kept the kids overnight when I was too sick."

"Yeah, I bet it was tough, Betty. Thanks for the coffee." Bobby tossed coins on the counter, hoping to make an impression with her and left the restaurant with a sinking feeling.

God Julia, where the hell are you? Was this payback for his miserable existence?

"Father, tell me what you think." Bobby knew how the real world worked. This truck driver snagged her, was raping her as they spoke, probably slashed her up, and threw her in a slough somewhere.

He'd shoot to kill when the prick was in his sight.

"Call for reinforcements." The priest's brows met seriously. "We can't jump to conclusions here, but we have to face the possibility that maybe she was kidnapped by this driver." Father held an even tone, clearly used to delivering bad news to people.

They walked out with their coffees. The bald man left his behind.

"Either that or she drove off irresponsibly, but that doesn't sound like our Julia," Father said.

"No. Julia isn't like that. She cares. See how the town is searching for her. Everybody knows something is wrong. She isn't the type of person to run off and leave people worried. She didn't have any reason to." Dammit. This town was getting to him. He could see himself with her forever, not as a pit stop.

The bald man left shaking his head. He walked away with his hands in his pockets and about halfway down the street he transformed into a bald eagle and flew away.

BOBBY

Bobby rubbed his eyes, trying hard to ignore what he saw. He'd always thought Mr. Eagle was creepy, but what was that? Was he supposed to ignore that?

His mind kept going back to what he'd seen.

Father nodded, but with his back to the man, he hadn't seen a thing and kept rambling on like a fool, "When her mother died I went to visit her a lot at first, expecting to see a break down, but she was so in control it made me relax. She said her dreams were peaceful and she found solace in them. Julia is one girl I've never had to worry about—until now." He sighed.

"I'll call you later. I..." Bobby was too shaken to even speak. He ran to his car, thinking about how James said there was weird shit going down on the prairies. Things a straight shooter like Bobby wouldn't understand. Magical shit he didn't need to know about. Then he'd laughed and said he'd taken care of it so Bobby wouldn't have to worry.

Now he'd seen a man turn into a bird. A bird.

His hand shook as he fumbled for his keys. He should call the station. He needed James. Where was that damn boy?

A cat was in front of his door and he kicked it away without thinking. It mewed as it went flying. Dammit. Hopefully no one saw that. Bobby glanced around but no one watched.

With a deep breath, he pulled himself together. Bobby wasn't sure what he'd seen but he needed to focus. He'd worked hard to build up his image in this town and one man turning into a bird wouldn't fluster him into ruining that.

Bobby's home base was two towns away, almost a half-an-hour drive. He needed to talk to the other two constables located there, and see if they could offer help, but he couldn't tell them about a man turning into a bird.

He'd stick to logical facts about the case. Keep his image sparkly. He tried the radio. It worked today so he talked to Officer Rodling while driving and paying close attention to the ditch, hunting for tracks with his eyes, bent grass; anything that looked like a car might have travelled.

The closest city was three hours away. Julia was missing for four hours. If she was in a semi, she'd be at a city, maybe even across the border.

Officer Rodling had a ton of questions. Bobby passed over the bridge and pulled over. "I'll radio the city police," he told Bobby. "Have them meet this semi. Worth a look, anyway."

Bobby thanked him and prepared to pull out, but something caught his attention. The grass wasn't right. Grass. He was so desperate he studied grass. An unused path led to an abandoned house. A low vehicle had driven over it. He put the car in park and slipped his camera in his pocket before he climbed out to walk the path. A thistle was crushed and many of the long grass stems were bent, but what caught his attention was the boot print.

Nothing magical about that. The ground was a bit damp by the river and there was a clear boot print in the mud.

Bobby walked around it, snapped a picture, then made his way to the house. He stayed in the long untouched grass, praying to God that Julia wasn't lying dead in the house. He didn't know if he could handle that.

Of course, he could. He was professional. He'd seen dead bodies before. Heck, he'd made dead bodies before. Still, inside he was just a man, hardly even that. He was a frightened boy falling hopelessly in love with a woman who couldn't meet his eyes for some unknown reason.

Yet he didn't lose a step. He was close now.

It wasn't Julia, but her car. Just her car with a bald eagle sitting on it. He could deal with her car, but the bald eagle made him want to run the other way. "Shoo."

The bird stayed, watching him as if curious what he'd do. Really, that was a good question. He could do a few things. The old Bobby had a few options. Of course, the new Bobby had to respond to the gripping anxiety inside him. The new Bobby didn't want to see the eagle shift into a man.

The keys were in the ignition and a recipe card was on the driver's seat with the word "Sorry" printed on it. Not even her handwriting. He knew her handwriting. It was crisp and sharp, hard to read. This was loopy, happy. Lying. The writer of this wasn't sorry at all.

He studied the ground, searching for footprints around the

car, but found nothing. Still, the bird watched while Bobby searched the house anyway, to be safe. Aside from a few rats, the place was empty. How did someone walk away from this car and not leave footprints?

Bobby should talk things out with James, that boy would see things he'd miss. Things were serious. Magic or not.

"You know the prick who took her?" Bobby shouted at the bird. "Because we're going hunting. Lead the way."

The bird took off. Soaring west. He watched the eagle, his orders ringing clear in his mind.

Shoot to kill.

Dammit. Something inside him didn't want to kill anyone, but he didn't understand why he had these conflicting desires.

Where the hell was James?

JAMES

James rolled over on the dry grass. He felt as if he was on the worst binge of his life. Not that he drank a heck of a lot in this life. Not with Jules to look after, but he'd been out enough. Enough to know how much a hangover sucked. Actually, now that he thought about it, he didn't remember having a hangover in this life. Were memories of his past lives haunting him? Why could he almost remember them?

He surveyed the fields. For some reason, when he peered down the road, he could almost make out the shape of his brother riding a horse and buggy, coming toward him. Only... he didn't have a brother in this life. He rubbed his head. It was getting worse. He hated dangling over Oblivion like this. He should be planted in *this* life.

The houses in this area were either too far off the road to see or far apart. He decided to run west, toward the city. He was in top shape, and could run twelve miles without a break; hopefully it wouldn't come to that but whatever. Hell with it. He was going after the truck, sticking with Jules.

About two miles down the road without meeting a car, he noticed that the dirt shoulder was disrupted. It was probably the semi that had pulled onto the shoulder. He searched the ditch to see if maybe Steve threw Jules out, too, but he found nothing. This guy was a real piece of work and when he put his hands on him, he was tearing him to pieces. Oh no. No. No. No. No. He'd toss him into the back of the sleeper and take him for a joy ride—that's what he'd do to Steve and his happy bloody annoying grin.

Another mile down the road it was clear the truck had turned down a gravel road headed north and James was ready to follow it when a police cruiser came into sight. He flagged him down, happy to catch a break.

"What are you doing out here?" The policeman asked when James opened the passenger door and peered in. "Training?"

James studied the officer carefully. He was young, probably a year or two older than James. Nervous. Then again, most people were nervous around James. He brought that out in them. Even cops wouldn't meet his eyes. This one looked ready to puke when James slid in the seat beside him. He had a hand on his weapon. Idiot. As if he was the danger.

"James Wyatt," he caught his breath in even strides so he came off relaxed and not like he might attack.

"Oh. Well." The officer swallowed and glanced at his radio bag then back at James.

"A truck, a semi was through here and there is a good bloody chance that my sister is in that semi. The guy had a gun. I have the licence plate." James pulled on his seatbelt. "Let's go. What the heck you waiting for? Move, officer." He lowered his voice to a whisper "*Comprends? Vas, vas, vas.*" He slapped the dash and the copper jumped.

"I'm supposed to bring you home. Someone is pretty hot and heavy searching for you." He peeled out as if his wheels were on fire, tossing gravel.

"Hell with that noise."

The cop sped down the gravel road, focused, but never called for backup. Still, they were moving. James could handle things on his own.

Damn right. As if they weren't going after the truck.

Copper clasped the wheel tightly as they moved for all it was worth.

"This radio still work?" James touched the bag radio. It might come in handy.

"Been nothing but static for the past ten minutes or so."

James checked the time. It was ten minutes past two. Yup. Right on cue the radios went down and the phones should be working. Only now there wasn't a blasted telephone in sight.

"You got a name, hero?"

Copper glanced over. "Martin, why?"

"Nice to know the guy you'll die with, is all." The car fishtailed on the gravel. "You can slow down. I do want to actually get there alive, cripes."

"Sorry, I'm not used to gravel roads." He didn't slow down, though.

Instead, he caught a heavy patch of gravel and the backend swung to the right. James gripped the door for impact, sure they'd roll. The front end slammed into the water on the opposite side of the road.

They sat in silence for a moment and James opened his

door. They were in a slough but the water wasn't deep. It rolled on his feet.

"You got a death wish, pinhead?"

Martin blinked and shook his head. "No. Just... something snapped in me to go fast. Go. Go. Faster the better."

James frowned. Wow. What was wrong with this guy? "See the town up ahead?" He grabbed the bag radio and stepped into the slough. The water was cold but not even up to his knees.

The cop scrambled out his door. "Nothing in that town. It's a ghost town. I studied the map closely because I didn't want to get lost out here."

Ghosts? Hmmm.

"Where does this road lead?"

"To Highway One. At the ghost town you can turn west or east and join up to other highways, number..." He paused, clearly trying to remember the numbers.

Steve could have gone in any direction. Wow. Everything fell into place perfectly. Almost as if he'd planned it. *For the love of knowledge*. Maybe he had.

"Not from around here, eh?"

Copper sighed. "This is my first day here. It's too quiet, everything makes me jumpy." His tone implied that he hated it and hoped the place blew off those maps he'd pretended to study.

"*Sacré*." James glanced around. "Your problem is that you don't care enough to try. I suggest you crawl back to a world you care about. Life is too short to sit with your feet wet. Get a grip of this life and enjoy it." He stormed out of the water and toward the ghost town. When Martin followed him, he kept right on yelling at him in his teaching way, "Everything in life happens for a reason, hero. Anyone could have stumbled on me running, yet it was you. So buck up and focus."

James stared at the old buildings in the ghost town and picked up his pace. Steve left him here for a reason, there was something to find.

Martin kept up to his even strides and put a hand on James' shoulder. James glanced at it as if considering breaking it.

With a tinge of concern to his voice, Martin asked, "Where

are you going? I told you there was nothing this way."

"Don't ask questions you don't want an honest answer to, hero. We'll make a call using this bag. I'll show you how we adapt on the prairies."

James turned it on as they jogged and it crackled but nothing happened.

James stopped running in front of the Hamilton Beach sign and dropped to his knees. "Watch what I'm doing. It's simple." He rested the bag radio on the road and opened the radio's brain with his knife. "Did you know, before the war people had cell phones?"

"What?"

"Never mind, the point is that the phones are working and this has the parts we need. It's a matter of connecting it to a land line. Every bag is equipped for hard hook-up. You need to know what you're doing."

Martin paced, ignoring James.

James got to his feet and stepped in front of him. "Just because you hate it here and would rather be home screwing your girl, don't ignore me. I'm teaching you something important. I'll show you how to hook it to the green box." James pointed to the green box by the sign.

Martin stopped pacing and got on his knees by the bag radio.

James was annoyed when people didn't want to learn. He knelt beside him and pulled the wires he needed out and hooked them to the adapter in the bag. He pulled the card from the fuel station from his pocket and showed it to the officer. "I'm going to leave this with you. You slip the adapter in the slot hidden under the box."

The officer searched with his fingers under the box for the slot as if he didn't believe there would be a spot there to hook it to. He nodded when he felt it in the cold metal.

"When you hook in, it links directly to someone and will ring. All these boxes are what I call a hard hook-up. They send you to the same place no matter if the phones are up or down and you'll talk to the freaks who control our communications. You'll be asked by a woman with a fairytale voice if you're a hero. Tell her you might know one in a pinch and give her the number on the card. Ask her to make a call with this message for Officer Bobby: 'Steve has a gun in his truck and it is possible he has a woman in the sleeper'." He showed him the number for the fuel station. "The kid there will be getting in contact with Officer Bobby. Only make the one call, make it quick and don't forget to mention the gun. If the woman asks for your name pull the hook-up out, count to ten and try again. She'll be more co-operative the second time around."

Martin grabbed the card and the radio. "I'm not leaving."

James glanced at the car in the slough. Clearly. "You like fun, right Martin? Or are you a tight-ass like Officer Bobby?"

"James, what are you planning?"

"If it happens to break any laws, I'll make sure you're unconscious."

"Messing with telephone lines might qualify. We were ordered to leave things alone until the viruses were under control."

The viruses were healed. Someone with a plan and a fairytale voice ran the show, but a guy like Martin lived with his head up his ass and did whatever he was told so James didn't bother explaining.

James checked his watch. It was late. The store attendant would have called in by now, Bobby would be talking to him. He needed this guy to make the call. Last time James used a hard hook-up when the radios were down, pricks showed up at the location of the hook-up days later asking questions about dreams. One even shadowed Jules, but that didn't last long because James didn't tolerate crap like that. Well, now he needed them.

Too many problems and everything he touched made more.

"I'll behave, Martin, promise." James flashed him a smile. "But tell me, do you believe in magic?"

"Like pulling rabbits out of hats?"

"Hmmm. No. I was thinking more along the lines of making dreams come true."

"Of course. Happens all the time."

"Yeah. I guess it does, doesn't it? Do you believe in soulmates?"

Martin chuckled. "Actually, I do. Met mine. The universe paused, creating this one dreamy moment, as if nothing else existed. Just us."

A cupid moment.

Hope swelled inside him, but James curled up his nose as if the idea sickened him. "Wow. I'm almost sorry I bloody asked. You are even weirder than the last guy I talked to today. What is wrong with you pricks?" James shook his head, but Martin glowed and this gave him hope.

BOBBY

Bobby got word that James left him a message at a fuel station and was on his way to hear it in person. He should be happy with this thought, but he was far from happy. It sounded like James was... being James.

What the heck was that boy doing in this remote, God forsaken, mosquito infested swamp land? How crazed was James? What would he do to anyone who hurt Julia? Would Bobby be able to stop him from killing this guy? Would he even try?

Bobby swallowed a hard lump down his suddenly dry throat.

That was the secret of it right there. He checked his speedometer. He wasn't driving fast enough. He wasn't trying hard, and he should at least make it *look* like he was trying and not hoping to hell to arrive to find the prick who'd taken her drawing his last breath. He'd better be, too. James had better have this asshole strung up when he got there. He'd swear up and down James was defending himself, that he had no choice. He could do that. James was smart. They'd make it look like self-defence or something.

Bobby ran a hand through his hair. He was too close to this. Was this what it was coming to? Would he ruin everything for this girl?

He thought of the bald guy on the sidewalk. *Shoot to kill.* Really, it was that easy. Rid the world of one more prick. Why not?

Bobby turned on his lights. He could talk to this witness and give James a few more minutes with the prick who stole Julia. Why not?

BOBBY

"Well, I mean, I trust Steve and all..." the scrawny, pimply faced boy behind the counter of the rundown fuel station went on and on as he confessed his every thought to Bobby. "More than this James guy who I don't know from a snowball in an igloo, but when I read the letter, well, look what he wrote."

Bobby took the paper. It was folded neatly. So unlike Julia who would have crumpled it. He recognized James' careful handwriting instantly. Now this was painfully honest handwriting. Blunt and to the point, even though it didn't make a lick of sense to Bobby.

Do not forget to entertain strangers, for by so doing some unwittingly entertained angels. -Hebrews 13:2

Yup. James. Bobby folded it and put it in his pocket. James drove him nuts. What did he mean by this message? Bobby studied the kid behind the counter. Maybe the message was for him. Got him to call now didn't it?

"Is he a priest or something? I mean a guy who quotes the Bible can't be all bad, right?"

Deceiving. Who knew what James was, but Bobby was still going with beyond genius.

"Those are the ones you watch out for, kid. Besides this is a message for me. Don't sweat it."

"Is he bad news?"

James? Bobby had no proof, not a smack-licking shred of evidence that the boy had ever hurt a soul or done anything against the law his entire life. Nope. As far as he could tell, he was too smart and needed to channel that somehow. Still, he knew what a guy could get away with if he was smart.

The phone rang. The kid picked it up and after a brief hello, he passed the receiver to Bobby.

"Officer Bobby."

"*Do you know a hero, Constable Robert Smith?*" The woman's voice was soothing. Bobby found himself leaning on the counter.

"In a pinch I might be one."

"*Hamilton Beach. Contain them all. We'll be there shortly.*"

"Who?"

"*What are the plans?*"

"I... I'm supposed to shoot to kill," he confessed, not sure why he wanted to tell this voice everything. "Steve is the target."

"*Learn to think for yourself. Steve is mine.*"

She hung up but Bobby held the receiver, thinking about her words. Was he letting Mr. Eagle dictate his life? Who'd meet him at Hamilton Beach and why?

The young guy behind the counter was talking, "I have the licence plate from Steve's truck. Hope Steve isn't in trouble."

"You like Steve?"

"Well, yeah. He's a good guy who believes dreams come true. Gotta like that."

How good was this guy at judging people? "You like me the same way?"

He looked down. "You're a policeman and all, but... ah... that's not the same as a guy like Steve. He's... the poor sap who gets a professional photo taken only to discover his fly was down. You know? You feel for him because he's always down on his luck, yet he tries."

"What did you think of James?"

"He says he dishes out trouble or something funny like that. I liked him. Anyway. That's all I know. Said he was bumming a ride though, and I know that's never a good thing to do, eh?"

"You did the right thing. Thanks. I know James, and he's a good kid."

James knew how to reach people. Bobby took out the letter and read it again. He was glad James was on this prick's tail. Whatever the boy did to this driver, Bobby would help him make it look like self-defence. He had to maintain this image, and he didn't want Julia to think him a tyrant, but her hero.

"Thanks again." Bobby headed out with these thoughts. He'd worked hard to maintain this good-guy image. No one needed to know he was a prick, least of all Julia. No, not when she was doing such nice things in the community. Going out of her way to help people.

He rubbed his gun. Maybe he'd hurry and help James. Looking like the hero in front of Julia appealed to him.

BOBBY

"James?" Bobby called down the deserted ghostly streets of Hamilton Beach. "Steve is in Regina. Come with me. Don't you want to be there when they search the truck? Why are you here? You're here, aren't you? I haven't heard a peep from you. Officer Martin? Is that your car in the slough? Hello!" Bobby snooped around the quiet streets. They had to be somewhere, but he didn't want to stop talking because the silence terrified him.

"Over here." A young cop caught his attention.

"Officer Martin? Nice meeting you. How's your first day?"

He leaned against an old building with a bait shop sign over his head but stepped forward to shake Bobby's hand. His grip was sweaty. "Don't even ask where the boy is."

The boy? Martin looked younger than James did. One of them book-type geeks. Bobby's eyes swept over Martin. No wonder James was running wild. He must have had a field day with this guy. Probably gave him a swirly and wedgies, too.

"This place is empty. Not a trace, yet he's bent on searching for something." Martin smirked. "I like him. He fixed my radio so it made a telephone call. You get my message?"

"If you tell me James made you happy to be stationed in this hellhole I will smoke you."

Martin's grin grew. "The guy's a genius on steroids."

Everyone loved James and he didn't try at all, in fact, he pretended he was dumber than shit and a real badass. "Yeah. Remember that." Bobby was serious. He pushed past him to scan the area. It was an old town. The buildings were intact but in decay. "I need to know where you saw him last, then you can scram. Take my car and vanish." Bobby didn't need this idiot here.

"Ah. Maybe I'll stick around." He pointed to the bait shop sign over his head. "He went in about ten minutes ago and hasn't come out. He's searching the area. Harmless."

Bobby went in. "James, it's me."

"Up here."

He found James peering out the window with binoculars. He had several pairs in front of him. "Found these in the old shop as if someone left them for me. This one has my name carved into it, yet for the love of problems, I do not remember owning eyes this sweet. I even found little messages." He pulled a bunch of papers out of his pocket. "Clues I left myself. More mucked up shit. Someone is messing with me, big time." He handed a pair of eyes to Bobby and made room but kept scanning. Then he made a mark on the wall in chalk. "Why did he stop here?"

"They'll search Steve's truck any minute," Bobby said. "Wanna come with me to talk to this guy? There's a house with a phone just down the road we can use."

James made another mark on the wall before he moved to another window.

"He stopped here for a reason. Help me before it gets too dark. I found six locations, already checked out two. That's not so bad. He moved through here fast."

Bobby was lost. "What exactly are you asking me to help you find?"

"I'm guessing, and I might be wrong, but I'd say the truck. He ditched his load and picked up a new one."

James thought Steve switched trucks? What?

Dammit. There was no way James was wrong about this. He needed to call the guys in the city.

STEVE

Steve pulled up to get his next load. Usually, he left the semi overnight and they loaded it so he could head out in the morning. He checked his watch. It was four. He had time to grab pizza for Julia.

First things first, he must clean the truck.

"I'll be in the truck if you guys need me." He smiled, happy it wasn't the night crew yet. He'd be out of here before they showed. Fewer people he interacted with the better.

"Hey, Steve." One of the guys rushed to him. "I got the job I told you about. Thanks for coaching me. The interview went great. I start in a week."

Steve nodded and whispered, *"Talk to your dad about a down payment for the house and you'll be set*. Living the dream."

Steve felt great as he polished his windshield. He wished he could be like James. Nothing scared that boy. It would be wild to be able to stare a gun in the face and not flinch. Who would have thought his whispers could make him impervious? Like stone. What went through his mind in those moments?

The truck was a disgrace. Unacceptable.

Steve was in full gear, scrubbing the floor when red and blue lights brought his attention back to reality. Cops.

They approached with their weapons drawn. Well. He hadn't expected this twist. Seems James hadn't thought of everything.

Steve climbed calmly from his truck, hands up.

"Don't move."

"I won't. What's this about anyway?"

"Step away from the truck."

Steve did as he was told. He was prepared to whisper, although he didn't think magic was needed. Actually, from his experiences, it rarely was. Sure he was a Whisperer, but Steve was usually just a man. That thought brought him comfort, even if there was an entire squad of guns on him.

"Is something wrong?"

"Don't move. We have reason to suspect you have a

concealed weapon. We will search your person and your vehicle."

Steve stayed still while someone frisked him. He couldn't see all the police cars, but he hoped James wasn't in one of them. He'd better be with Julia. If James was in one of them cars, he'd kill him. It would be the first person he killed, but dammit, he was sure he would.

Who had called the cops? He knew it wouldn't have been James, he'd be busy searching for Julia, and there were no phones at Hamilton Beach. No phones, no radios, nothing but nature forcing him right to her.

A man in a suit approached. "What were you doing in the truck?"

"Cleaning it before I turn in for the night. You see I got myself a dog and she made quite the mess."

The dog barked right on cue. What a sweetie. He couldn't wait for Julia to meet her. A Border Collie pup. He felt bad for not bringing her along today. Julia had clearly wanted to meet her.

They searched his truck for an hour and questioned him endlessly. They kept saying they were looking for a weapon. They pulled everything out. They must have come up empty because they left apologising.

He didn't whisper once.

Things were working out smoothly. He was glad he'd gone by the lake and swapped his truck for his old rig. It was a brilliant part of the plan. He had to hand it to James—the guy came in handy. How could he see every possibility? It was incredible.

Hopefully, he was half as smart awake as he was asleep and he pulled off his end of the deal. Steve checked his watch. He'd never make it back to the cottage tonight. Not now. Not with the police watching him.

Yet Steve couldn't leave Julia alone for the night. What if James didn't make it? He didn't like all these ifs to James' plans. He'd have to find her in her sleep. He climbed in the cab of the truck.

"Butterflies, fly me to Julia." Steve let the butterflies whisk his soul to Julia, but the meds still had her in a heavy sleep. She was unconscious and tied to the chair. He stood and

watched her sleep for a moment. The butterflies scattered along the wall, waiting for him.

He hadn't tied her up nearly as good as he should have. Where was James? Why wasn't he here already? Steve walked around her and loosened the tape on her hand a little more. What was taking James so long?

"Butterflies, fly me to James."

He was whisked to James who peered out the window from the bait shop in the deserted town. The dweeb stood behind James.

What was James doing with the cop?

Was this the prick who had turned him?

The cop moved for his gun the moment Steve swooshed in beside him. He even glanced at Steve as if he could sense him hovering there, glaring at him. Then he returned his focus on James.

This changed everything. James had switched sides. It meant he had to get Julia away from him and it explained why he hadn't found her yet.

Frustrated, Steve whispered for the butterflies to return him to his body. He had to get to Julia. If James was out of the equation, he'd scrap the plans and do things his way. Hell with him.

When he opened his eyes, Steve was shocked that Al stood over him. The door to the truck was open. He pulled Steve out and tossed him on the floor of the warehouse. Steve glanced around for help but everyone was gone.

Al leapt on him and punched Steve in the gut. "Fucking pansy. Where is she? I have pricks from Utopia on my ass now. You like to pull shit like this?"

"Utopia? What?"

"They want that boy."

"James?"

"It'll be you next. You think they plan to let you walk around with god-like powers?"

"Calm down. I want to unbind the magic, my way." Steve scrambled to his feet.

Al shook his head. "You're a goddamn liar. All you'll do is fuck her until you both die and you know this. I see she's not with you, means you have to go to her."

No. James was supposed to find her. He regretted it the moment the thought flashed through his mind.

"So then I'll find her via the boy," Al answered, reading his thoughts.

Steve got goosebumps. He was so close to his dream, he wouldn't let Al ruin it. He rushed to the car he stored by the warehouse, hoping he could beat Al there, but he was already nowhere in sight.

Steve searched the skies. An eagle flew off and vanished. Dammit. He'd never arrive in time.

JAMES

James wasn't sure where Bobby had vanished to, but he'd been gone for a good ten minutes.

With four more sheds in the area big enough to hold Steve's rig, James had a place to start—four places to be exact and a few hours before dusk. He'd been looking for a stone cottage but didn't see one. It took longer than he liked, but he didn't want to have to come back again. He was sure now. He glanced at the map he'd drawn on the wall and memorized it. He hated the wilderness, liked open areas where he could see the enemy coming. Water was the worst. He shivered at the thought of the wild creatures lurking in the dark. The bloody lake looked about a mile long, too. What if Steve killed her and tossed her in? His index finger shook wildly at the possibility. *Merde.* Steve said to trust him. Said some other lunatic was after her who they should hide from. He said James was compromised. For some reason that made sense.

James headed toward the steps to find Bobby while thinking about Steve. He didn't get a bad vibe from Steve. Sure he was a nutso, but he wasn't dangerous, just afraid. Scared people did dumbass things. Still, James might push each of his eyeballs out and make him eat them anyway. That's what he'd do if Jules was hurt.

James ran down the steps. Right into Bobby.

Hmmm. So the guy building an image shows up right on cue. James studied him, his finger twitching. Clearly, Bobby had learnt something interesting. The question was, how much would the big phoney share and how much would he keep for himself so he came off the hero?

Bobby had his hand on his gun. Frankly, that was the first time James noticed him acknowledge it. "You were right. Not the truck. Had a dog with him. Plates were out by one number. Same freight company, same type of truck you described."

James stared at him blankly. "Tell me something I don't know, moron."

"Like?"

"How would you find that out? Radios are down."

"Could we say a birdie told me?"

Hmmm. As in an eagle? A wall snapped up between him and Bobby. "The gun?"

"None." Bobby was firm.

"Then he left it for me. Where?"

"Why leave you a gun?"

"Because there's a bloody lunatic after my sister. A big bald pinhead, you see him?"

"What?"

James watched fear flash across Bobby's face. Actual fear. He'd never seen Bobby afraid.

"What happened, Bobby? *Parle, maudit.*"

"Nothing to talk about. It was a dream."

Dream? James glanced around. Did that mean those pricks were already here because of the hook-up he'd had Officer Martin do? What did they want? "I said, talk, dammit. Tell me about the dream."

"It was silly, but a man, a bald man wearing this plaid shirt had these odd tattoos on his arm, and he turned into a bald eagle and flew away. I knew him, but I didn't know he could shift like that. Impossible, eh? Dreams are stupid that way."

"Hmmm. You dream this shit up while you were awake or at home snuggled in your bed?"

Bobby studied his feet. James knew his tells and that meant he was about to lie. James didn't give him a chance. Instead, he put a hand on Bobby's shoulder and said, "An eagle, a bald one, was circling this town earlier. Where did it go?"

"I followed it here. He flies fast. Been to the city and back already."

"Magic." James sighed. "I've tossed around improbable and probable solutions for hours. If I accept the possibility of magic, my improbable solutions make sense. This means you're the dick who made me forget who Steve was."

"I hate it when you talk gibberish. Who is this Steve? What does that shit mean? I've been nothing but nice to you, and I can think of a few times when I should have set you straight."

James eyed Bobby. "I want to find my sister. I talked to you about magic before. I've seen and dealt with it. I have no problem believing in magic, do you?"

"Magic. I mean come on, James. Magic?"

"I believe my soul is alive. I believe my dreams are real. Why not believe a man shifted into a bird and flies at the speed of light? You saw it with your own eyes, yet you question it. How can you doubt what you saw with your own eyes? How can you call it a dream when we both know you were wide-awake? I believe it and I didn't even see it. I see the bird circling the town, searching for God knows what. Did this freak whisper to you?"

Bobby closed his eyes.

"Find her, Bobby. You make me sick sometimes. I keep thinking I want you to be the one for Jules, and I have no idea why I want something so stupid. She clearly won't warm up to you. When you can't even wrap your mind around a simple reality I wonder why I even bother setting things up between you and her. Makes me think I don't want this, some other prick does."

"Did your sister agree to go out with me?"

"Really? I'm beginning to understand why Jules can't get a spark from you. Somewhere along the road, you died and you need to find yourself. I hope you do, because it must be pretty boring to live this pretend life you got going on."

Bobby took in a deep breath and followed James out the door. "What does that mean?"

"I'm on to you," James mumbled. "I know this is an image. None of this is real. It can't be. No one sucks at living life this bad. No wonder Jules thinks you're a stranger—you don't even know yourself. Now, fight off whatever he said to you, forget Jules. Focus on getting this prick with me. I've put together possible scenarios, and the one I'm going with involves magic. You in?"

"You asking me to trust you instead of my own common sense?"

"Your common sense is compromised." James kept walking. He refused to beg this moron for help. Either he trusted him or he didn't.

Bobby caught up to him. "Tell me what to do, James. I trust you with Julia's life."

"Hmmm. Too bad I don't trust you with mine."

"You used to."

James glanced over his shoulder at him while they walked. No, he never did, just some pinhead wanted him to. He wouldn't let this guy win. "Keep your eyes on the eagle up in the sky, but if he lands, you let me deal with him when the time comes. Steve says he's a monster, and magical creatures are not for pinheads like you to be messing around with, *comprends?*"

"No, James, I never understand your rules, and I believe in magic, but that doesn't help me."

That's what James liked about Bobby. He made his own rules. Like a real man.

"We have no proof whatsoever that she was ever with this Steve," Bobby reasoned, as if James hadn't thought of that. He signaled for Martin to join them, but James kept walking, on a mission. "Nothing, unless you saw her with him. Did you?"

"Steve? This is who worries you. Steve?" James looked him square in the eyes. He stopped 'cause he suddenly didn't want Bobby following him. "I was in that truck. I sat beside Steve. Frankly, I trust him with her more than I trust you. I heard her plain as day. I heard my own sister moaning for Steve to satisfy her in her sleep." Bobby winced, but James pushed on. "It was muffled and it was faint, but I didn't even have to move toward the door to hear her. I listened with my soul, and I swear to you on my mother's grave that I heard my sister making sex noises in the back of the truck and I know this because nothing angers me quicker than that sound. No idea why, it just triggers my rage. Now you tell me, Officer Bobby, if a guy like me would even dream up *merde* like that in his worst bloody nightmares?"

Bobby swallowed and rubbed his hands on his slacks. "No, I suppose not."

"Now. Regardless, if I tell you Steve is not the problem, the... bald eagle you saw is, you'd better believe me, because I'm already sick and tired of your crap. He's not even all the problems. To send you the message I made a hard hook-up to the telephone lines. For some reason when I do that, crazies come out to play. Be on the lookout for nutjobs. You feel like you're in a dream now, wait until they whisper to you."

"This makes me awfully nervous, is all. I'd prefer if the

eagle were on our side. He did lead me here."

"Hmmm. He leads you to water and you jump in? Is that how it works in your rose-coloured world, Bobby? Because in mine, when someone leads me to water I shove the pinheads in to test it out first."

"The dreamy voice on the phone said I had to contain everyone and wait."

"Yeah, we're contained, Bobby. Look around. This is exactly what they want."

Bobby rubbed his forehead. "Tell me what you know. I'll decide for myself who to trust."

"You see, Steve is keeping her away from this bald eagle character. Like a game of cat and mouse. Somehow, we're in the middle, brought in by the two players. Me from Steve's side, you from Baldy's side. We're standing at an impasse. Do we join sides or do we part ways? *Comprends?* I won't go to your side so the choice is yours."

"And these crazies?"

"They want me or Jules, not sure why but it has to do with the Green Revolution."

"Them *Get Naked and Muddy* freaks? You figured this out?"

"Of course. It pisses me off that you can't. It's plain as day, staring you in the face."

"Let's bring them down. Why let them use us?"

"Hmmm. We could. But I decided to like Steve. So did Jules, hence the sex noises that piss us both off. I realize that puts Steve on your *merde* list, but you can't think with your pecker on this one. Jules has an incredible sense of who to trust. If she trusts Steve, so do I."

"I see," Bobby said. "So you think we should save Steve and kill Mr. Eagle? What if I disagree?"

James took a deep breath and thought about this. "Do you?"

He looked torn. "Yes." The word was tortured from his lips.

Then the rules changed. Bobby was compromised and couldn't fight it. James let the next actions fall into place in his mind. Bobby chose his own fate and he couldn't help him.

Officer Martin joined them, but he grouped him with Bobby now—the enemy, and there was only one thing to do with the enemy—send them searching for the pot of gold at the end of the rainbow.

"It's getting dark but I want to search a few places. I saw seven barns," he lied. "Each one could house a semi." James drew them a map in the dirt. "Not much movement around any of these places so we're going in. We'll ask questions later."

Martin opened the driver's door on Bobby's car. "We'll start with the two to the north." Bobby motioned for James to get in his car, but there was no way James was going with Bobby.

"It'll be faster if I jog to these." James pointed to the ones around the lake. He was sure they were the suckers anyway. The road there led out to Number One Highway. The house was by the lake and the barn well concealed in the trees. Lots of playing room if he wanted to hide her. He looked to both cops, not sure why they couldn't see the obvious. Not his problem. He wanted his five minutes alone with the area. That's all he'd need to find the gun Steve had left him anyway.

He took off toward the lake before either could object. He didn't have time for them to figure out their own incompetency.

He watched the sky. Sure enough, the bird stuck with him. Good. He'd deal with him, too.

JULIA

Julia's heart fluttered when her arm slipped along the duct tape. Her hands were free and in the one was a juice box. She bent to take a sip as thirst overpowered her. She drank it all and sat still, afraid that if she tried to break free while excited she might damage the progress she'd made. The wooden chair was uncomfortable underneath her.

Light peeked in through the cracks in the thin walls and she could hear birds outside. A spiderweb over the boarded up window to her left glimmered in the dim light. The door to her right was locked with a chain.

She took a deep breath and slowly slipped her right arm up. It was free. She was free. The tape had sweated off in the heat. She ripped the binds off her legs. She wasn't well taped up. It was almost as if Steve wanted her to get free. Huh. Maybe he did. Steve was so confusing to her. She didn't mope around figuring him out, though. Never in her life was she so happy to be free.

She needed water. The juice wasn't enough and she tossed the juice box on the floor.

Julia surveyed the tiny room. Light filtered in through the cracks, giving the room a desolate feel.

Hopeful, she tried the door. It was locked but old. Using her weight, she rammed into it. The door shattered and she landed in the middle of the splinters. She was okay. She could do this.

Collecting herself she got to her feet and an overwhelming sense of thirst hit her. Her lips were cracked. The next room had a sink and she dashed to it, turning on the rusty taps.

A mouse had made a nest by one of the taps and watched her, fearful. At first, orange water splattered into the sink, but it quickly sputtered to a stop. The sink itself was in rough shape. Mice turds and dead flies lined the bottom. Julia turned the tap on higher, but nothing else came out.

Would she die out here? Seeing the useless water at the bottom of the sink was devastating. She needed out of here.

She flung open the front door. The sun was setting but there was enough light for her to make out her surroundings.

This wasn't so bad. Trees clustered around the house, and she smelt water. Lots of it.

Julia had no idea when Steve would return. What if he didn't? Where had he gone? Why was he keeping her in the dark? A part of her wanted to hide out and wait for him but the logical side of her screamed, *Run!* Argh. It was confusing.

She rushed into the yard. There wasn't much of a path. Most of it was overgrown. She glanced over her shoulder and was surprised to see that the rooms she'd left were nothing but a workshop tucked away in the trees. It would be easy to overlook.

Beside it was a shadow. No. She looked closer. It was a beautiful cottage made of stones, only... was it really there? It shimmered in the light from the setting sun as it played an illusion. The cottage was small, yet... perfect. Homey. She ran to the veranda, almost stumbling through the light, not sure if she'd find steps or air. The moment her foot touched the staircase the house in front of her came to life. It was real. She stood on the stoop and looked out at the lake. The rest of the world looked like a mirage now. The light was very strange here. Too bright in spots.

She banged on the door, screaming for help.

It swung open easily, inviting her. She was light-headed, dreamy, but walked in, entranced by the familiar.

This was the house from her dreams. Literally. How could it be? How was that possible?

As she walked in, the air changed and shifted as if she suddenly had new eyes. She touched the door frame. It was warm under her fingers. Had she been here before? Why did she feel like she was walking into a new world?

First things first. Finding the kitchen exactly where it should be, she drank. Water. Delicious clear water poured from the tap. It flowed so sweet she drank it straight from the faucet, her head bent over as she'd seen her brother do countless times.

Then she snooped through the cottage as if she had every right to wander this house. Maybe she did. She belonged here. This was her dream.

Was this a dream? Would she wake up tied somewhere

unsafe?

Everything was exactly the way it should be. Night after night, she came to this house. She ran a finger lightly over the dishes with a smirk. Steve had brought them in. One set was blue glass, the other was white with blue flowers. He'd asked her to pick which ones she wanted, and like a happy couple, they settled on both. Her smile deepened. They were happy in this dream.

Upstairs she avoided the big comfortable bed, dismissing it with a quick glance. The rest of the room smelt like him. Pine trees. The familiar pillow was on the floor. She'd tossed it at him this morning. A dream. Yet it was on the floor where they'd left it. How? Picking it up, she smelt it, too. More Steve. Her stomach ached, deep inside. A deep, longing ache.

The closet door was open a touch and one of her shirts caught her eye. She pulled open the door. Her clothes were there, taken right from her clothesline. Things she'd been missing. Not many of her things, but enough to get by for a few days.

Had Steve been by her place? Had he taken her knickers right off her clothesline? She walked the room in a daze. It was home. So familiar she couldn't freak out, she couldn't be angry. It was... perfect. He even had photos of the two of them, not together of course, but Julia in her frame, and Steve in his, smiling at each other, so happy.

Oh Steve. She touched the picture of him, confused. Why was this so messed up?

Julia turned toward the big bed. Their bed, the one they started in last night in her dream. Lingerie nestled in the middle. She ignored it and left the room in a hurry, too afraid to touch anything else, because if she did, she might never leave, and she couldn't wait for him. Could she? Was this what he expected her to do?

Why tape me to the chair and not leave me lovingly in the bed? If he was saving her from Al, isn't that what he should have done? Or was being tied to a chair protecting her from something else? Again, confusing. Why didn't he say things?

Maybe he was nuts and she needed to get far away from this guy.

She rushed downstairs, stood on the veranda, and studied

the path. It was blurry but it split in two directions. The first led to the water she smelt and the other she assumed led to the road.

Stepping off the veranda and back into that distorted world was hard. The moment her foot touched the ground, the world came back around her in vivid colours and details. She stepped toward the path leading to the lake. It was overgrown and hadn't seen life in a long time, yet Julia was drawn by the promise of water this close to the cottage.

The lake wasn't big, about a hundred feet across and a mile long. She glanced back at the cottage but it was now out of focus.

The old boat dock looked like it had seen better days.

Nothing was familiar, but by the beaten dock, she found an old sign, like a road sign with the name Hamilton Beach and an arrow pointing south. She'd never heard of the place, obviously not many people had.

The sun would set soon, and she needed to escape these trees and find someone to help her. A stranger. She sighed, not comfortable with the idea, but needing help just the same. Really, she could sit and wait for Steve, or get help herself. Of the two solutions, a stranger was the best option. Clearly, Steve was insane. Al pushed him over the deep end. Stealing her undies. What was wrong with some people? Still, she smirked. For some reason, she liked the idea of him going out of his way to set things up for her. Maybe she was crazy, too.

Yet... he'd made her a home she liked, and it was perfect. She'd never admit that to him, but inside, to herself, she couldn't lie. This dream he'd created for her was theirs and no one could steal that away.

Julia followed the path and her thoughts cleared slowly. It was like waking from a dream. She was more aware of herself. Her breath tasted rank. She'd never take her toothbrush for granted again... if she got home. Maybe she should have grabbed a toothbrush at the cottage.

She glanced at the stone cottage as she walked the path to the lake. Everything was ghostly. Why didn't it feel weird? Probably because she'd seen it so many times in her dreams. It was home. She'd live in this cottage in a minute. With Steve.

This wasn't home, her logic reminded her. Home was with Max and James. No, not anymore. James was moving out. It wouldn't be home without him. Besides, Max would love this place by the lake. What dog wouldn't?

Was James searching for her?

Julia had no idea if anyone even knew where she was yet or if anyone was even searching.

Oh, she missed Bobby, too. Not in the same way, because she tolerated Bobby for James. The safety he created was a nice thought right about now. She wanted something safer than these woods. She felt alone. She pictured Bobby, but slowly the image faded into one of Steve.

She wanted... Steve. Not Bobby. Not James. Not Max. That was the truth, and she could think about her dog or her brother or about the policeman who was probably going nuts with worry, but at the end of each thought, she wanted the guy she ran from. Why? Why did she feel safe with him? Because it was Al they were fighting, and no matter what Bobby did, he would never be able to protect her from a guy who could be Uncle Jackson one minute and a bald monster the next. How could she have forgotten and why were these memories clear to her now?

I'll always protect you, Julia. Trust that.

She looked around. Despite this, there was a new longing inside her Steve created with his safe cottage and lusty dreams. Pine trees. She took a deep whiff of them. *He is nuts and kidnapped me today,* she reminded herself. Yet that wasn't what had happened. He wanted to protect her from something she didn't understand and he couldn't seem to explain to her properly. *Oh Steve.*

She wiped her tears and headed down the path. She couldn't stay here. She needed James.

She pushed herself harder and jogged up the path toward the dirt road. She followed it unsure where it would lead. It wound around trees and she came face to face with a fox.

The fox's hair went up along his neck and it growled. Under normal circumstances she would have simply turned around and prayed it didn't follow her, but she needed to get by, and the weird eagle circling the sky was freaking her out a bit. She wanted to stay along the trees.

She heard a yelp from the bush along the ditch and knew why this fox was so protective. "I promise I won't touch your babies, but I need by." She took a step forward. The fox growled louder, and she noticed blood on its fur. This wouldn't work.

The bush along the side of the road was thick but she managed to push her way through it a hundred yards off or so, then returned to the path. The fox watched her, but didn't move.

"Stupid fox." She cursed to herself, but she was back on the path with minor scratches. It was growing darker. Thankfully, there would be a bright moon soon.

The bush ripped at her pants and she ignored the scrapes on her arms. Julia forced herself to keep moving, even if she wasn't making much progress at this point.

She had no idea how long she'd run. Maybe this wasn't even running. She moved, but not fast. She considered curling up along the side of the road when she noticed a light in the distance. Maybe half a mile ahead.

Sore and tired, she rushed to it, promising herself that she was alive.

JAMES

Merde. James tossed the empty juice box back on the shed floor. He'd missed her. If that fox hadn't attacked him, he might have found her.

Where had Jules gone? He glanced around trying not to disrupt the scene. Steve had taped her to a chair. Clearly not well, but she should be here so he could rescue her. Only reason to do that was if Steve had to leave her and didn't want her wandering off alone because there were more than foxes in these woods. *Like eagles who shifted into creeps.* That much was clear. Everything was clear, as if he walked through motions he'd practised a dozen times.

James followed her tracks in the dust. They ran around the room. First to the shop sink; she was thirsty.

His arm bled from the fox bite so he needed water, too. He tried the taps. No water. Not a drop. Hmmm. He passed his hand over his face. He was too angry. He needed control of the rage. He wasn't thinking clearly. His finger twitched.

Breathe. Focus.

She would be searching for safety. Familiar items. Nothing was familiar. So where would she go? He stood back. It grew dim, but he swept the flashlight he'd found over the room. The old door was rotten and broken, almost as if someone had charged through it. A pamphlet was tossed casually on the floor, and...

Wait.

Steve would not toss anything on the floor. Not that clean freak.

James picked it up.

It was for tunnels around the lake. Well, now he was getting somewhere. He smirked. Maybe Steve was on his side. His index finger ran over it smoothly and he was surprised to see it not twitching. Hmmm.

Forgotten tunnels under a lake would take care of his AI problem. An unexpected cave-in felt about right.

But what about Jules? Where could she be? Why hadn't he seen her?

He wiped the blood from his arm using his T-shirt, then he

headed back into the darkening night.

She couldn't be far.

"Jules?" he called into the shadows. Maybe she went in this house. Strange that he hadn't noticed it during his search. Lights were on inside. He climbed the steps and ran his hand over the carvings in the wooden railing. James shone the flashlight on them and did a double take. Neat. Someone had carved monsters in the wood. He examined each spindle. Each one had a carved creature on it. As his hands ran over them, his world shifted, as if he was suddenly drunk.

Had Steve made this? Amazing. What were these creatures? One was a horse with wings, another was a giant man made of stones. Some even looked like butterflies. He'd never seen anything so wicked. No. Not wicked—demonic. Facts about demons rushed at him and James shook his head to clear it.

He knocked on the door and again paused at the masonry. Things were clearer. The dizziness he'd experienced on the steps was gone. This house was built by hand. Each rock put in place, lovingly. He felt the pride put into it as if he'd done it himself. No wonder Steve was in such good shape.

He opened the door. "Hello? *Bonjour?*"

The cottage was empty, but he walked in. The place was nice. Way cleaner than their place. Julia would go nuts in something this perfect, yet... it did scream her touch. Better, it held a safe quality to it they didn't have in their home. This was a place where dreams protected him from the harsh cruel world.

He was home.

James cleaned up in the bathroom and, as he left, he paused in the living room at the photo on the wall. What the hell? It was his sister. Was this Steve's house? James was intrigued. Even more so when he spotted a photo of him and Jules from years ago. It was the most interesting place he'd ever visited. It was almost as if Jules herself had decorated it. How...

James inspected each room, one by one. Finally, he sat on the edge of the big bed. Lingerie was nestled on the comforter with an engagement ring snuggled in it. He picked up the ring and studied it. He didn't know much about diamonds, but it looked decent.

Hmmm.

This was a lot for Jules to hide from him. He didn't like this. Was Steve delusional? Living in a fantasy?

Magic.

I'm a Dream Whisperer.

Men turning into bald eagles.

Moaning in her dreams.

Demons on spindles.

Jules was in serious trouble. His finger went nuts with the possibilities.

Bottom line was that Jules was missing, and she wasn't safe until she was with James. *Comprends?* Yeah. That he understood. That much, his brain wouldn't let go.

He went to the shed to search the semi for the gun. He was sure he'd find it there. Steve was leaving him a trail of breadcrumbs. He didn't like this but didn't see a way off the path he was stumbling on.

JULIA

Julia peered through the trees at the old houses in the abandoned town. They were intact but in shambles. A few windows were broken or boarded.

She didn't feel safe and thought about returning to the cottage. At least there, she felt love.

The only light came from a running police cruiser at the end of the street. It shone on the deserted town. A truck had been left in the middle of the dirt road, but other than this, there was no sign of life.

Was that Bobby's cruiser? The idea terrified her. Before she could decide if it was a good thing that he'd come for her, someone breathed on her neck. She hadn't even heard footsteps. How could this be? Had they swooped in beside her?

She turned. A tall bald man held a finger to his lips.

Al.

She scrambled back, ready to scream, but when he whispered, the oddest sensation came over her. *Floating.*

How was this possible? Her insides were on fire and she could no longer feel her body as it fell to the ground, helpless. She stood, staring at her body as it collapsed on the grass. Why wasn't she in her body?

Panicked, she glanced at Al. The world came to life in front of her in vivid colours. Cold fright washed over her.

"STEVE," she screamed. Yes, she needed Steve. "STEVE!" her soul screamed so loud she was sure even James would hear her.

STEVE

"Julia?" Steve heard her as if she was beside him, screaming in panic. He pulled over to the side of the road. He was too far from Hamilton Beach.

A police car wasn't shy about following him and pulled in behind him. Once at Hamilton Beach he'd whisper for him to forget and send him on his way.

But was he too late? What had happened to Julia?

Terror invaded every tiny fibre of his soul.

Julia.

He was too far from her. He wanted to be with her instantly. What was happening there? The weight of everything he had to lose fell on his shoulders.

In his rear-view mirror, he saw shadows diving at the police car. Something was definitely wrong.

His soul ached. Why?

The police officer scrambled out of his car and stumbled into the ditch as if something was chasing him. Steve climbed out of the car, too. An overwhelming sense of fear smashed into him. He knew what caused that type of feeling; a fear demon was near. Hell, Al. What a prick. First the cops, now this. Steve wasn't trained to whisper to disturbed demons.

Then again, Steve wasn't trained to whisper in dreams but he was good at that, plus Satan probably wouldn't mind if Steve whispered to his demons, as long as he treated them with the respect they deserved. Mischief had always been there for him, and he believed that if given a chance, all demons could be that reliable.

The shadow crept along the ditch and slipped in his car. The puppy howled.

Great. If Al controlled this demon, it would be nasty.

"You okay?" He called to the cop.

"What was that?"

"Fear demon. *Get in your car and drive home. Sleep, dream of being a hero, and forget everything that upset you today.*"

"'Kay. You be safe now."

"You beware."

The cop actually got in his car, did a U-turn right on the deserted highway, and headed back to the city.

Steve climbed in his car to calm the puppy. He could handle this. The shadow reappeared in the backseat. This time, in the mess of darkness, he saw Julia locked in a silent scream.

Not Julia—her soul. No wonder his soul ached.

Hell.

Steve dived for the shadow only to watch it melt into the seat. The puppy trembled by the water dish he'd set on the floor of the backseat. Why dive when he could have whispered? He was always doing that. No wonder Al was winning. It was instinct on his part to respond as a man. He slammed his hand into the seat then reached for the dog to calm her.

How would he find Julia if she was mixed up with a fear demon?

"Mischief."

Mischief appeared in the seat beside him. "*You look like shit, man. What's going on? Thought you were bringing your gal home today. I got her a gift.*" He showed Steve the tiny red orb in his hand. It was beautiful but he had no idea what it was for.

"Some stupid-ass demon took off with her soul."

"*Shit. I'll hang out in Hell and if she shows I will haul her back.*"

"What'll he do to her?"

"*Well...*" Mischief took in several deep breaths and his glossy black chest rose and fell in even sweeps. The puppy climbed on Mischief's lap and snuggled in for a nap. "*Depends who whispered to him.*"

Steve pulled out and headed toward Hamilton Beach.

"A safe guess would be Al."

"*Then... well...*" Mischief petted the puppy, his long fingers mingling in her fur.

Steve glanced at his friend. "Spit it out."

"*He's known to ask demons to carry a soul to other realms with them.*"

"Where is her body? Can she live out of it?" Hopefully, her body was at the cottage.

The black slits in Mischief's yellow eyes blinked out. "*You invite her through her door and into Dreamland with you and she survives. She will be fine.*"

"Yeah, but she's with *me* in Dreamland."

"*How long she will last out of her body depends on the realm they dumped her off at.*"

"I need to be with her. Can I use the butterflies to visit other realms?"

"*I could help you, if you insist on following her. But you need to come up with a better plan. This one sucks.*"

"I thought you could only travel to Hell." Steve pulled into the town where he grew up. A police cruiser was in the middle of the street, still running, but he couldn't see anyone. He drove slowly and parked by Al's old truck. He'd left it in the middle of the road as if he still owned this town.

"*I do have other friends, you know. Geesh. What we need is a tracker. A demon who can blow your soul from realm to realm. Sit back, I'll summon Hawk. This might blow up in our faces, but it's worth the try.*"

Steve turned the car off and locked the door. The puppy was on Mischief so he left the door open, this way the puppy could run in and out. Steve glanced over the seat. Her bowl still had water. Hopefully he wouldn't be out of his body for long. He looked at her long and hard trying to summon some courage. James was right, calling her Julia wouldn't work if Julia was going to live with them. And she had to. Maybe Julia would come up with a better name.

While Steve distracted himself with these thoughts, Mischief snapped his fingers and a strong wind rushed at them. Suddenly, Steve was blown from his body and out of the car. A huge bird was before him. Like a prairie hawk only eight feet tall and well... slightly see-through. His eyes were yellow like Mischief's, only more so.

Steve waited. He knew better than to talk to a demon he didn't know.

Mischief slipped out of the car. "*His soulmate was taken. He needs to catch up to her. She is kind of girly looking.*" Mischief made an hour glass figure with his hands. "*Goes by Julia and when she is scared she screams like this—*" He screamed Steve's name like a girl.

Hawk flapped his wings once, twice and the wind pushed into Steve's soul.

The freedom was intoxicating. If he lost Julia, he didn't plan to return to his body anyway. Still, as he floated from it, he knew the truth, she could be anywhere. How would he find her?

"STEVE!"

The wind picked up and everything blurred around him as he left the Mortal Realm.

STEVE

Steve had no idea he could be this afraid. He was on a new realm that looked like a snow cave. He dropped the ball of snow he'd picked up and called out into the looming tunnels.

"Julia? Are you here?"

"Steve!" she yelled from somewhere overhead. He looked up. Shadows lined the top of the cave. He had no idea where he was, what any of these realms were called, or who lived on them. This was the third one, and it at least made a bit of sense. Although he wasn't sure why light came from under his feet.

The shadows moved along the ice wall.

"Julia, I'm coming for you." He gripped the cold wall and climbed. He scurried up the side of the cave, his hands searching for any grip to hoist himself up. His soul ached where his muscles were on his mortal body, as if he were in it. It was a strange sensation. The walls were so cold his fingers grew numb. He saw shadows run along the top of the cave. With no idea how he'd pull her out of them, Steve continued his climb. He'd worry about that once he got to her. Maybe he'd become one with her and they could return to the heavens like a whispering god. Al wouldn't be able to mess with them then.

He flung himself up higher. Shadows scurried to his left so he switched direction but they rushed toward him. His grip slipped. *His grip*... the cold wall under his fingers crumbled.

Steve fell.

Julia screamed as the wind picked up and blew him into a new world. He rolled in... sand?

Grains of sand pelted into his mouth and eyes. It blew on him like rain, making a horrible crashing sound as if it were a thunderstorm. Everything felt more real than on the Mortal Realm. The sand pelted his face, burning and soppy.

He faced the new world he'd been blown into. He couldn't see a blasted thing through the whirling sand. Where was he now? Squinting he tried to see her, but sight was clearly not the sense he needed on this realm. He blocked the sand from his face and took in a deep breath. Her lilac perfume wafted toward him from the right. Steve wandered that way. Fear increased with each step. He was closer. Closer. He stumbled in the sand. It was cold under his fingers. Feeling like a blind fool, he got up. Everything was out of focus as the sand whisked around him madly. He trudged on. Suddenly, right in front of him, her face appeared.

"Julia." Steve reached out for her but her face transformed into a fanged beast and he pulled away. "Julia?" He spit out the mouthful of sand he'd inhaled.

It was impossible to hear anything over the roaring of the sandstorm.

Then the blowing sand fell and the sky was pink around him. Three suns lit the world. He was in a barren desert. No sound. No movement. Alone.

He couldn't keep doing this.

His panic deepened. He needed a better plan. "*Butterflies, find James. Mischief, I need magic that will allow James to see me.*"

JAMES

James walked out of the shed while loading the gun Steve had pointed at him earlier. He'd found the bullets in the glove box of the truck.

The idiot hadn't even loaded the bloody gun. Probably didn't know how this piece worked. James was mortified. *Sacré. Moron.* After slipping the gun inside the backpack he'd found full of flashlights and supplies, he went hunting for the tunnels. It took him longer than he'd hoped, but the entrance was in the woods, the path to it well-worn. He flipped open the cellar door.

Going underground was probably safer than walking through the woods anyway. He shivered at the idea of facing wildcats.

James climbed down the ladder to the tunnel and tasted the dust in his mouth as it made sludge behind his teeth.

Suddenly, Steve appeared before him. Well, he looked like Steve, but when James put the flashlight on him... he was kind of see-through and surrounded by... butterflies? This guy kept getting weirder and weirder. James got in for a closer look. Hmmm. So this was magic. "You plan to say something or just freak the *merde* out of me with your butterflies?"

"I'm soul travelling. The longer I do this, the less likely I am to return to my body so I don't have long. Al used a demon to steal Julia's soul. She's trapped on a spiritual realm somewhere in this universe. She could be anywhere. Anywhere, James. On hundreds of realms. Anywhere. I need help. When I get to where she is, he moves her. How do I find her in the universe without him knowing I've found her?"

Yup. Sounded like Steve, blubbering and confused about things that had simple solutions. Why did he let this Al guy freak him out? Still, James could see how dedicated he was to his sister, and well, James liked that.

"Can you whisper to this demon who has her?"

"Doubt it."

"Then it's Al you want, not the demon. Go to him directly.

Make him bring her to you."

"He won't do that. He just won."

"Make him think like a man. Why doesn't he want you with my sister?"

"He linked our souls and can't undo it. He wants me to stay away from her until the bond wears off."

"Really?" James was doubtful. "Could it be that maybe, just maybe the two of you are his ticket outta here? Could the two of you have powers to send him packing? Or perhaps do damage he won't survive?"

"What? You think Julia can kill Al?"

"It's a possibility. One of several. But not alone. Clearly. It would take you and Jules. That's why he's keeping you apart. He's looking out for his own ass."

The swirls of pinks, yellows, and blues that were Steve exploded and the butterflies went in and out.

"Damn, James. I wanted to unbind my soul from hers." Steve actually looked troubled.

James shrugged. "I call 'em as I see 'em, and you can't unbind with her because she's your other half, you're linked, end of story. Why else would he be keeping you apart? Think a little. He brought you together because he needed a power of some sort, took it, then realized he couldn't use it."

"Most times if a power belongs to someone more powerful they call it back."

"Exactly. So now she has this freaky power and he has to keep the two of you apart so you don't use it on him."

"If I undo the ritual, I won't be able to use her magic."

"You won't undo it. Don't lie to me. You want to be one with my sister forever. It's what I'd want if I found my soulmate."

"I can't ask her to help me destroy him. Have you met your sister? She's so... good."

"Like you're not."

"I've gone my entire life trying not to kill or hurt anyone with my poisonous whispers, but I know deep down that if Al hurts Julia, I don't care if he's my own flesh and blood, I will send him to Afterlight. And I don't need her to do that."

"But you don't want to?"

"Of course not, he's sick. I'd like to help him. He's smart, he's dedicated, and in his own way, he was always there for me. I mean, damn, he's my dad."

"And you don't want Jules to do it?" James studied Steve's shining light. Was this his soul? It was kind of dreamy—in a macho way.

"Julia? James, I've watched Al kill. He gets a rush as the soul moves on to Afterlight, but killing Al would scar our souls, turn us horribly dark. I'd rather spend my life undoing his work."

"That's working out real well, isn't it? Running from him will only get you so far, Steve. Show him what you can do. *Vas-y.*"

STEVE

The puppy was on Steve's lap when he came back to his body. The bald eagle circling the skies in the moonlight made his skin crawl. It grew dark, already a few stars sprinkled the skies while the sun set. He put the puppy on the passenger seat and climbed out of the car, leaving the door open. The dog followed.

The muscles in his shoulders ached and Steve stretched them out.

Two policemen rushed forward with their guns drawn as if he was the threat, their souls were a freaked-out mess. Clearly, Al had whispered to them. He looked down at the dog with a heavy sigh. "That gangly one is the one I was warning you about," he told the dog. "Annoying how he's always after our Julia."

Steve faced the cops. "I'm here for Al." He clenched his fists, ready to knock the pricks out if they had her.

"Who?" they asked together.

Steve pointed to the eagle as it swooped toward them. "I assume that's Mr. Eagle."

Al shifted beside the cops into a man. They backed up. The dog barked and backed behind Steve with a little growl.

"Son. You're looking... annoyed. See you're having a bit of a problem staying away from the enemy. No worries, she's contained."

"I want her back."

The pup yelped in support.

"Yeah, and I want you to activate this magic I received during the bonding ritual years ago. Doesn't mean we get what we want."

So he still had the magic. Well, he was going to start by getting it away from Al. "I propose a challenge."

The cops were agitated and stopped listening to sweep their weapons around nervously from one to the other. Al faced them. "*Sleep.*" They fell to the ground like Raggedy Ann dolls.

Al rubbed his hands. "Go on, you mentioned a challenge. I'm curious what you have in mind."

"Bullfight in Hell. I'll be the matador. Since you seem to like shifting into animals, you be the bull. Mischief is setting things up as we speak."

Al's right eyebrow went up playfully. "Oh I love this. Winner keeps the girl."

It annoyed Steve that Al thought of women as possessions. Over the years, he'd gotten to know her well, and Julia was like him. She stood her ground. She was smart, funny... "She watches from the crowd, free, while we play for her soul. But I get a moment alone with her before we fight, that's all I want, one moment to say good-bye."

"Then I want one of your powers if I win."

Steve frowned and glanced at the dog. She was sitting beside him, a little braver. "Which one?"

"You'll find out when you lose."

Steve checked his wrist as if expecting his magic to disagree with this offer, yet the power for sending a soul to Afterlight throbbed toward Al. The word he needed tickled his tongue he was so eager to use it. "You want the ability to send a soul to Afterlight with one little word?"

Al grinned. "Then it's settled, by the witness of the gods, that's the power we play for." The earth rumbled in agreement. "There something you want to play for, son?" Al waited.

Steve bent to scratch the dog behind the ears. "I told you, all I want is a moment with her."

"Oh I'll give you that for free. It'll motivate you to play dirty. What ability do you want from me? All my powers are yours for the taking. Choose wisely." He offered up his wrist as if it was a huge honour to feel his magic.

Steve forgot how Al could shift from nasty to nice in a breath. He took a step back. "You think I stand a chance, Dad?"

"All's fair in love and war, or so they tell me. State your prize." He stared intently at Steve, folding his arms in front of him.

"Well. When things went wrong, you took Julia's powers, but... they belong to her. If you lose you should give them to her before you move on."

Al stepped forward. "She wants this magic? All of it? I

asked for one power."

Steve had no idea if she wanted them, or what she would say if she knew Steve asked for them. They were safer with Julia. That much he knew. "Do you agree?"

"Well." Al's jaw was firm as he paced in the light from Steve's car, ignoring the coppers at his feet. "This might work." He nodded. "Last thing I wanted, Steve, was to have to kill you. Heck yeah, that works for me." His grin was tight-lipped as he pulled his entire face into a weird elated smile. "You sure you have the guts to play me this challenge, pansy?"

Steve nodded.

"If you back out halfway, I'll kill James."

Steve stepped forward. "If you back out halfway I'll haunt your sleep."

Al nodded. "It's a deal, son. See you in Hell." He whispered for a demon to merge with him and his soul whisked off to Hell.

"Stay. I'll be right back," Steve said to the dog. "Mischief, bring me to Hell."

JULIA

Julia's soul was one with the fearful demon as she blinked from place to place. Not only did he share his thoughts about each new place with her—one was too hot, one too crowded, one smelt like the inside of a shoe—she shared his hope and his fear with each movement he took. It was strange. She was still her, she knew all she always knew, yet she knew more. She knew things from the beginning of time, from before people existed and gods travelled the heavens. She knew the Whisperers who had taken this demon's powers and how he was frustrated with Steve for not listening to Al.

When she saw Steve, she shared the demon's elation at seeing him. This was a fun game to him. He was proud that he played it with Steve, because Steve was a Chosen One. Satan had big plans for Steve.

He shared this in his happy way and as scared as she was, there was nothing scary about being one with this demon. She wanted to stop moving. To stand on her own and she pleaded the demon to stop for a minute so she could pull herself together.

Suddenly, he did.

She was in the middle of a crowd of strange creatures. The fear demon ripped away from her. Elbows and... *branches?* were in her face. Julia glanced to her left, feeling an intense presence bear into her.

Steve.

She flung around excited. His handsome features stood out from among the strange beasts. He was a greyish light with a swirling rainbow at its core. She locked on his face. He had the saddest eyes. She was sure Steve would stand out anywhere, but why was he grey and... see-through? More than anything, she was drawn to the rainbow-light that flashed in his core. It made her want to be naughty.

Then he vanished and she felt the tingle of Steve's hand against her waist and spun around to see him, but he flashed out and was against her other side.

"Shh," he breathed against her ear as she stepped against his greyish see-throughness, grasping for the rainbow calling out to her from inside him. "I've challenged Al to a whispering duel for your soul's freedom. Well, there's a power exchange involved, too."

Julia stepped closer to him and the light coming from her rubbed against his, flaming up in a colourful rainbow trimmed in grey. "Steve, I'm scared. Why do I feel so alive? I saw my body fall. I was one with a demon who adores you."

"Our bodies are at Hamilton Beach, waiting for us. This is Hell but your soul is still linked to your body. See the thread coming out of it? You can go back as long as the link isn't severed." He looked down at her, ready to melt right into her. "As souls we can become one." The desperation in his eyes made her edge in closer. "But there might be no undoing that. It might not be something we can return from, but... Julia, I want to." The crowd pushed around them.

It was loud and noisy, but she didn't care. "I feel real."

"Oh we're real, like in the dreams. It's that we're more alive. We're pure energy and if we combine the energy, it'd be a rush."

Like she'd done with the demon. "Can others do this?" she wondered.

"You can't mingle your soul with just anyone. Demons sure, but not other mortals, it's because of that ritual we did when we were sixteen."

"If we unbind our souls, will we be able to do this?"

"Probably not," he admitted. "Becoming one would be impossible with our souls. Physically, yeah, but not with our souls. The ritual allows it, it opens the walls. Unless of course..."

"What?"

"They say soulmates have this bond naturally since this is who you were one with at the dawn of existence and it is who you must unite with to return to the heavens."

"How do you know we aren't soulmates?"

He winced. "Al said we aren't. James thinks we are. I don't know. I wonder myself sometimes. I even looked it up in sacred Notebooks, and it said that when soulmates meet, a rainbow springs to life in their souls." He swallowed. "I mean, it's wishful thinking, but your soul has this beautiful rainbow light that pulsates in the center of you. Sometimes, I lie to myself at night and dream that it might be a rainbow just for me. A rainbow. Stupid, but since I read that, I want to see it so desperately in you, I actually do."

Steve was dressed in jeans and the familiar *Get Naked and Muddy* T-shirt from her dreams. His swirling rainbow was strong and pulled her toward him. She stepped into it, letting the crowd push them together as if by accident. He gasped but she moaned, feeling the intensity of his grey light smear into hers. It was the most warmth she'd ever felt inside her. She was herself. Yet... the rainbows that were Steve cuddled her. She knew all he knew. Shared the rush of their emotions, their knowledge, their magic, their love, his... fear.

She pulled away from him. She had no idea he was afraid of what he could do. He wouldn't be able to fight Al this terrified of his powers.

"You pulled away." He gasped, clutching her as if she might run. "How? Hell, Julia. I was so entranced by you I couldn't move. Where do you hide that love? How is it possible to love so much? So deeply?"

"Of course I pulled away. Like you did from my body. It's possible. You fear for nothing, Steve. Think of it like sex. It might feel like we'll never be able to satisfy each other but that moment will come when we know all we can stand to learn and we pull away."

"Promise?" The distress showed in his rigid jaw.

"Steve, is this what troubles you? That you'll in some way..."

He studied her face. "Absorb your soul, turn you evil, make you into the monster I am." He looked to the side, not seeing her. "Yeah. I don't want you to end up like me."

She forgot about the weird creatures around her and thought about what the fear demon had taught her. "Look at my soul. Does it look frail?"

"No. It's beautiful, pure, and strong. It smells like lilacs." He had a lusty glare to his eyes. "Can we... do that again? It was the most exciting thing I've ever experienced."

"If I am bonded to you as your soulmate, this makes me your equal. Trust me, Steve. I can stand up with you against Al."

"Please don't. You're not a Whisperer. You're not a part of

this world."

"Steve. Neither are you. You're a man who whispers to me in my sleep. You're just a good guy."

He touched her hair and sent tingles through her entire soul. "I'll be fine, Julia. Sit here and wait for me. Al is an idiot who agreed to a bullfight as the bull."

"Why does that make him an idiot?"

Steve was grim. "The bull always dies."

"Always? You sure?" She was afraid for him. "You're talking about ancient bullfights that were set up. This is very real and you don't have any advantages." A part of her never wanted to be without Steve.

"My advantage is that I think like a man. He wants to be a beast, let him. James said this is the best type of fight for me to win. I trust him."

"James said that?"

A monster made of solid rock led Steve to the field and prepared him for battle by giving him a sword and armour, even a cape.

She tried her best to ignore the monsters around her. Not that they paid her attention. They acted like fans at a ball game.

The crowd waited for the competitor, for Al. Clearly, he was the one they came to see. He didn't disappoint either. He stomped out. The largest beast Julia had ever seen. A monster to defeat all monsters. He was at least twenty feet high, solid black. Her heart sank because there was no way Steve and his little sword could defeat this giant beast.

Cheers erupted as he strutted around the arena. Julia was knocked forward. She glanced back, surprised that these creatures could push her around when she was a soul. Everything was weird. She wanted to go home. Not her big empty house either, she wanted that cozy cottage. Home.

Julia scrambled to find a better place so she could see what Steve was doing, but he stood calmly on the sidelines and watched Al putting on a show.

Al paraded around, huffing and puffing, stomping and proving to the crowd that he was in fact the bull.

If the monstrous bull was supposed to die, he didn't know this. Given his size and speed, Julia didn't see how it was possible for Steve to kill this thing. Could he kill his dad? Julia had been one with Steve, and there was no way she'd felt that inside him. He was afraid for his father. Her heart raced and she touched a hand to her chest. She felt so real. One stomp and he was dead. Could you kill a spirit? She'd felt real when shoved a moment ago.

Julia pushed her way through the crowd, closer to Steve, until she was along the railing. "Steve."

He flung around to face her. "Julia?"

"Be safe." It was all she could say.

He smirked and with a light bow, he said, "Beware." His hand rubbed her cheek gently. "Julia, don't be afraid. I have a simple target. I know how to wear him down. James and I simulate battles in our dreams all the time, well... when I'm not with you. Your brother knows weird shit. Does he do this in real life?"

"Ah no, mostly he gives me grief." She felt better. If James taught him what to do, he'd be fine. James knew how to fight. She'd never actually seen him fight a bull with a sword, but she was sure he could survive in this ring blindfolded. Yeah. James was a survivor, if there was a way, he'd find it.

The crowd fell silent.

Julia scanned the area to see why. The bull stopped showing off and fixated on Steve. His target.

"Guess that's my cue." Steve walked to the center of the field and waited.

No one breathed. The air even shifted, layering itself as if the tension was too deep for this spiritual world.

Then Steve broke into a run with his sword drawn.

The bull charged.

Within moments, he stomped over Steve. Julia leaned on the railing, her entire soul in a knot as she searched the dust for him. *Please don't let him be hurt*, she prayed.

The crowd went breathless with her.

When the dust settled, Steve was motionless in the sand.

Screams of excitement came from behind her, but Julia could hardly hear the crowd, her heart beat so fast. How could it make that much noise when she was nothing but a spirit?

Without thinking, she jumped the railing and ran to him.

Steve hadn't moved and the bull turned for a second stomp.
"Steve, wake up. Wake up," she screamed, picking up speed.
The bull changed his course, headed her way.

STEVE

Julia?

Steve must be dreaming. Julia ran toward him across the battlefield? He assessed the situation. Al, in bull form, charged. Julia ignored the bull and rushed to Steve, yelling for him to get up.

"Time, still," Steve whispered, not sure how powerful the magic was on this realm or how long time would stand still. Did time exist here? It was an ability he rarely used on the Mortal Realm, forget in Hell.

Everything around him froze, even Julia. She was moments from being crushed by Al's horns and hooves. Steve dashed to her, tackling her to the ground. The world unfroze as they rolled together, their souls blended for a moment and Al charged on with a victorious bellow. Steve felt the whoosh as a hoof planted inches from them.

"Julia." The warmth of her soul gave him hope. She was safe. "What are you doing? Get back in the stands."

"Steve, I thought I lost you."

"I'm not that easy to kill. Mischief is with me. He won't let Al kill me." Mischief tensed against his soul. He didn't like to merge with him completely, but he latched on to his soul like a leech.

She recoiled.

"You on the other hand would be toast. Go."

The bull changed direction to survey the damage and came for them again as they scrambled to their feet.

"Run, Julia."

"Your sword." She glanced at the sword and it flew to him.

"Cool. You whispered to my sword. Run." He shoved her, but she clasped his hand. "Go. Mischief can't project us both out." Yet he couldn't let her hand go either. It would have to be her who pulled away.

"Tell me what to do. I'm not leaving."

He didn't have time to argue with her. He rushed toward his cape, dragging her behind. "We won't make it. Whisper for the cape to cover his eyes."

"I... How?"

"Like with the sword. Believe. Want. Whisper."

"*Oh Steve, I do want that cape to cover his eyes*," she said in a quick breath as they ran. His whispering magic flowed from his hand to hers. Weird. He had no idea his magic could do things like that. Maybe Al was right and those powers were rightfully hers. The cape magically flung itself at the charging bull and Steve reversed his run, Julia in tow. They dashed toward the bull. Al was frantically shaking his head, caught in the run, but slowing to collect his bearings.

Steve's entire focus was Al's front left leg. The tattoo he wanted would be there. If he cut Al from his powers, it was all he needed to do. Those powers would be free to return to their rightful owners. "Let go of my hand," he told her.

She did and Steve clutched the sword with both hands charging for the leg. She was tight against him. He wanted to tell her not to touch him while he did this but he felt her already arguing with him as her soul gripped his. *She wasn't letting him go*.

Al shook the cape free as the sword pierced the tattoo announcing him as a Soul Whisperer. The magic seared into the weapon and passed through Steve. It settled in Julia who had her arms around him in a bear hug.

Noooooo!

Julia stumbled into Steve, pushing the sword in deeper.

"*I want us back by our bodies*," Julia whispered, and just like that, Steve was sucked from the demon realm and back to the real world, in the woods.

Nooooo!

"We have to go back. We have to go back." Steve was frantic. He was close to winning. "Hell. Hell. Mischief, whisk me to Hell." He was snapped back to Hell, but Al was gone, the crowd was gone. The ring was empty.

He dropped to his knees.

"*I'm sorry*," Mischief said. "*She whispered to your souls, there was nothing I could do*." He pointed to the sky where the suns shone far apart. "*In accordance with the Mortal Realm's timeline, time flies when the suns pull apart and stands still when they touch. Everyone has gone. We must get back. I sense your Julia's panic and I do not like it*."

Al would think he opted out. Meant he'd be hunting James.

STEVE

Steve went back to Julia. She was gaping at her lifeless body as morning light streamed in through the forest. They'd been gone all night, and it had felt like only a few hours.

He had no idea how deep in the woods they were, but the trees were denser to the north which meant they were probably close to town.

"How do I get in my body?" She was frantic.

Steve understood her panic. He'd lived it himself too many times.

"We have to hurry. Your brother is in trouble. Try stepping into it," he told her. "It hurts, so sorry. It burns and stings, and feels like you're being sucked into a vacuum. This might not work." Then again, Julia's soul came to him every evening. Maybe she was used to this. "Pretend you're waking up."

She rested on her fallen body. He offered to hold her hand but she didn't grab it. No, not his Julia. What a brave girl. He watched her soul as it struggled with the weirdness of merging with her body again. The rainbow light in her soul reached out like a hand and pulled him closer. He leaned over her.

Finally, she sank into her body and reconnected with it.

"You're right," she mumbled, her eyes closed. "It was like falling into myself, kind of like waking from a dream. I almost reached for you at the last moment, but I felt the comfort of my own aches and gave in."

She touched him. Her soul clutched his when her fingers grazed his cheek.

"How do you feel?"

She had her eyes closed. He caressed her face, her hair.

"For a soul, you feel real," she said.

Suddenly through the trees the dog came crashing at them. She dived for Steve, knocking him off Julia, slopping kisses all over him, pinning his soul to the ground.

"I am real." Steve chuckled and pushed the dog off him.

Julia got on her knees beside him and rubbed the dog's head. "She's adorable." The pup licked Julia. "A little scruffy brat."

Steve met her eyes, the dog between them. "Julia, how do you feel? You... you took in Al's powers." He forced a swallow down. "He'll come for you." *And James.* Gosh. He couldn't say that aloud.

"Cold and damp. Moments ago I was so alive and warm, and now... the realness of the world rushes at me."

"You're a Whisperer, now. One without a tattoo. That means the magic coursing through your soul is unpredictable, unstable, and very dangerous. I need to find my body. James is in danger and so are you. Any idea where we are?"

"Outside of town. I was looking at a police cruiser when I was ripped from my body." She jumped to her feet easily and faced his soul.

Steve peeked through the bushes to the south. Sure enough, his car was parked in front of the fancy house his pa grew up in.

"Julia, do you want me to try to break the connection between us? I see the link, I could whisper to it. If it works, then you can turn around and run to my car and never look back."

She peered through the leaves at the car in the middle of town with him. "Look at it, waiting for me."

He turned up his wrist, prepared to whisper to the link connecting their souls. It was a thread of a line, but seeing it always made him feel better. How painful would it be to break the link?

Julia went to grip his wrist and pulled away when her hand went right through him. "Sorry, I forgot you aren't real."

"I am real," he repeated. Why didn't she understand that his soul was real?

"Say the words and I'll do it, Julia. You'll have your freedom. Al won't be able to bother you. You have to request this. I won't make this decision for you."

"Will it remove the magic I did? Will I be me again?" she demanded.

He shook his head. "No. Unless Al calls the abilities back, they won't leave you. Even then, the gods decide who is worthy of it. You can't un-be a Whisperer. If you never get a tattoo, those powers coursing in your body will make you mad, turn you evil, and eventually destroy you. A tattoo like mine," he showed her his wrist, "helps control the magic. Kind of like a recipe book that stores it for you. You take it out when you need it. You'll learn to whisper to souls with it, all kinds. The energy in objects like blades and the souls in humans."

"Whisper to souls? That sounds horribly evil." She shook lightly and he watched an ability leave her and snap back to Al.

"That was the power to shift. He called it back." Steve glanced through the bushes, the dog peeked with him. Al was by the truck where they usually did their rituals, calling on the magic. How many more would she lose?

She took a deep breath as the truth set in. Steve sighed. Would she hate him for making her into this monster? Already, he noticed grey clouding her once light soul. He was polluting her.

Julia wouldn't meet his eyes, yet he continued to explain. "I have no idea what will happen if I unbind my soul from yours, but you'll be able to forget about me if I whisper this. We're running out of time, decide if you want me in your life or out."

"So I wouldn't feel the connection to you?"

He studied her, forgetting about Al.

She bit her bottom lip. Slowly the sun rose through the trees, bringing the world to life around them. The gentle light from her soul made her shimmer beside him. *Like a goddess.*

"Is it terrible?" Her voice shook.

She looked ready to run and he had no idea what she meant. It was all bad. Al was out there, calling her powers back. He wouldn't have time to try anything.

"The tingling?" Her voice was soft.

"You feel that?" He grabbed her shoulder. "That's not magic, that's you. The light rainbow in your soul is reaching out for me. It creates the rush between us."

"Why don't you want to be linked to me?" She glared at him now, anger in her soul and it took him off guard.

The dog yelped and they jumped.

"Me? I... I want..." He looked at the pup, he had no idea what he wanted.

Julia ran from him into the open where Al would surely see her.

Steve called after her, "This isn't about what I want, Julia." What did he want? The dog barked, urging him to go after her.

For so long he wanted to give her freedom it never occurred to him how that would affect him. Would he even survive if he couldn't go with her to Dreamland each night? If he couldn't feel the tingle between them?

The longing he had for her was crippling as the distance between them grew. She glanced back when he whispered her name but ran away from him.

Right to Al.

Al spotted her as she fell into the open area and stopped summoning her powers to charge for her. She noticed him too late and swerved back to the woods.

His arm was still bleeding but he'd clearly live.

Panicked, Steve rushed for his body by the car. The puppy ran to Julia, barking and growling.

Julia and Al rolled to the ground.

"Thought you'd sneak away?" Al mumbled against her hair loud enough for Steve to hear as he whipped by. "Give me my magic back. It's dangerous. You have no idea what you're doing with it." He restrained her.

Steve didn't take time to adjust to his body as the butterflies pushed him toward it, stumbling over the dog who dived then backed up, terrified then brave.

He ran to Julia as Al pulled out a knife. "In the name of the whispering gods," Al said. "I cut off your wrist to return their most sacred of powers until another shall be worthy." Julia squirmed under him.

Al raised the knife.

Steve wouldn't make it in time. "No!"

The knife came down.

The pup leapt for his arm.

"Stupid dog!" Al tossed her into the trees. Mischief caught her, appearing out of thin air. He set her down gently and rushed for Al. Al glanced up as Mischief dived, taking him in a tackle. They rolled off Julia and into the long grass by the forest. Steve rushed to Mischief as Al plunged the knife in his stomach.

"No!" Steve screamed, but Mischief shimmered out, bringing Al to Hell with him.

When Steve turned to help Julia, she was gone.

JULIA

Julia started the sports car, eager to run from it all. The pup had jumped in with her.

Her stomach growled, reminding Julia that she hadn't eaten all day or night. The pup edged toward her when she slipped behind the steering wheel.

She avoided looking at Steve, but she knew exactly where he was, as if his presence was a giant bulging, beating heart demanding her attention. She put the car in gear.

Finally, unable to resist the pull, Julia glanced at Steve. *Please Julia,* his eyes begged as he ran toward her. Why was he chasing her when moments ago he wanted to unbind with her so they could go their separate ways?

Al materialized out of thin air behind Steve. She screamed and stepped on the accelerator. The car lurched forward and a photo fell off the dashboard. She ignored it, taking the dirt road at a wild speed. The puppy whined. Julia glanced over as the dog nuzzled beside the picture of the cottage by the lake. Home.

STEVE

"Take me to Mischief." Steve swung at Al who ducked in his lightning-fast way. They'd been fighting now for a few minutes and they were by one of the abandoned houses in the deserted town. Al rammed into Steve, landing them through the old wooden veranda. The wood smashed under their weight.

Steve was quick to his feet, brushing off the debris. Frantic.

Julia was gone. Mischief was hurt. His dad would be going after James next. He felt like everything around him was falling apart. How could he contain him?

Al snapped Steve against the old house with a roar. "Give me back the power to raise the dead."

Raise the dead? Al thought he had the power to raise the dead? He didn't. And why did this power freak him out so much anyway?

Movement from the woods made them both turn. James ran out of the woods, like a ghost. He moved so fast Steve could hardly make him out. His soul was almost one with the hazy morning light as he expanded out and snapped back to his body.

"Where did you come from?" It's what Steve wanted to say but he wasn't sure it came out that way because James had him and Al pinned to the house by their throats before either could comprehend how Wild he was.

James' entire focus was on Al as if there was no one else on the entire planet. He trapped Steve, too, but Steve was sure it was for show. He hoped so anyway. He didn't want to be on James' shit list, or *merde* list as he was sure to call it.

"I wanted a chance to watch you boys cut off body parts you hold dear. And I was hoping to whisper to see how that worked out for me." When James made the threat, Al's eyes shifted to James' un-inked wrist.

"You ain't a Whisperer," Al said.

James pushed harder on his neck and his soul focused in and expanded out again. "Sounds like a dare to me."

Steve felt the pressure of James' index finger not twitching against his neck.

Come on James, get control.

"You willing to take that chance?" James said as he let Steve go so he could punch Al.

Steve caught his breath in short gasps. Al moved into the punch, letting the air out so his pain was minimized.

James pushed Steve and he stumbled on the messed veranda steps and scrambled up them to escape James' reach. James was already on Al. He tossed him at Steve and rushed up the steps at them.

James' soul steadied itself and caught fire. He hit Al again. Damn, the kid could hit. Al didn't hit back, not yet. Not this time. He let James believe he was in control for a few minutes. All part of the illusion. Steve knew how Al worked. James wouldn't win this.

Before Steve could intervene, one of the policemen appeared along the side of the house with a gun pointed at Steve. Great. Where did he come from? "In the house," he ordered. "I can't let you do this, James. They aren't worth it. Let me take them in."

James tensed and tossed Al in the house when the copper stepped aside. "Bobby, get outta here."

"*Shoot*," Al whispered from in the house. "*Shoot them both.*"

"*Time, still*," Steve whispered at the same time, and Steve actually heard the bullet from Bobby's gun as it soared. The world slowed. He dived for James and pushed him into Al who had scrambled to his feet.

The bullet caught where he'd been a moment before and blew a hole in the wall.

Steve ran into the house. This was a trap. They were luring James into the house and he needed to get him out of there. James was in a heap over Al. Neither moved. Why weren't they moving? What was wrong?

Their souls were gone.

Steve grabbed James' shoulder and flipped his body over. "Mischief, how do I get him back?" Steve was hysterical. "Mischief," he called desperately. How hurt was his friend? What if Al stole his powers for shifting to Hell? He thought about how he'd materialized. How the knife had pierced his friend.

"Don't move," the police officer shouted, the gun on Steve as he came into the house.

Steve ploughed Bobby over, into the broken veranda. He expected a few more shots, but without Al to whisper for them, they didn't come.

The gun flew from Bobby's hands and landed softly in the grass by the veranda.

Bobby's soul was tarnished, full of swirling yucky bronze clouds. He'd never seen that colour in a soul and it annoyed him that this soul was even near Julia.

Bobby was a much better fighter than Steve, that was clear when he restrained Steve to the ground, delivering blow after blow.

Gasping for air, Steve whispered, *"Off me."* Bobby flew back and landed through the door to the house, not far from Al and James. He was quick to scramble to his feet, and took on a defensive pose, but Steve was slow to his feet.

He walked to Bobby who trembled and Bobby said, "What... I mean how did you do that?"

"Dream time," he whispered again, and Bobby collapsed in a nice coma in the doorway to the empty house. Steve pulled him by the collar to sneak a better look at the creep who was after his girl.

Bobby had blood streaming from his nose, but other than that, he was fine. He pulled the knife from Bobby's hands, not sure when he'd taken it out. Dirty bugger.

"Steve?"

Steve turned to see Julia's soul flash a horrified orange. "Julia?" She came back!

He dropped the knife when her eyes went from Bobby to it.

"What did you do to Bobby? And James?" She gasped and the orange melted out of her soul in a quick sweep.

"It's not what it looks like," Steve stammered.

"You *are* a monster." She ran.

STEVE

Steve scrambled to his feet, chasing after Julia. *She came back,* it was all his mind shouted, reliving the moment. What good was seeing souls when he had no idea what anything he saw meant? Why did the confusion melt out of her soul?

Could he fix this?

"Julia," he called after her. She pushed through the trees and he rushed in after her in the morning light. Hunting her like a savage beast. "Mischief, stop her. Julia, stop! Wait. Let me explain." He glanced around for the puppy. She hated being alone. Where was she?

Steve chased Julia, her soul cried as he closed in on her. She glanced back at him and frantically ran harder, leaping over stumps and pushing aside branches.

"Leave me alone."

"I can't, Julia. Leaving you is the only thing I can't do. Please don't cry." The tears were tiny streams of pain his soul couldn't bear. He had to stop them before they killed her. Him. Them.

He ran in front of her and snagged her in his arms. At first, she struggled, hitting him with her fists but when her tears turned into sobbing, she rested her head against his chest, giving up.

"He's sleeping, Julia." Steve clutched her. "It's how I protect idiots to keep them out of harm's way. He'll wake in a few minutes."

"Sleeping?" she spoke against his chest.

"Yeah." Steve stroked her hair. "I'm a Dream Whisperer, Julia. I make people fall asleep with two words. Do you see why I hate to whisper? I have to be careful. I change free will. I... I am a monster."

She pulled away to say something but the tears started again. It was unlike her. He pulled her against him so his soul could bear the burden for her.

"Steve," she looked up at him, "even when I walked in and thought you killed the two most important people in my life, I still loved you." She pulled away from him and put her hands on the closest tree, as if touching it would make him vanish. "I'm the bloody monster. Why does it terrify me to think about unbinding our souls? I can't. Please don't ask me to."

She loved him?

"I didn't kill anyone. So forget that. If we can get to the cottage, we'll be safe there and we can summon James to Dreamland. He'll know what we should do." He swallowed as her soul went a multitude of colours, from pink to purple, he couldn't even pretend to understand. He wrapped his arms around her, burying his head against her neck. Forgetting about this mess for a moment. "If I could undo one thing in my life, it would be the ritual," he admitted. "Not because I don't want to be linked to you, but because I don't want to see you turn into a monster like me."

"You're not a monster."

"You think otherwise."

"Even if you get in my mind, my soul, you can't know what I feel. I feel like the monster." They were silent for a moment, holding each other. "Steve?"

"Yeah?"

"Can you wake James up? Is he okay?"

"No, he's far from safe. His soul is gone. I need my friend Mischief to find out where he is, but twice I called him and he didn't answer. Where did you leave my car? My dog?"

"Your bratty dog is fine." She smirked briefly. "I... I brought her home and got stuck behind the bait shop."

Home? His home? She was at the cottage then got stuck? Where was she going?

Oh. She hadn't come back for him. He pulled away from her. Here he thought she'd made a decision that she'd stay by his side. He'd been foolish to jump to that conclusion. Clearly. The crying, the confusion, it meant she wasn't any closer to figuring things out.

He knew how thin the line between love and hate was, he felt it all the time with Al.

He focused on her. "Al probably sucked your brother to Hell. I'm sure if anyone can have fun in Hell it's James, but I have to get you to safety so I can go after him, okay? Mischief?" He scanned the trees. "Where is he? Let's get you to the cottage. Julia, are you hurt? You don't have a bra on.

Did someone take it off you?" He came behind her and she tensed. He couldn't remember if he'd felt a bra earlier.

"Ah... Steve. My lack of a bra is not your business."

He wanted it to be. "Come, I'll carry you home." He scooped her up. "I want to make sure he didn't touch you, because if he did, I happen to know a god who hates him, and I'll hand him over to his demons. So yeah, your lack of a bra is my business." It sounded like a pout when he said it, but too bad.

She tried to break free from his arms. "Let me go."

"Did he touch you?" His grip around her was firm as he carried her off.

"No, Steve. I was late and upset yesterday morning and couldn't find it, okay?"

He watched her soul for a lie but it never wavered. "Oh. Sorry."

"Put me down."

"I want to carry you. You're upset and it makes me upset. I need to take care of you."

"I'm not a child," she said.

"I know, believe me, I know. When I'm upset, I expect you to take care of me, and I want to do the same. It's what good partners do, no?"

She leaned against his chest. Funny, but the tiny gesture made him feel better.

"Steve, Al doesn't want us together."

Julia was light in his arms, as his adrenalin pumped full force. "I know."

"Why not? Nothing happened when our souls were one," she said against his chest.

"What do you mean nothing happened?" Steve stopped running and his eyes swept over her body. "Stuff happened inside me. I don't imagine that counts to anyone else. But I felt... alive, even more drawn to you if that's possible."

"I meant nothing happened to him. For some reason, I thought it would. Put me down." She scrambled from his arms and faced him. The trees were tightly packed, yet enough light came from her soul for him to see every detail of her face. The energy between them increased again.

She ran her hands along his arms and held his wrists. His

magic coursed into her, deepening the rainbow in the middle part of her soul. Why was she able to share his powers? Was he corrupting her with a simple touch?

Like an idiot he spoke, not sure where he was going with his thoughts yet knowing he had to speak them. "This is where the tunnel..."

She took a step closer so their bodies touched.

Hell.

He forgot what he wanted to say and stood there like an idiot at her mercy, ready to please her, his eyes on her lips. She ran her finger along his jaw and the touch was electrifying. It invaded him in waves that weakened his knees and he dropped on them, kneeling before her, clutching her waist with his head against her stomach.

"I can't fight it, Steve." She ran her hands in his hair as she pulled him tighter against her.

"Mmmm." He slipped up her shirt and on his knees he licked her stomach then unbuttoned her pants. Teasing smells invited him in. He moaned as he worked her pants off her. Why wasn't he moving faster?

He moved too fast. He needed to enjoy her.

"There's a tunnel under my feet that runs along the lake to the barn and to our cottage. We're safe there. It's where we need to go. One of us has to pull away." He grazed her ankles as he ran his jaw up her bare legs. "James was right," Steve was almost pleading as he peeled off his shirt. "We need to stay away from each other. Back away. Your brother needs us."

"Julia?" Bobby hollered.

"Gee. Do you want Mr. Boring to find you without pants?" Steve kneaded her undies, wondering if he should rip them or slide them down gently. He wanted to do both. Desperately. How much time did they have? Did he really care if Bobby stumbled on them?

Her breaths deepened as his jaw rubbed her belly. Her shirt was off.

"Julia, answer or pull away so we can get in these tunnels." He kicked open the trapdoor with his foot, while he kept his hands on her. It was unlocked. Why was it unlocked? He felt out of focus, as if they were in a dream. Had he unlocked it?

No.

James. James had been here. He studied Julia, snapping his hands off her. "For James we need to control ourselves."

"For James." She nodded. "Bobby, I'm with Steve. Can you hear me? Go home. Leave me alone. Just leave me alone."

Her hips pushed against Steve. He brought his hands back to her body, lightly, and leaned in to kiss her neck.

"I hear ya," Bobby answered not far away. Lost in the trees. "I'm coming to save you, Julia."

"Julia?" Steve pulled her close, eyes closed. He swallowed hard. "Come with me to the tunnels." He drew her with him, shaking. She ran her hands down his pants and clutched against him tightly. Could she feel how ready he was for her? Nothing was stopping him.

He continued his journey exploring along her body with his hands. His jaw rubbed her cheeks. She was crying again.

He stepped away.

"Don't stop, Steve."

"You say that, but your tears scream that you haven't picked me yet, Julia. I can't. I... You have to vow to love me, Julia, as deeply and completely as I love you." He reached down and grabbed her clothes. "Get dressed. Maybe this Bobby guy can protect you while I go after James."

"You're leaving me with Bobby?"

"Clearly you're thinking about going with him. I thought you came back for me, not that you ditched my dog and got stuck while you left me." His pout annoyed him. Why was he always acting like a baby around her?

"But Steve..." Again, tears cut her off.

He grabbed her hands and put her clothes in them. "Stop crying, it's not like you."

"I can't help it. I've never experienced emotions this deep before, they're... drowning me. I have to release them."

"Yeah, whatever. It's clear you're not telling me something. So get dressed, and when Bobby shows, ask him to bring you home. I can't believe I'm even saying this. You'll be safer than with me. All I want to do is haul you down this hole to attack you in the mud."

"I'm the one attacking you, and I already am."

"Am what?"

"Home, you fool. That's why I came back. I was going home and realized I was already there. I brought our dog home and… I wanted you there with us."

Our dog…

"These tears have nothing to do with you, they're for another life I could have. Somehow, there was no choice to make, and this pisses me off." She slid her undies off and dangled them. "I want you."

He leapt at her, trapping her against a tree with his entire body as he stood over her. He wore too many clothes. Why was he wearing anything? He slipped her underwear in his pocket so she couldn't put it back on, then he undid his button. She helped him out of his jeans as if he wasn't moving fast enough. She was a drug that sucked him in, and within moments, their naked bodies hugged the tree.

"Marry me," he pleaded with kisses.

"You want me to marry you?"

He wanted to sweep her away in kisses but they were already kissing. How could they kiss more? "Can I kiss you forever? Forget what I said about Bobby. Pick me. Always pick me. Do you feel your body responding to mine? Don't fight it, Julia. Give in. It's pleasure. Passion. Delight." He worked her legs apart and brought the one up and around him, so his body pinned her to the tree. "Satisfy me."

"I... Steve. You asked me to marry you while we're both naked."

"I'm doing this wrong." He rested his head against her shoulder. Breathing. His body brushed hers. He trembled from wanting her so wildly.

"Julia?" Bobby was to their left. If they called out he'd find them in the bush.

"We need to get somewhere safe so I can find James. Or clothes. We need clothes, walls between us. Parkas." Despite his words, Steve brought her against him.

Julia checked over her shoulder, and for a moment, he thought she might actually call out to Bobby. Her hand settled on his chest and he watched it touch him lightly. Too lightly.

She was about to open her mouth when Bobby pushed

through the bush, gun drawn.

"Steve, hands up."

He didn't have time to think. Bobby pulled the trigger.

JAMES

What kind of hell had he fallen into now? One second they were in an abandoned house fighting and the next they were in… some type of hell.

James tumbled into this new world and surveyed the area. The flames around him melted into the earth and with it all the warmth. He wasn't sure why, but he was hungry for ice cream.

He wiped his chest, taking in his surroundings. His eyes stopped on yellow eyes in the trees. What was watching him? He felt a familiar pang in his gut but he didn't know why. He hated not knowing everything.

If there was one thing he didn't like, it was to waste time, no matter where he was.

Al didn't squander his time looking around the swampy lands either. He clearly knew where they were so James stepped closer to him, his ticket outta this place.

Al flashed his wrist toward the pinkish grey sky and whispered, "*Nightlies, come to me.*"

James studied the odd sky with him. Hadn't it been morning? Two moons gave off light. Hmmm. Clearly, they weren't in Saskatchewan. "What kinda hell did we stumble into? What's a Nightlie?" James asked.

Al watched the sky. A loud squawk came from overhead, then from out of thin air, two giant flying horses landed by Al. James got in for a closer look.

"Step back. You want to be eaten?" Al said in his gruff voice. "What's wrong with you? You're in Hell, boy, at least pretend to be afraid of its demons."

"Hell?" James glanced at the swamplands, which didn't look any more intimidating than these weird flying horses. "Am I dead?" He didn't feel dead, he felt very much alive. Too alive.

"Nope. Just soul travelling. I had a demon bring us here so I could have a conversation with you. You calm now?"

"I guess. Did you do that, too? Because I should kill you yet I feel peaceful inside."

"No insides, this is your soul you're dealing with. Anger

ain't allowed in Hell."

This made perfectly good sense to James so he nodded. "Steve's soul was bright when it came to me, yours is... no offense man, but it's kind of crappy looking."

"Fuck you, prick." Al climbed on the horse. "You coming?"

"I... really?" James wanted to fly with this strange creature in the worst way, yet he knew he shouldn't trust Al. "First, let's talk, man to whatever the heck you are. What's the deal with you and my sister? Steve says you're always between them and I won't put up with you harassing my sister, *comprends?*"

"No, I don't understand your French whispers." He whispered something, and James leaned in to catch the words but they were too soft. "Coming now?"

"Sure." Kicking Al's ass wasn't the brightest idea, since he needed his help.

"Climb on, I'll show you, James, why your sister is a menace, then once you know the truth, you'll work with me."

James climbed on his own bird-horse, entranced. Something splashed in the water not far from the woods. He glanced that way, but saw nothing.

He could hear Al out. Maybe he was right. Steve and Julia were clearly experiencing some type of strange connection that had them afraid to be alone together.

"I feel like I'm in a movie or something. Is this creature real?"

"Very much so. Welcome to Hell, James. *Fly.*"

The horses took off and James grabbed the mane, surprised to feel feathers.

Al soared in, closer to James. "Pay attention, boy. I have a lot to teach you if you plan to defeat a Whisperer like Steven. That boy is so powerful now, only way he dies is if his soulmate gets recycled and he chooses to go after her. He has to choose to die. Can you imagine being that close to god-like? Did you know he flies without horses? He let you in on his secrets?"

"Defeat Steve?" The idea was absurd. Steve wasn't a threat to anyone. Was he?

"Yeah, once I show you what's real, you'll be making

damn sure he stays away from your sister. Trust me."

"You're the one ruining lives. Steve is just... freaked out."

"It might look that way on the outside, but I know the truth."

"And what is the truth?"

"You see, I am immortal. And the only way I can die is with a very special power. It's two pieces, one piece gives immortality, the other takes it. On the surface they look like opposite powers. The power that gives immortality does so by raising the dead. The power that removes it, does so by freeing the soul from the body. They must be used in that order each life cycle."

James nodded. "Let me guess, Steve and Julia have these abilities."

"Afraid so. They got their powers mixed up during a ritual I did. But point is, I am the last of the immortals. I will do everything in my power to keep Julia from making more."

"Wait a minute. Are you not telling me that Steve has to kill you? I'm sorry, but have you met Steve? That boy wouldn't kill a butterfly."

"It gets worse. He merged with her soul during the ritual. They're linked for eternity. And since Steven can't use that power until she does, and I can't kill her or he dies taking the power... I'm screwed. I have no way of destroying the power that creates immortals and Steven can't free me, until it's gone. Now fly toward that mud bog. I have a lair there we can chat in."

JULIA

Steve's breath tickled her neck. "*Speed.*" He yanked Julia to the ground with him so fast the world was a blur. She caught her breath, controlling at least one thing. Could Steve move as fast as a bullet? Had he sped up time for them or something?

The explosion hit the tree where they stood, not a moment ago, yet Steve's hands wandered her body super-fast, checking if she was hurt, then he put distance between them, leaving her alone.

She crouched against the tree, searching for her top. "Bobby, put the gun away," she said, determined to help him.

Steve was in front of the tunnel entrance, naked as can be, facing Bobby, challenging him boldly. Sunlight peeked through the trees and highlighted him perfectly. Wow. She let her eyes wander his tattoos and was surprised when Steve kicked her pants toward her.

"I'm unarmed, Bobby. Julia came with me willingly. She was running, hiding from a lunatic who's after her."

"You're the lunatic," Bobby snapped.

"What did Al whisper to you? Let me undo it so you think for yourself. *See what's real, Bobby.* I'm going down this tunnel, and I trust you to bring Julia to safety, far from Al. Okay? Protect her."

"I do protect her—from you."

"Julia, run. I'm making things worse, feeding the whisper already in play. He'll snap and this might not be good."

"No," Julia panicked. "You have to save him. You can't hurt Bobby. He's a victim to that maniac. It's your duty to save him."

Steve winced. "What if I can't?"

"You must." She pulled his shirt over her head and tugged it down.

Steve ogled her.

Where did her underwear get to? She searched the ground frantically. "I won't talk to you unless you put away the gun, Bobby. Steve is unarmed. You can't kill an unarmed man. You told me you felt like you were getting a second chance at life, yet you won't give this same courtesy to others? Snap out of it, you're a good guy, Bobby, I know this."

He pointed the gun at Steve. Steve was still gaping at her. He didn't act uncomfortable. The morning light bounced off his body perfectly. She had a hard time looking away from him. Was he waiting for her to run to him? It would set Bobby off again. She picked up his pants and walked to him. He could save himself, yet he didn't leave. He faced the gun, grounded and focused.

"Steve? He has a gun…"

"A gun makes you put what's important in your life in perspective, and seeing you in nothing but my shirt is probably the only image I ever need. My gosh, you're sexy."

She handed Steve his jeans. He clutched them, eyes on her. "Who are you going with?" Even his tone requested she jump down the tunnel with him.

She dived toward him and he scooped her in his arms, dropping them into the tunnel, with his hand around her waist, his pants left behind. She didn't feel them land on the draughty tunnel floor. It was as if they flew.

It was dark. "*Light*," she whispered and a swirling light appeared before her.

Steve didn't comment. He ran, clutching her hand. The light followed them and exploded upwards when Bobby dropped into the tunnel behind them.

"Mischief? Where are you?" Steve snapped the light aside with his hand. "*Dark*." He pushed her against the tunnel wall and a bullet exploded off the wall up ahead. She smelt the horrible stench of the explosion as if death itself had found her. Steve's whisper slowed the world.

Pain exploded in her. Deep. At first, she couldn't identify where. It was as if her soul ached…

"He's firing at us." She breathed against Steve. The pain settled in her shoulder. "Am I shot?"

"I am. Shoulder." He groaned. "I can heal this but I need time. Get rid of him." Steve collapsed in her arms.

The pain was so intense she fell with him.

"Stop, Bobby. I'm hurt," she yelled. "Our souls are linked. If you hurt Steve, you hurt me. Stop."

Steve was at her feet. She felt him against her leg but

couldn't see anything. Before Julia could move, warm hands came around her. Bobby scooped her up and ran the other way with her. She felt vulnerable in his clumsy hands as they slipped under the shirt and gripped her skin.

She struggled, but he was strong. James taught her how to break free from attackers, but Bobby knew her moves before she made them and he kept her tight.

When she could breathe again she screamed, "Let me go. What's wrong with you?"

"Climb." Bobby pointed up the ladder to the woods above. How much time did Steve need? Her shoulder throbbed.

Bobby followed her up, too close, but she broke away from him and stumbled into the woods.

He was on her instantly and tackled her into the leaves, his body pinning hers. His breath warmed her face, and she turned away from the coffee stench.

"Julia, I saved you. You're my girl. I won't hurt you." His voice was soft, pleading, but his body was heavy on hers and she wanted him off her.

"Bobby, you listen to me." She glared at him and wiggled.

He let her go.

Quickly, she rested against a tree before he changed his mind. She spotted her pants and considered going for them but he sat beside her. Softly, he ran his hand over her arm. She snagged his hand, returning it to his lap.

"My soul belongs to Steve and you shot him."

"How can that loser come between us in one day?"

"You ever hear of the fairytale where the prince decides he's going to win over the princess? He's sure she belongs with him because daily she watches him train. He fights valiantly for her kingdom and always she looks dreamily when he's around. Then one day, when he's sure she'll say yes, he goes to ask her hand in marriage. Only she pushes pass him and walks off with the servant who looks after his horses. All this time, she wasn't watching him, but his servant. The prince can't figure out what he did wrong. She should be with him. He's brave and wealthy. What is she doing with a servant?"

Her shoulder throbbed violently and she clutched it. "Do you understand, Bobby? He did nothing wrong. He just wasn't the guy."

She rested her head against the tree. "God, I hurt." She rubbed her shoulder.

Steve shouldn't be in this much pain alone. She needed to get to him, but she had no idea how to break free from Bobby. "James is hurt at the house we were at. The old one with the broken veranda. Can you find him? I can't move. Go."

"I won't leave you."

"You shot me. Back away from me."

Bobby closed his eyes. "Dammit, where? Show me where."

"In my... soulmate." She rubbed her sore shoulder.

"What?"

"I can't explain it. I hurt. James will know what to do. Find him."

He paled.

"Julia? Bobby? Where are you guys?" James yelled, his voice hardly audible he was so far.

Bobby scrambled to his feet. "He's coming." He scanned the scene as if making sure everything looked good. "Tell him I saved you."

"He can't find you here with me half-naked. Go get him while I dress." She closed her eyes and much to her surprise, Bobby ran toward James' voice.

She pushed herself to her feet and dashed for the tunnel after snagging her pants.

Steve needed her.

JULIA

Steve was on the tunnel floor, unconscious, when Julia found him. She whispered for light and slinked it over his entire body. Not a hole in him. Julia wasn't sure if he was sleeping or if his soul was off searching for James. She passed the light over him a second time. A third. A fourth.

Steve looked peaceful.

She crouched beside him. Warmth came from him and she realized how cold it was in this tunnel. He needed his clothes. She lightly touched his chest. Eyes closed, Steve snagged her wrist.

"James is safe. He was calling for us," she told him.

Steve moved her hand over his pounding heart. "Skin against skin," he mumbled. "I had no idea your skin would be so consuming. Keep your soul to yourself and touch me. Please."

The idea was incredible and she slipped off the T-shirt and dropped her pants beside it on the dirt floor.

Steve jumped to his feet in seconds. "What are you doing?"

"Skin against skin." She pushed tight against Steve. His body was warm. His heartbeat responded to her touch. She rubbed her cold hands against his hot chest. Skin.

"Julia?" He breathed against her neck as he kissed it. "Where are my pants?"

"I doubt you need them," she teased.

He brought her to the ground with him. They breathed as one, panting, their bodies touching in every possible way, searching each other for heat.

Eyes closed, Steve pushed inside her. Julia let out a painful gasp and backed off.

"What the hell happened?" He sat up, cradling her on his lap.

She huffed as heat shot through her like lightning. She'd expected pleasure. Always in the dreams rushing at her, flooding her memories, there was nothing but pleasure when they came together. Why was there burning? She gripped his arms.

"Julia. Holy hell. I'm sorry. I... damn it. We were together so many times in our dreams it never once entered my mind it wasn't real. Did I hurt you?"

She didn't want to look at him. She rested her head on his shoulder, unsure if they should try that again. "I'm on fire inside."

The burning passed while he held her. Safe. She was safe.

"We need to do this slower." He kissed her shoulder and leisurely worked his way along her neck. She was warm in his arms and let him. *"Focus on how each kiss makes you feel,"* his whisper sent warm tingles down her spine. His hands explored her body and she relaxed.

"I want this," she confessed, suddenly craving the heat inside her.

"We'll go slower. Slow. So slow I'll drive myself nuts." He brushed against her, not just with his finger, but with his lips, his legs, his toes, all of him teased her. "I'll bring our souls together. Ready?"

She breathed against his sweaty, dirty chest, her hips meeting his endlessly, softly. She caressed him. Each stroke satisfied the burning inside with a soothing thrill. She traced his skin so lightly as if memorizing him.

And finally, they melted together.

JULIA

Julia rested on Steve, spent. He pulled her into his arms. Their souls were one and she knew Steve's thoughts. He wanted to carry her to the cottage. Thank God. She couldn't walk. She felt like oozing mud.

She was cold and it was damp in the tunnel. The cottage was a good idea. No words were spoken, only this knowledge they shared between souls. She liked being one with him and didn't ask to pull away. He gathered her in his arms, and she let him, too weak, too tired to argue. She'd seen too much today. Julia rested against him, sharing his love for her. Her hands explored. It wasn't long before their touching bodies were too much for him to endure again. Their soul-light let off a faint glow that wasn't doing much good.

He set her down and pinned her against the chilly tunnel wall. With only him for warmth, the cold from the wall made her push back against his heat. They stood breathing, just gasping together, while they fought the urge to attack each other.

Julia ran a finger along his jaw, feeding the tension.

She said, "Channel your energy into the world around us. This is what you're afraid of, that this energy between us is unnatural so send it back to nature. It's around us. Limit our touches."

Without a word, he grabbed her thighs and pulled them up, using the wall to balance her. He massaged them, sending a rush of orgasmic tingles through her. She moaned with her hands on the wall, taking her own advice. The wall responded with a light vibration, full of life behind her.

Steve pressed in. "Julia." His breath warmed her lips and she kissed him, soaking up his body.

Slowly, he entered her, pulling away from her lips. She waited for the burn, but this time it was a need that devoured her. She wrapped her legs around him while he held her hands over her head, pushing them into the wall. They could hardly see each other in the dim light. Every touch was long and deep. The wall groaned and moaned with the movements, leaving them to recover between breaths.

Steve explored her body as she heaved to meet his fingertips, enjoying the tickle. She was overcome between the hot and cold, between the tingles and the want, that she pushed away and dropped her feet.

He panted and gripped her, his warmth melting on her shoulder as he came closer. "Julia?"

She turned around, grabbing his hands and pulling him against her.

"Hell, Julia." Firm hands grabbed her around the hips. This time, he came at her harder and deeper. Pure delight as his hands travelled down to her thighs. Her breasts pushed into the cold tunnel wall while he tasted her neck. The release came like waves of freedom built up during the last five years of prison. An explosion of souls. With it, the ground shifted.

They fell straight down into a dark chasm.

JULIA

The earth moved. Not only under Julia, but around her as Steve was torn from her and she fell with it.

Darkness enveloped them as she dropped in a void.

"*Butterflies*," Steve whispered, snagging her wrist tightly and bringing her to a jarring halt.

Just her wrist. Their only connection. The rest of her dangled in the frigid air. Dirt tickled her skin as thousands of butterflies gathered, holding her up.

God knew what Steve held on to.

"Julia, you alive?"

"Yeah. What the heck happened?"

He chuckled. "Best orgasm in the universe would be my guess. Even the walls felt it. I'll fly you up."

"How can you laugh at a time like this? I thought we were dead."

"I'm not that easy to kill." He hauled her up, and as stupid as it was, when his second hand came around her arm below the elbow, the tingling was as intense as ever and it shot jolts of thrilling joy through her body. Was she flying?

Every time their skin brushed even slightly as he reeled her in, her entire body experienced the rush of it.

"I whispered," he told her, "and it actually felt nice. No guilt. Strange."

"What the hell was that?" Julia rolled on top of him, excited. "An earthquake in Saskatchewan?"

"Sink hole, I guess. We're along a lake. The ground's unstable. It happened to me once before when I was six, and I lost a toe because of it." Firm hands came around her, checking her for injuries.

"Really? A rock fell on it or something?" Using her feet, she felt his toes. Sure enough, he was missing one.

"No, nothing like that, but cool part was that I flew out of the hole." His hands explored her and his words were warm against her cold skin. "I was so excited that I could use the butterflies to fly, I told Al. He went nuts because I was late for his training session and cut off my toe."

Julia fought back a gasp. His father had done that to him

and he still tried so blasted hard to save him?

"He told me only tinkerbells flew and he'd better never catch me doing that shit."

She touched his lips. "He didn't want you to fly? That's strange. Makes you wonder what that guy hides, eh?" She let him hold her. "Do you really know you can fly yet never do?"

"Yeah. I hate magic." He stopped exploring and held her tight against him as if he was afraid to lose her again. "Try not to panic when that happens. Whisper to the world around you. I'll make you a whispering tattoo, 'cause these abilities are dangerous if they infect our souls. Each tattoo allows you to store a new ability without it affecting the world around you unless you whisper it back. The world will listen to your whispers and respond."

"Like we were doing with the transfer of energy from our bodies?"

"Yeah," Steve said. "I guess I released too much and made a bit of an explosion. Sorry, you had me excited." He gripped her tighter. "I can do a lot of cool things. I slow time, stop bullets. I always thought a Whisperer does whatever they want, but Al says no, Whisperers have to earn their powers."

"How did we end up like this? I feel like an ordinary person."

"I wish I did. I feel like such a freak."

She rubbed his forehead. It was tense. "Is that because Al made you feel this way? Maybe you aren't bad, Steve. I sure don't feel anything evil when I'm with you. I feel... free."

"I'm from a family of Dark Whisperers, our goal is to ruin people's lives. Al is a dumbass. If you ask me, Whisperers were created with a better purpose."

"Did you help me when my pa died? Is that why I always woke up feeling peaceful even though I was angry the rest of the day?"

"I sent you dreams about the wind. You seem to like wind."

"Those dreams. You could do that for others. Whisper to them in their sleep."

Steve smirked. "A Dream Whisperer for the grieving. Yeah, I suppose so. That would be noble. You always make things seem easy, like James does. Why do I overthink things?"

She snuggled tighter against his chest and kissed his neck, safe in his arms.

She wasn't sure at what point their souls returned, but she wasn't one with him anymore. The emotions inside her were her own.

"I love you, Julia."

A light blinded her, she winced, hoping to see who had found them in this murky tunnel.

A gun clicked.

"I'm too late, ain't I? By the looks of things." James panted as if he'd run from town. She'd never heard him pant. James normally had excellent stamina.

"Oh good, you found the gun I left you," Steve said.

"And the bullets, pansy."

STEVE

Steve watched for the finger against the flashlight. He waited for James' familiar tic, for his happy soul to reach out, but it was hard to see it with the light blinding him. He couldn't confront James unless he knew he was calm, and if that finger wasn't twitching, he should keep his mouth shut. He gripped Julia tighter, her naked body against his.

Still, James' soul was wild in the dim light. What happened with Al to cloud up his soul like that?

"Where is Al?" Steve wanted to know.

"Dead."

"What? How?" Steve asked confused. "Show me." He wouldn't believe it until he saw it. He was supposed to help him. *You only have to help one to be a hero.* One.

"I don't care if your brain splatters on her, Steven, I will shoot you. Let her go." Again, there should be the *comprends?* Steve was used to.

It didn't come.

Something was wrong. Even Julia shifted, uncomfortable. Maybe seeing his sister in the arms of a guy pushed him to this point and James would calm in a moment and be James again. James was a good guy, but he was slightly nuts, Steve reminded himself.

"James, breathe, man. Calm down."

"I will not calm down. Get your bloody hands off my sister, now." James was on his knees. "I'll shoot him down here, Julia. I'll toss him in the hole fate made for me."

"If you kill me, your sister dies."

Julia stood in front of James, naked. "You will not shoot him," she said. Steve covered her breasts with his hands, instinct on his part, brother pointing a gun at him or not. His body had a mind of its own around this woman.

How entranced was James? He clearly wasn't himself, but how deep had Al gotten? Steve squinted when the bright light shone on his face, as he searched for that finger. James hid it against his jeans. He couldn't tell if it was twitching. He had no idea how dead he was.

"Move, Julia," James said.

"No."

"Then bring him with you. Fucking brilliant plan. We'll keep little Steven prisoner at our place, Julia. Show him what kidnapping you will get him. Oh yes we will. Find your clothes for Pete's sake. It's disgusting. Come on, pansy."

James grabbed Steve by the hair and pulled him after him, pushing the cold steel against his ribs.

STEVE

Two days later—

Steve watched James work in the basement of their farmhouse. Apparently, he was building Steve a cage. He was going to keep him prisoner until he figured out how to unlink their souls then he was going to kill Steve. Or so he said.

Steve's puppy was at the window, sleeping. He missed playing with her, but at least she was safe. After settling on the name, Brat, Julia brought her over. She loved playing with Max.

He heard Bobby upstairs, which meant Julia entertained while Steve was stuck in the cellar with this psychopath he couldn't even reach in his sleep. Steve had no idea what Al did to James but he began to lose hope.

Even his soul wasn't acting the same.

While he built the cage, the gun was tucked along his back the way his old man always wore his. It was strange, but he never fancied James for a guy who'd stick his gun in his pants like that. Not sure where he thought he'd keep it, but along his back wasn't it.

His last two days with James had been interesting to say the least. Like usual he asked Steve a million questions about his powers, not so much how they worked but how he activated them.

"So you like building things?" Steve asked.

"Of course." James was working well with the tools, but James did everything well. It was almost annoying.

"My dad works with tools, too. Or worked. Are you sure he's dead? It doesn't feel like it. I mean... when my mom died I felt it deep in my soul like a part of me went with her."

James stopped working to look at him. He didn't say anything but the look, it was... fatherly, and he hadn't seen a look like that in years.

"Maybe there was nothing good to the prick," James offered.

"No. There is or was. There's good in everyone."

"There's evil in everyone, too. Evil is easier to feed, takes less work, and is much more rewarding."

Steve was shocked. "Are you listening to yourself?"

"Nope, I'm listening to Bobby get it on with your girl upstairs. Must be driving you nuts, eh?"

"That's your sister."

"Hmmm. Listen to them go at it. Must make you want to kill someone eh?" he teased Steve.

Steve was chained to the wall like a dog, sitting on the floor. Yeah, he heard Julia above them, but in his mind, she ran away from Bobby. She could look after herself around Bobby, but it was Steve's instinct to want to protect her. He tugged at the chains, frustrated.

He could walk out at any time, but he was humouring James, figuring out how to get him back. Because the James he trained in his dreams would never say evil was an easy way out. James might be nuts, but he was pure at heart—a hero. Whatever Al did to him could be undone.

From upstairs, he heard Julia chuckle. Why was she laughing with Bobby? He didn't like that. Steve took his eyes off James for a moment to glance at the steps, as if they knew why she laughed with that creep. His brain was mush. All Steve could concentrate on were her footsteps above him. Pacing around the table. Bobby was too close, trailing her.

"Want me to help, James? I can help. I'd much rather be in this cozy cage you're building, snuggled up to Julia than chained to the floor."

"You do not go near her. She's dating Bobby. Is that clear?"

Is that clear? Since when did James speak like Al? Wow, Al really did a number on this guy.

"Mr. Boring? Come on, James. As if. Look at me. *Regardez-moi*. What happened to you and Al in Hell? Talk to me. If you killed him, and his soul merged with yours, it would explain why you're doing things like him. You have to fight it."

James snapped his head to glare at him. "Al showed me the truth. You and Julia can never be. Can you pull those powers out of her and give them to me? Show me how to use them?"

"What? He's got you wigging out, brainwashed, James.

You're not thinking. You're not..." Steve paused.

James held the hammer, his index finger relaxed against it. Ah hell.

How had he missed that? Al could shift into other people? It was one thing to shift into a bird... but people? That was probably the darkest power he'd ever heard of. Who would do *that*?

Where was James?

He hadn't been able to reach him in his sleep...

"Forget it," Steve said. "Whatever he did to you is probably an improvement. So if you don't need my help, I'll take a nap. Keep it down."

"Whatever, hope you can sleep while your girl gets it on upstairs with Mr. Boring."

Yeah, like Steve was worried about that loser now. If Al was secretly running the show, it wasn't good. He needed to find the real James and fast, without letting on to Al that he knew it was him.

Two days. Two days. If James was out of his body for two days it was probably too late. He wouldn't want to come back. Could he come back?

Damn it.

Steve was sick as he watched the Fake-James work. His avoidance of Al over the years cost James his life. They'd screwed up, but he wouldn't let Al win. No.

"Mischief. Where are you?"

JAMES

James slapped his hand in the thick mud. The yellow eyed creature glared at him. "Can you help me get out of here?"

It slunk away.

"No. Don't go. Stay. Talk to me. Are you hurt?"

The eyes blinked as the creature peered over the edge. "*I must go, Steve calls.*"

"You know Steve? What's your name?"

"*I have many names, Hero. You know this. Now I go by Mischief, which you called me when I ruined your farm.*"

"I'm James, and I swear you didn't ruin my farm."

"*Yes. I remember. It was many, many nights ago. You were very mad. I was very bad. Disappointed you. Not good to disappoint Hero.*"

"Okay, okay, so we have history, that's cool. I'm trapped. Help me get out of here."

"*I cannot undo the immortal's whispers. I must go to Steve. Must not disappoint, Steve. But I am weak. I hurt.*"

"Well, if you can't go to him, bring him to you." James tried not to move 'cause every time he did he sank lower in the mud.

Mischief was gone.

"*Nightlies, I could use someplace safe,*" James whispered but nothing appeared. "*Branches, I could use help.*" They didn't lower. "*Steve, you weenie, if you hear me I could use your magical whispers right about now.*"

"Yeah, I'd say. Your whispers only work in French. I don't know why. How did you end up in a soul sucking mud bog?" Steve peered from the ledge, which was slightly out of reach.

"Get me out of here."

"James, your soul has been out of your body for two days."

James looked up at Steve. He was see-through.

"You mean I've been in here for two days? As if. Does time stand still here or something?"

"Every realm sucks away time differently, but trust me, it's too late, you're dead, man. Your heart probably gave up, and your brain died. We thought you were alive and torturing me so we never went to check. I'm sorry, but I'm here to bring you to Afterlight. What will we tell Julia?"

"I don't feel dead, so I'm not."

"Yeah well, it don't feel like the earth is round either, but it is. Trust me. You're dead."

"I'm alive, stop telling me I'm dead. Can you help me?"

"You don't have a body to go back to. I don't know how it works but the fine grey line that should connect you to your gut is damaged in several places."

"Shit. Take me back, I gotta see this," James insisted.

"Of course. *Foolish soul, get the hell out of the mud and come here.*"

James blinked from the mud and appeared beside Steve. "Smartass."

"I'll whisper to your soul to find your body and I'll meet you there, okay? Don't do anything until I arrive."

"Steve?"

"Yeah?"

"Thanks for finding me."

"Thank Mischief for sticking with you. He normally runs from Al, so he was very brave." Steve's greyish soul flashed a deep brown. "Sorry it took so long. I should have noticed the first night that it wasn't you, *mon ami*. A better friend would have noticed."

"Yeah, well, we can't all be brilliant." James smirked. "At least you found me. I can't believe Al ditched me. Actually, I can't believe he entranced me enough for me to climb on that flying horse. *Merde eh?* I must be weak. Can you show me how to fight off a whisper from a moron like that?"

"Yeah, James, break his jaw so he can't whisper. Think like a man. He won't see it coming."

"That'll work perfectly," James agreed.

JAMES

James found his body hidden in a closet in the abandoned house at Hamilton Beach. He looked dead. Steve was right.

Why the heck did he feel so alive if he was dead? How would he explain a screw up this big to his sister? Could he even explain it? He was a spirit. Dead.

How did James lose? Entranced, he'd climbed on a flying horse, like some fool. It was weird, but like with the seatbelt, it had felt like his idea.

When Steve appeared, James didn't bother with pleasantries, "Did you know that Al thinks Julia can raise the dead with whispers?"

"Oh hell." Steve looked ready to puke. "That's what all this is about? My whole life that guy was paranoid about that power. I was supposed to kill anyone who I met with it."

"Well, you can't kill Julia."

Steve ran a hand through his blond hair.

They were silent.

Finally, Steve said what they were both thinking. "She could bring you back."

"Apparently, that's not a good idea. Besides, it's been days."

"Two days, the legends say we have three. I need to make her a whispering tattoo so she has control of her magic. Getting her away from Bobby and the Fake-James is my first priority, then I'll get her here. I'll have to show her what to do before the end of day three."

"Calm down, I'm dead anyway. It really isn't so bad. But I do agree that you need to get her away from that freak. I'll wait here with my body, until you come back."

"I have a day."

"Really, don't worry about it. I'm fine. I've never felt so alive. Maybe I don't want to come back. Al was pretty horny about destroying that power. Can we do that?"

Steve shrugged. "I'll know more once I mark her and the power settles in the tattoo."

"So where is Al keeping you?"

"In your cellar tied up like a dog. He's making me a cage. I thought I could walk out at any time, that I humoured him, but Al will have the place protected with whispers. This means I'm screwed."

James paced, his finger twitching madly while he pieced this together. "Well, go make sure Julia is okay. *Comprends?*"

"I can't believe I thought Al was you. I feel horrible."

James grinned. "Too bad, because I feel fantastic."

STEVE

When Steve snapped from his trance, Julia was coming down the basement steps and Fake-James was gone. Steve did a double take. She wore high heels and a long silver dress that glistened against her skin as if she were a dream.

Hell. Maybe she was.

"James said I could bring you food now that you were all secure and cozy down here. What are we gonna do? He's snapped a biscuit. He says we're breaking the bond tonight. He's pulling out all sorts of old Notebooks and has them all over the table upstairs, pacing around them as if one of them has the answer."

Steve hadn't even noticed the food. He jumped from the bed and made his way to the bars of the cage surrounding him. Fake-James had done a nice job on his pen.

"Julia, we need to talk."

She set his food so he could reach it. It was a sandwich but he had so much to tell her and Fake-James could be back any moment that he didn't bother with it even though he was starving.

"Bobby is getting worse. He's so corrupt his eyes gloss over when he looks at me, as if I'm dead to him. It's creepy."

"You wore that for him? Hell, Julia. What the heck for? You look like a dream."

Her hair was done up in a fancy bun and she pulled it out as he said this… probably to drive him nuts.

"Don't be stupid, I wore this for you. I knew you were alone all day, and I was so excited when he told me I could finally see you."

The idea made his shoulders shake against the bars. "Not alone. Your fake brother kept me company."

"Fake? What does that mean?"

Fake-James stormed down the steps. "Time to see if we can get you two back to normal." He held tattoo making items, and a Notebook that were very familiar.

Head against the railing and his hand around a bar, Steve kept his eyes closed because he was dying without her touch. Physically dying. This connection was at its peak; he could no longer be without Julia. Breaking their bond was probably impossible. Maybe it had always been impossible.

Her dainty hands wrapped around his, and thrilling sparks shot threw him. He wanted more, and kissed her forehead. Much to his surprise, she moved and her lips were there. He met them through the bars.

Her lips shook against his as they touched gently and she pulled away.

He had something important to tell her, but hell if he could remember what.

"You seriously plan to kiss this pansy with me watching?" James interrupted in a crisp firm voice. She melted into Steve when James spoke. No, not James. Fake-James. It took Fake-James to physically pull them apart and send a fist flying his way before Steve took his hands off her.

Julia ran upstairs.

Steve stayed on the floor, his nose bleeding and achy. The punch hadn't helped. He needed her, but at least he remembered what he wanted to tell Julia.

"Julia, you know your brother," he called after her.

She paused at the top of the steps.

"Talk to him. He'll know what to do," Steve said.

"Don't make me put you down like the dog you are, pansy."

It was always these games with Al. Why keep him alive? James always said to seek the simplest answer. Which would be...?

Al couldn't kill him. Dammit. Why hadn't he realized that? Al needed him out of the way but he couldn't kill him. Why not? Was it a son-father bond or was it just that he wasn't powerful enough to kill him?

"I could make her a tattoo to block her magic," Steve offered.

Fake-James looked at the Notebook in his hand. "Really? You can do that?"

Of course he couldn't, but if Steve could make her a tattoo to house her powers, she could bring James back to life. He traced an upside down teardrop tattoo she needed to house life restoring magic. "If I don't colour in her tattoo, the magic will be trapped there." This might be true, Steve had no idea.

"Bring her back. I'll do my best."

"It's worth a shot. If you could block her magic, I wouldn't have to kill you." He smirked.

"I'm not so sure you can, *James*."

JULIA

"Julia?"

She cried in her room. She wouldn't look at James when he stormed in.

"Let me explain something to you." James paced her room. "You and Steven cannot happen. There is a prophecy that you will create a demonic immortal being. Is this what you want? To mother a demonic child? Stay away from him. Is this clear?"

Julia's hands flew to her mouth. "What?" Why had no one told her? They'd already been together.

James paced.

Julia glanced up at him. "I can't explain it, James. I need to be with him."

"Of course you do. It's the devil at work, pulling you together. Stay away." He sat beside her and held her hand. She waited for his familiar, *"Je t'aime"*. When it didn't come, it was a slap to the face.

She contemplated their linked hands then pulled away. "James, I have power inside me. Dark magic. Steve says he can make me a whispering tattoo to control it. That might help get the tingling under control."

"Think you could use your powers to destroy him?"

She took a deep breath. "You want me to kill Steve?"

He sat on the bed. "Explain the tingling." James always wanted to know how things worked, felt. "Is it in your soul, body, or does it ignite this magic?"

She thought about this. "All of the above."

"He kidnapped you, or did you forget that? We kidnapped him. Or did you forget that? It was supposed to be payback for what he did to you, but we're in some twisted twilight zone where you kiss him. I don't like this." He paced, rubbed his hand over his eyes. "Julia, don't let him toy with your emotions like this, walk away from him. Can you?"

"No," she admitted.

"Do you understand how important it is for you to stay away from him?"

'Do you understand'? When did he stop saying

'*comprends*'?

"I can't."

"Then let's use this link." He told her so matter-of-fact. So like James.

"How?"

"He has a weakness, you should be able to sense it via your connection."

His weakness? "Steve's weakness is his dad. He wants to save him. He believes he only has to save one to be a hero instead of the monster he was raised to be."

James closed his eyes with a painful sigh. "You sure that's still his weakness?" His voice was just a breath. Then he suddenly pulled himself back to the present and cleared his throat. "I mean, the prick is dead. He must have another weakness."

"I'll pay closer attention."

"*It's time you give in to Bobby.*"

His whisper was like a wave of dizziness seducing her. Like when Al whispered to her. It triggered her rage.

How dare he whisper to her.

"I never once said I didn't like Bobby."

James' index finger was calm, but it should have been going nuts. He growled. "What went wrong? This connection should be severed. I did everything in my power. Everything! Yet you're linked to his soul like some type of soulma..." He paused and met her eyes. "Pisses me off that I missed this. We might have to do this another way."

"What does that mean?"

"Will you try with Bobby?" He checked to see if his whisper had worked.

Why not break it to him? "No. Never."

"Then Steven will have to make the tattoo. I will stand and watch so you don't end up kissing him. We do it through the bars. Meet me down there when you're ready. Wear normal clothes." He stormed out and she changed into a tank top and jeans.

The door to the cellar was open and she listened to them banter back and forth. Steve was discussing the tools he'd need for the ceremony. James disagreed on several but Steve was firm.

"Julia." Steve watched her come down the steps as if she were a goddess.

Her heart beat fast.

Would he sever the link?

"Sit," James ordered.

Steve examined her new clothes as she stumbled before him. She grabbed the bars and he instantly had his hands over hers. She noticed that he'd eaten the sandwich. He stood gaping at her. Softly, he said, "Tonight we make you a real Whisperer."

"Do you know many?" she asked.

"I met one once, a Dream Whisperer."

James stopped with a jar of ink in his hands and looked at Steve. "Did he tell you anything? I want to know everything he said. Where did you meet him?"

"Calm down over there, *James*. It was a long time ago." Steve kept his eyes on hers.

"This tattoo I plan to make is only going to be an outline, just a little symbol that looks like an upside-down teardrop. It will block your magic until I colour it in. This will protect you from using it and hurting anyone. James says this is for the best."

"Steve. Am I evil? Is this dark magic I feel inside me?"

He shrugged. "Might be." He rubbed the cross she wore around her neck. "They say Jesus was raised from the dead. Do you believe that was evil magic?"

She smirked. "Well..."

"Couldn't magic just be magic?" He gave her a hopeful look. "I want to use my powers for good, Julia. I don't want to be a monster."

She clasped his hands firmly in hers, yet he pulled one free to run it along her waist. Even with the bars between them, he was all over her.

James placed a tattoo making needle in Steve's hand. "Now." He sat Julia in front of him and hovered over her, his arms crossed. Steve set right to work. He pushed the needle under her skin. Julia wasn't sure this was safe, but he clearly knew what he was doing. She didn't watch but kept her eyes on his.

"Steve. James told me... he told me I'd have a demon

child."

James stood his ground, arms crossed and silent.

"You saw demons. They're not dangerous, but they aren't like us either." Steve shook his head. "As if. I bet we have cute kids with long brown hair like you."

"Or beautiful blue eyes like you."

He grinned. "Yeah. Brats."

The heat between them increased. Julia wanted to be closer to him but if she moved in he'd get excited again, and Steve was hard to refuse once he got going.

He gripped her wrist and it throbbed while he worked. James watched very closely. "You're making the symbol for Spirit Whisperer," he said coolly.

"Of course, she whispers to spirits. Ideally, her magic should restore souls to their bodies. A giver of life. I'll whisper that all abilities for giving life find a home in this symbol and they will come to Julia. No matter where they are."

"And they'll be trapped until you finish her tattoo?" James checked.

Steve nodded.

But Julia wanted to know, "You'll steal abilities from other Whisperers?"

"Probably demons, too. Don't know where these powers might come from, but if you're a stronger Whisperer, they won't be able to summon them back. If the demons like you, they'll let you keep them and shadow you, like Mischief does to me, but if they don't like you or don't find you worthy, they will challenge you for this magic. You might lose it."

"You ever lose a power?"

"No. Doubt there are many Whisperers around. Like I said, I only ever met one."

"Was he nice?"

"He was confused, lost. Slumber the Dream Whisperer."

"Like you?"

"Yeah." He pushed the needle into her skin.

"Steve, have you ever given a tattoo?"

"To Al, to myself. Sure. We don't have time to worry about it Julia. Worst thing that will happen is that it gets infected and the nurses yell at us. Okay? Look at me, Julia. Not at what I'm doing."

She did. She met his blue eyes. Too blue. "Steve."

"Yes, Julia?"

She wanted to tell him how she felt but she didn't know any words to express it. Nothing was deep enough to let Steve know how much she cared for him. "*Je t'aime*," she blurted out, aware of how James felt. It was as if the first words she'd learnt were the only ones deep enough to express the depth of her passion.

Steve closed his eyes and smiled, not touching her. "*Je t'aime, toujours*."

His words touched a part of her soul she didn't know existed until that very moment. It felt so... eternal.

The tattoo turned out not bad. It was very faint and very small. He'd added three wavy lines around the teardrop, and really it looked more like a ghost to her than a teardrop. Julia didn't feel anything though when he whispered the powers to her. She wasn't sure what to expect.

"Go on. Try them out," James encouraged her. "See if it worked."

"But I didn't feel anything."

"Still, they should be there. Here." He handed her a fly he'd found on the floor. Dead. "Whisper to it. See if you can bring the living back from the dead."

"You want me to raise a fly?" She looked at Steve for support and he shrugged. "What do I whisper?"

"Your magic should be blocked," James pointed out.

The door burst open to the cellar and Bobby charged in, gun in hand, he descended the steps, the gun on Steve. "I knew that Steve prick was here." He fired at Steve and James dived in front of him taking the bullet.

He fell against the cage and to her horror his body shifted into Al.

Al?

Julia stood over him, shocked.

"*Dream time,*" Steve whispered and Bobby fell.

"Julia! Focus. Get me out of here. Al set the keys in the toolbox."

Julia ran for them. "Is he dead?"

"No. He'll catch his breath in a few and whisper himself better. He's a Body Whisperer. Your brother is in trouble. We have to get to him. Let's tie these two up and drag them in the cage. It won't keep Al for long, but maybe we'll have enough time to get to Hamilton Beach and save your brother."

"Is James hurt?"

"Something like that."

JAMES

James stood on the steps of the old house where his body hid. He looked around at the dreary day. He felt so great, he couldn't believe the weather didn't reflect his mood.

A man stumbled out of the woods.

James sat on the steps, curious why this scrawny prick was in the woods.

"Hey!" he shouted to James. "You there! My wife, my sexy, incredible, fairytale wife said I had to find you and bring you to Utopia, but man, you are one hard prick to find. Where do you go at night?"

At night?

James glanced around and shot to his feet. Could this pimple-face see him? Wasn't he like a ghost or something?

"I mean, shit. I wait outside your door in Dreamland every blasted evening and never see you. It's like you have a fucking backdoor I don't know about."

Another weirdo. James waited for him to approach. This guy was a toothpick. He squinted at James, his mouth making an ugly curled up pinch that showed off his buckteeth.

"You see me?" James asked. "Do I know you?"

"Slumber, a Dream Whisperer, but someone has you blocked from me so I had to find you in person. Although, I didn't expect to find you so... um... ghostly."

"Why?"

He shrugged. "My wife, did I mention how fucking fairytale-hot she was? Well, she needs the best counsellor and that is apparently you. We're all set, ready to unleash our whispers to get this world back to nature."

James nodded as if it made sense. "The culprits behind the *Get Naked and Muddy Revolution*."

"Guilty. So you are clearly Hero."

"That means nothing to me."

"You know, Hero. Heracles... the idiot who paired up with a Love Whisperer so he could win over his sexy cupid soulmate... nothing?"

James shook his head, but he was listening now.

"You are the guy who counsels Grey Whisperers with this

incredible wisdom that spans from knowing every life you've lived. You are the only Whisperer, alive or dead, who always remembers his past lives. My brother would have loved to meet you."

"Well, I ain't a Whisperer. I met one. He was kind of weird. Another tumbled me to Hell, that sucked, and I'm told my sister might be one now. Not sure what I think about that."

"You mean you don't know you're a Whisperer? That means what?"

James frowned. "Clearly, it means I'm not. Can't you see I'm dead?"

"The dead don't hold on to mortal bodies, they hang out in Afterlight."

"I really didn't know what to do, so I thought I'd just sit here and think. This prick told me raising the dead is not cool, yet it's a power my sister has, and she's a wonderful person. So I'm confused."

Slumber chuckled and pushed up his sleeves, revealing pin marks of a serious drug addiction. "Yup, sounds like the asshole I'm supposed to recruit. Listen, if you're dead, well, *c'est la vie*. It's not healthy to hold on. You need to hit Afterlight. But..." He cleared his throat and stepped in closer as if he might ask James if he sold drugs. "If a Spirit Whisperer wants to give you immortality, take it. It's not permanent. Her soulmate will be able to kill you anytime. So listen... There is Wild magic in the air, some type of link I sense between this realm and Dreamland that might give a guy like me a rush." His bushy eyebrows shot up. "Tell me who's messing with Wild magic, 'cause I could use me some of that shit."

"Not me, I'm wasting my life. I hate Wild magic. Makes me want to smash my fist into..." Mainly Steve. "Someone."

"Sounds like a dark whisper." He squinted his eyes. "I cannot believe you let a Dark Whisperer near you. I'm going to whisper, just listen to my words, they are to help you, and I do not want you lighting my soul on fire because I'm whispering to you."

James nodded. "Go ahead. What more could go wrong?"

"Next time you feel the urge to smash your fist into this someone, look at your hands and remember the good things

those hands could do instead."

James rubbed his jaw. Hadn't Steve said something similar to him?

"This is weird. Everyone was sure you'd have summoned some cupid magic by now, since you were so attached to those powers your last life."

"Cupid powers?" James smirked. "Sounds a little girly."

"Yeah, well if you want to impress the girls, you need to be prepared. What about your interpreting abilities?"

"You mean how I can figure things out rather quickly?"

"Well, at least you got those with you. So, what's the name you go by if you aren't Whisperer Hero yet?"

"James." James walked in the house and Slumber followed.

"What you holding on for, James? It's really not like you."

"Jules."

"The Wild cat or the cupid?" Slumber asked, not the least bit interested.

James wasn't sure. "My sister. She is Wild though, annoyingly so. I don't like her like that." He tightened his fists, thinking about her stupid sex dreams.

"Focus on those hands. Relax. Fill me in. Why would someone want you to kill your Wild sister?"

"Not her, her stupid soulmate, Steve." James studied the guy. "I like him, but when he gets talking about Jules, something snaps inside me and I..." He glanced at his hands. They were made to do good things. "Maybe you can help him since I clearly can't?"

"Depends. I guide other Whisperers, but we have to follow certain rules."

"Rules?" James chuckled. "You don't look like a guy who follows rules."

Slumber smirked and slapped him on his back as if he were real. "Tell me what you know, and we'll start by getting you back to normal. We'll summon cupid powers for you to mess around with, see if that counters the dark whisper you're fighting. 'Cause the cupids I know, when they see soulmates, they turn into sparkling idiots."

"You know Love Whisperers?" James was suddenly excited.

"Aie. They are dying to meet you. Sorry, no pun intended."

JAMES

James was in what Slumber called a training circle with candles lit around them when Jules and Steve rushed into the abandoned house like the devil himself was after them.

Slumber shot to his feet and took on the traditional whispering greeting pose he'd shown James. With his wrist up, James felt the dreamy-type magic Slumber pushed into the room. Very cool.

Steve and Jules gaped at them.

Steve said, "What are you doing, James, throwing a party? Oh it's you," he pointed to Slumber. "Finally decided waiting around Dreamland wasn't the brightest plan?" His body was almost plastered against Jules and even as a spirit, James had this urge to snap him in two.

Luckily, Slumber stood between them, keeping them calm. "Look at your hands. Wow, that's some intense Wild magic at work here, Steve. You summon that, James? Whoa, James. Eyes on your hands. Those are the hands of someone with work to do. Feel my words. *Wild magic is healing.* You believe this. You know this. Cupids use these abilities to heal the darkest of souls. You used this magic to help this sorry sap and it's pissing you off because someone is using you, playing you. Don't you think for yourself?"

Wild magic is healing. James stood back and relaxed. Yeah. It was healing, so why did it piss him off to see his sister a victim to it? Had someone whispered to him? Now that was frustrating. He wasn't about to be victim to some stupid whisper.

"What is Wild magic?" Steve asked innocently.

"You two are infected with Wild magic by the cupid here. It's triggered whenever you touch." Slumber pointed to their linked hands. "Trust me, I love anything that gives me a rush. Someone with a sense of humour whispered to James here. Someone who thought it would be funny to see a cupid kill his parties."

"His parties?"

"Yeah, the couples he's brought together. He wants James to kill anyone enjoying the rush of Wild magic, even though he's the idiot who probably sprung it on you in the first place. Good news is that it's healing your soul, Steve. You look good enough to be a god and really, it's about time."

"How do you know that?" Julia asked.

Slumber smirked at James, waiting for him to say something.

Frustrated, James said, "Jules, you know better. Don't ask how someone knows things when you can trust they only announce things they are sure about."

Slumber laughed. "Yup, that's about how you usually say it. You feeling your memories coming back?"

James nodded. He felt great. It was time to leave this life and try again in a new one.

"Is my soul really good?" Steve looked worried.

"Good enough. I'd like to undo the Wild magic. Join us in Utopia, and I'll show you how."

"Utopia? Ah hell." Steve sounded annoyed. "Al hates that realm."

"Al? The immortal?"

Steve frowned. "No, Al my dad, the annoying."

"You whisper to help others?" Jules asked Slumber.

"Of course. I can help you. The Wild magic isn't needed and I'd like to remove it. Might help James calm down, too." Slumber lifted his left eyebrow playfully. "Coming?"

Steve looked down as if guilty as heck. "I don't want to undo this connection and no, I'm not worthy of a place like Utopia."

Slumber let out a long puff of air. "I used Wild magic once. It was a fun escape—while I was Wild. Now I wish I would have saved myself for my soulmate. I should be getting back to her. Coming James?"

"That's what's pissing me off," James said finally putting his finger on the trigger. "Their dream sex. They're wasting their lives in some type of fantasy."

"No. It's not like that," Steve stammered.

Slumber showed fangs like a beast and growled. James came forward expecting Steve to panic but he didn't even flinch at the sight of those fangs. Clearly, he'd seen worse. Or... no... he was gone. His soul was gone and so was Jules'.

"Yup." Slumber said to James. "When faced with conflict,

he snags her soul and whisks her off to Dreamland. There they live free and happy—Wild. It's healing and a lot of fun, but he needs to face his fears if he's to evolve and stop ticking you off." Slumber grabbed Jules' arm while they were entranced.

Steve snapped back and shoved Slumber. "Hands off, shape-shifter."

Slumber turned Jules' wrist up anyway and the moment her wrist was up Slumber dropped to his knees.

James had the urge to bow, too.

"Welcome home," Slumber said, humbly. Then to James, he said, "This is a traditional greeting between Whisperers, and whenever a Whisperer has power blessed by gods like they do, we bow."

Steve backed out of the room with his arms around Jules, ready to bolt, yet he lingered in the doorway, as if torn between leaving James and staying.

James reassured him, "He's harmless, Steve. Weird, but so are you. I like him. Hear him out. If he wants you to stop going Wild, I think you should. Be a man and face your fears."

"I'm afraid of nothing." Steve was clearly lying. James could see his fears all over his face.

"James, why are you see-through?" Jules asked.

"I'm good," James was quick to say.

"He's dead," Steve said. "You have to bring him back, that's why I made you that tattoo. Can you feel the power in it?"

Jules stumbled into Steve. "What?"

The pain on her face was enough to kill him. James didn't want her to suffer anymore.

Steve gently pushed her to her feet. "It's fine, Julia, whisper to his soul and he'll return to his body. He will rise again within three days. You can do this."

She studied her brother. "James?"

He wanted to tell her that he was fine. That he felt alive and didn't want to come back, yet he couldn't disappoint her. He looked to Slumber, not sure what to say. Al had been clear that she shouldn't raise the dead. He had been very clear on that.

Slumber said, "You were given this power so you could learn what it is to be a goddess. The responsibility is beyond what we imagine. You must make this decision on your own. Will you raise your brother from the dead or let me walk him to Afterlight? Either way is acceptable, it's what you choose to live with. James should be in agreement of your choice, as all Whisperers respect free will. Well, the good ones do. "

"I..." Jules was confused.

"I must apologise, but your tattoo is poorly made, please allow me the honour of remaking it when I get you to Utopia. You'll have much more control of your magic if I colour in the details and link your powers to your soulmate's with his symbols."

"No. Stay away from us." Steve was right panicked but James wasn't sure which parts confused him.

Julia added, "Steve said it would block my magic."

"I lied," Steve mumbled. "It will only make your powers harder to control, but they're there. Guys like Slumber who study in Utopia would be able to use your magic if you let them fill it in. Don't."

Trying to be helpful, James asked, "What is Utopia?"

"Another realm that is home for all Whisperers. Everyone is welcome."

"Not everyone," Steve insisted.

"These days Whisperers visit the Mortal Realm to guide others or to learn. The odd ones get sent to live among the mortals when they request this." Slumber grinned. "Like James here. He always amuses us. Look at the mess he got himself into this time, and still, he manages to find himself a Whisperer to bring him back. Amazing."

"So then I should?" Jules looked relieved and James sighed.

Would he really agree to this?

"Train Steve to whisper properly," James said. "I'm not worried about whispering, but Steve thinks himself a disappointment and it annoys me. Give him confidence or something."

"No. I don't want to whisper at all," Steve said.

"That's the coward's way out, Steve," James reminded him. "You think that by not whispering, you won't have to face your dad. But you do. You know you do, and the minute Jules brings me back, you won't have a choice."

It was dim in the room, but James found that as a spirit he could see beyond his normal eyes, even in the dark. It was as if all things glowed, especially Slumber. Man, did he ever have a gloss to him.

"You don't want to help people?" Slumber was in Steve's face. "You can't ignore or change who you are. Embrace it."

"Help people?" Steve had mixed feelings. "Whisperers satisfy their own desires. Back away from me."

Slumber pointed to Jules and Steve. "I sense your desire to give things life. One of you spiritual life and the other physical. Together you and your wife could whisper a dying field back to life. Steve, wake up. You are a Whisperer, stop dreaming about being a man. There has to be something inside you that grounds your beliefs and makes you want to help others. Focus on this need."

"I'm not his wife."

Steve let go of her hand and clenched his fists. He looked ready to smoke Slumber, but instead he turned around and spoke low to her, but James could hear. "Whisperers believe that when souls link, they are husband and wife. He doesn't understand that we were linked in a ritual and aren't whispering soulmates." Steve left, banging the door behind him.

Oh. That's what was bothering him. He thought Slumber was going to think him a phoney and unlink their souls and he'd be left alone. James held his sister back because she was ready to run after Steve. This overwhelming urge came over him to fix this. Steve was his sister's soulmate. They belonged together. He didn't know about any ritual, but he knew this to be fact.

He glanced at his hands as they sparkled. "Jules." James felt so alive. "It's time you tried something or said good-bye. I'm feeling strange."

Slumber was at his side in an instant. "That's your cupid senses. Seeing Steve troubled summoned cupid magic. Feels weird, eh? My powers make me all tingly, too."

Jules ran to his body and knelt beside it. "Lay on your body, James."

He went to look at himself with her. He looked so relaxed. He couldn't have been dead long. There was still a fine grey cord coming from his body to his soul. It was severed in places, but it was there. "Will it hurt?"

"Yes. You'll feel a sucking, a burning, but think of it as waking from a dream."

At least she was honest. He rested on his body not feeling it at all.

"Jules, I'm not sure about this. I like being dead. I know that sounds stupid, but I'm free. The emotions are vast, too much to feel. The knowledge is all, too much to know." He sighed, content. "Perfect."

Her face twisted into grief and he reached for her arm, "I'm ready. Whisper."

Slumber knelt beside him. "Once she does this, only her soulmate will be able to kill you. The Whisperer with the opposite power."

James thought about this. "I'll be invincible?"

"Maybe this is why Al wants our powers. He wants me to use it on him," Julia said but James had his doubts. Al was pretty bent on no one using her power.

"She can only use it once," Slumber said so matter-of-fact. "The choice is hers."

Julia glanced up at him. "Once? Are you sure?"

"Very. Once per life cycle. You bring one soul back, then Steve will be required to take one since the powers are soulmate bound. The gods are funny that way."

"What happens to our magic after we use it?"

"Moves on to new soulmates, depends who the gods choose. They will learn, and the cycle continues. If you bring him back, make sure Steve knows he can use his power once and that he has to use it to send James to Afterlight. Otherwise, your brother will be immortal until the power comes back. And it becomes a vicious cycle because he can't use it until you do. Unless we link it via a tattoo, then either of you would control it. In Utopia, we're good at getting around the rules the gods set." He winked at Jules.

James didn't want to be immortal. He wasn't even sure he wanted to come back. He'd talk to Steve himself.

Jules touched his lifeless body, moved the curls on his

forehead as she always did. "Ready?"

James nodded. "Al needs his jaw broken so he can't whisper, and I'm the guy to do it."

She ran her hand over his chest. "*Unite*," she whispered and instantly he felt the heaviness of his body. He'd been so light moments ago, and now he was heavy. It pulled at him, making him drown. He wanted to fly. Why would he let it weigh him down? He'd been free.

"He's fighting it. Why would he fight it?" Jules asked Slumber. "*James, breathe. Feel your body with your soul, live in it, become one with it again. This is your body. Live as a mortal again.*"

Hmmm. Perhaps she was right. This wasn't forever. It was his body for a bit. He slipped into it like a glove but she was wrong, there was no sucking, no burning, it was more like a yucky heaviness. He wanted the freedom he'd experienced moments ago.

"Give him a moment. James is much more evolved—soul-wise—than most. Living as a mortal to learn or to teach something is difficult." Slumber taught Jules but she didn't look at him, she glared at James and he met her eyes, trying not to show her how afraid he was.

He thought about what Slumber said. James liked the idea of being an advanced soul. It made him proud yet at the same time, it gave him a huge responsibility he'd never be able to live out. He stretched into his body. He wasn't staying in it for long.

"*For the love of facts*, you did it, Jules. You raised me from the dead. Now that is magic. Wow." James glanced around. His body was heavy against his soul. "I owe Al time in Hell, I do."

"I need air." Julia ran outside.

"So what do you want to learn now?" Slumber was quick to remind him that they'd summoned his powers. "Want help finding your soulmate?"

"Hmmm. Outta my way. I told you, train Steve, he wants to learn your *merde*, and he's off feeling sorry for himself. Your dark magic is not for me. I'll find my own woman. I don't need your help, thank you very much."

Still, something told him he was going hunting. Really,

what if he could find someone who his soul could bind to? The idea made him eager to live for a few more breaths. It would be his reward for helping Jules and Steve with their issues.

"I'm not talking about any woman, James." Slumber cut him off, too. "I'm talking about a warrior. A goddess who would be your equal in intelligence, a spiritual being who would evolve with you as a Whisperer and let go with you as a whispering conscience, a supreme being. Someone as nasty as you, but as good, too."

Let go as an immortal god? He stretched, seeing the possibilities instantly. Why would he have to die? He was already immortal. "I'm listening, teach me, but go faster, my brain processes quickly. You know what? Keep your mouth shut and stand still. I'll rub against your soul and absorb your knowledge that way."

Slumber bowed. "It's nice to have our hero back."

"Good to be back. So, Steve mentioned a realm full of knowledge. Show me how to get there."

"Come to Utopia and learn for yourself. We have this information documented in sacred Notebooks about past lives. The Guardian of the Notebooks will be excited to meet a legend such as yourself."

James thought about how afraid Steve was of Utopia. "Why would Steve be afraid of a place full of sacred books?"

Slumber shrugged. "Good question. I'd guess that Al has those answers. You see, over the years, many Notebooks were stolen from the Guardian..."

"We help or kill guys like him?"

"We're here to help Dark Whisperers evolve, too. Somehow, Steve found enlightenment. He healed himself. Normally we teach them, we study them, observe, and the odd one is healed, but it takes a special Whisperer. Guys like you have clear rules—stay away from Dark Whisperers. You're too close to the end of evolution to muck this up, James."

James' finger went nuts. No. That was wrong. He was here to help Al. He knew that much. He couldn't watch Steve screw this up. He looked at the other Whisperer. Oh, crap. The truth hit him like a tractor on a rampage. It wasn't Steve whispering to him in his sleep. It was James whispering to Steve. All this time. "Well, I'll be. I came to save Steve. Why?"

"Well…" Slumber smirked. "Turning a Dark Whisperer into a Light Whisperer with no magic, well... that would be a god-like mission, don't ya think?"

Clearly.

James asked, "What would have happened to Jules if Steve was her soulmate and he was evil?"

"Ultimately, she'd turn dark," Slumber said.

"So I saved my sister's soulmate." James sat on the dusty old sofa, too jolted to stand. His soul knew this truth all along. "I'm not here for my soulmate, I came to save my sister's," he told Slumber. "Why would I come back for that?"

"Why not? Grey Whisperers believe that we only have to save one soul to be a hero." Slumber sat beside him. "This is what you do. You help others become gods. You did well, they look happy. You did a good thing. But James, maybe it's time we help you become a whispering god."

"Hmmm."

"Steve healed himself, means there is good in everyone." Slumber stayed by James on the crappy sofa like an old friend. "I mean really, if there is hope for assholes like him and me, there is hope for all on the Mortal Realm. Come to Utopia with me. Teach us what you learnt."

Tempting. But if James was to be a god, he had work to do.

"Wanna come with me to break Al's jaw before we head to your peaceful realm?"

"Someone needs to keep an eye on you. Let's go, Cupid."

STEVE

Steve stood in front of the cottage, overwhelmed. The lights from his car shone on the rock walls. He'd made this house for Julia. Built the place himself. He wanted desperately to give this to her. This. He didn't know what *this* was. It was something she'd dreamed up, something she wanted every evening in her sleep since he found her and he had no idea why or what it meant. How he even fit into the Wild dream of hers was beyond him but he'd worked his way in.

He ran up the steps to their room, turning lights on along the way. Their room. He shook his head with that thought, because they'd never actually been here together, yet it was theirs every blasted night.

He searched the bed and snagged the ring.

He'd worked his way into her dreams and ended up in this room with Julia, yet in real life they couldn't seem to get here.

It was nothing but a dream.

He clenched the ring.

He'd make things right for a change.

Determined to fix things he rushed back to the car.

Bobby was there, his gun drawn. "Hands up." He had the door to his car open, his gun over it, ready to shoot.

Steve dropped the ring, it rolled on the cement walk and settled in the grass. Shining in the setting sunlight.

"Not sure where you materialized from." Bobby scanned the area, the cottage invisible to him. "Pretty sure you won't be able to move faster than this bullet, Steve my boy," Bobby said coldly as he pulled the trigger.

"*Bullet, return,*" Steve whispered to the bullet, as he dived for cover. The gun fired and Steve was sure he was dead.

He had to be.

He waited on the ground for a second shot. When it didn't come he got to his feet. Bobby leaned against the car.

The familiar pains were there. Steve was alive. The shot had missed.

Hell, that was close.

He got ready to attack Bobby but there was no movement.

He just leaned there, his face serene, his soul ecstatic.

Steve prepared for an attack.

"Bobby. Are you calm? Listen, man." He had no idea how Bobby even found his place.

Steve walked up to him, his eyes on the gun he held over the roof of the car. He came along Bobby's side.

"Bobby?" He touched his shoulder, ready for a fight but Bobby slipped down the car. "Hell. Bobby?" Blood warmed his hand. Panicked, Steve watched him slip along the car. With a gasp, his soul vanished into the world around him.

"Damn, Bobby. No. No. Stick with your body for a moment. Give me one blasted moment to whisper to your body. I can fix this." He could fix this.

What the heck had happened? The gun. The bullet went through backwards and into Bobby.

What the hell had he whispered?

Bobby's soul melted into the light around them, reminding him of that butterfly's soul five years ago. No calling him back.

Steve slumped beside his empty body. What would he tell Julia? How would he tell a woman who believed in life so strongly that she could raise the dead that he took the life of someone she'd clearly wanted to save?

What had he done? A good Whisperer like Slumber would have frozen him, would have stopped time, and healed things. No, not Steve. Oh no, he made things worse. No way to avoid the evil inside him. Would Julia ever forgive him? Did he deserve forgiveness? He bowed his head. That was the secret. He'd wanted Bobby out of the way. So many times, he'd thought this.

Now he was.

He took a deep breath but had no idea how to fix things.

JULIA

Worried about Steve, Julia paced in front of the old house they'd been in. Where was he? Why did she feel guilty and sad inside? "James, I have to search for Steve. He went toward the cottage. Something's wrong."

"Sure. Meet you at home." James followed Slumber into the woods.

"Where are you going?" He planned to leave her alone?

"Slumber'll show me how to use Utopia to travel. I'll meet you at home, it's fine. He's family. Yell for him if you need anything, he'll zap us to you."

Slumber chuckled. "That's not how it works, moron." They waved her off and vanished in the trees.

"It's in my nature not to trust strangers," she called after them, but they were gone. Everyone had left her.

She walked the dirt road toward the cottage, cursing Steve for leaving her, and James for putting his stupid need to learn weird things above her safety.

Why had Steve left?

The sky was grey as night approached. The dirt road wasn't half as far to the cottage as the woods were and she stumbled in front of the house in the dim light within five minutes. She was amazed at the beauty. She wanted to live in this house. Every window had the perfect view. Every rock told a story. No other place in the world was this full of love.

Steve's car was out front. So was Bobby's. Great. Were they fighting? Bobby was pretty messed up. Clearly whatever Al was whispering to him had him nuts.

"Steve," she called as she opened the door and walked in.

The house was empty, so she left it and stood in front of the cottage, studying the yard. The moon and sun were both out, the moon high in the sky, the sun setting, almost gone. A shine in the grass caught her attention so she picked it up. A ring? A wedding band.

"Steve?" Her voice was a whisper.

"Don't come back here."

She rushed toward his voice. He was behind the house. Shovel in hand, digging with his soul-light illuminating the night.

"Julia, stay back. I..."

She glanced down. Bobby was crumpled in the long grass.

"I have to bury him."

"What happened?" she stammered.

"I whispered." Steve looked up at her, his cheeks stained with tears, his hands covered in dirty blood.

"Can I bring him back?" She rushed to Bobby and fell beside him. With both hands on his body she whispered, "*Live*." She waited for some sign that her magic would work, but the pull she'd felt when she'd whispered to James was gone. No magic existed for her to whisper to.

The distress radiating off Steve spoke volumes. Bobby was gone. He knelt beside her, "*Live* is the whisper I must use to activate the magic I have that sends someone to Afterlight. That won't work."

"It did work on James."

Steve nodded, thoughtful. Then he wiped his sleeve against his cheek. "I whispered. Why did I whisper?" He bowed his head shamefully and waited for her to say something, but there was nothing to say. What good was magic if she was powerless when it counted?

His fear was very real to her. They had powers coursing through them they had no idea how to control or contain, and it was only a matter of time before something like this happened. She still wasn't even sure that bringing James back was such a good idea.

She held his hand and placed the ring in it. "All this scares me, too. But maybe Slumber can help us."

He got defensive, putting up imaginary walls between them. "He can't undo what I whispered." His jaw was tight. "Just go. Get out of here. I don't want to feel how much I disappoint you."

Head down, she did leave, taking Bobby's car. She was determined to find James because Steve might be afraid of Slumber and Al and even himself, but James would know how to help them.

JULIA

When Julia pulled up to her family home, the air was full of dread. The place felt foreign, like a hiding spot, not a home. Even the dogs looked miserable here. It was hard not to whisk them off to the cottage with her.

She knew that in that house was nothing but misplaced items, hidden weapons meant to protect her.

She didn't need protection anymore. Power surged through her with every breath. She had no idea what to do with it, but it was magic others were after and she'd protect it.

Julia understood how Steve felt. She didn't know what she was capable of and the idea of ending up digging a grave for someone she wanted to help terrified her. She had to talk to Slumber and James, find a way to use this magic pulsating in her wrist for good things. Steve said it was like a recipe book but it was more like words tickling her tongue that she needed to blurt out.

She stormed into the house with this determination but was surprised to see James tossing knives at Al. Al was tied up but he deflected each one with words.

"Kind of neat to see how he whispers to the knives," James told her without looking up. He almost sounded bored. "He whispered to me, but it didn't work. Now that I have magic whipping around in me, I'm almighty. Where is that weirdo boyfriend of yours?"

"He needs your help. He whispered something that killed Bobby and he's afraid."

James shot up to pace the living room between the coffee table and the couch. It looked so crowded she almost left. "Can you bring him back?"

Al was tied up tightly but spoke fiercely, "No! Don't use that ability. Whatever you do, don't."

James smirked. "Why not? It's not so bad to give people life."

"I'm the last of the immortals. If she makes more, Steven won't be able to become a god until he returns to clean up that mess, too. That's the goddamn catch: once per life cycle for each of the ancient powers. And that power, it seeks out very special Whisperers. Steven will always be first on that list now."

James frowned, clearly reading more into what Al was saying than she did. "I'll call on the magic and give it to her again," James said.

"You can't summon half an ability. The complete power is forbidding life to move on and permitting it. It gets split between soulmates."

Julia sat with her hands clenched. When he said it like that, she was a monster. She'd kept her brother from dying. Something he'd wanted to do. He needed to do.

Julia shivered. The magic wasn't to restore life, but to trap it. This wasn't her belief at all, it was Steve's. She believed in life after death. In spiritual existence. "I used Steve's life restoring magic. Means he has my power that frees immortals. We must have got our powers mixed up somehow."

Al was stern. "What do you mean used?"

She felt like puking.

"Ah fuck. Who is the next immortal?"

James took a deep breath. "Jules. Al needs to move on. There is no decision to make. You must use the power for Steve. If it's rightfully yours, you can call on it right now."

"And Steven needs to be a god. He's too powerful, the magic will always find him," Al insisted. "There can be no more immortals. Who is it? I have to talk with them right now."

Julia looked at her brother horrified. Steve would never be able to kill either of them. She knew this. She'd felt his strong will to hold onto everyone in this life. Death was hard on him. He would never do it. He would not see this as a good thing.

Could she? Would he forgive her if she killed his father?

"You were planning to ask him to kill me," James reminded her.

"Ah shit. I'm screwed again." Al banged his head back and it hit the wall. "I covered my fucking bases. What happened? He didn't go to Utopia, did he? Those idiots think your power is wonderful."

Julia thought about how Slumber knelt to her.

James sighed. "Jules, Al can't go another 500 years. Look at him, he's snapped. He needs the healing light of Afterlight. You know this."

Al shut his eyes. "It's not me I worry about. That boy, he has to live through this hell again and his soul gets more troubled every bloody time. He's the god of dreams and needs to move on, but he's so powerful, that stupid power will keep finding him, life after life. He's the one soul I was destined to save. All this work for nothing. He's tied to her now, and tied to the powers. The cycle will never end. He'll have to return to free one of us."

"Maybe you should have told him the truth," James mumbled.

"Yeah, because the truth has worked out for me before."

"So..." Jules looked directly in Al's eyes. "Did I make you immortal?"

"Not exactly. You're right about having his powers, must have happened during the ritual, but it was attracted to others before Steven and you. They moved on, became gods."

That explained why Slumber wanted to make her a tattoo of the magic Steve had. It was rightfully hers, and he didn't know how to use it. No wonder he felt guilty when he whispered.

Meant she could do it.

"*Freedom*." Al's binds fell loose and he leapt up, diving for James.

They flew over the couch locked together, and became a blur as they struggled.

Whispers coursed through the air until James fell limp and Al pulled away. "That should keep him out of my way for a bit," Al said.

She rushed to James. "What did you do to my brother?"

Al shoved her. Julia fell over the coffee table and into the mess of magazines she kept on the floor. There was a knife in them. She clicked a small switchblade open. Al looked at it, amused.

"*Speed*," he whispered and the next thing she knew he held the knife against her throat.

"*Live*," she whispered for the magic Steve had that should be rightfully hers. "*Live. Live. Live.*"

STEVE

Steve held the door to his car, studying the monstrous house Julia lived in. He rubbed his wrist. His powers warmed. Was Julia calling his magic? Why? He let out a long breath of air.

His pup rushed to him and Max stayed back but looked mighty pleased he was there. "Hey. You two behaving?" Max gave him a bored look. Brat did a lot of jumping until finally Steve bent to pet her.

"I want to go in the house but I'm not sure I can explain what happened to Julia. You think she's gonna throw me out?" His gut clenched. "I killed a guy," he confessed to them. "It was so easy, too. I don't even know what I whispered to make his gun do that. It was fast."

Max listened, so Steve gave him a pet, too.

He got up and went toward the house. He had the ring in his hand.

He had no idea what to say to her, but he had to say it anyway.

Paint peeled on the wood siding. He'd have to fix the place if she planned to stay here. The idea was impossible. She had to live with him in their cottage but he had no idea if she'd come with him now that he was a murderer. Accident or not, it was his magic that had killed someone. Someone he'd promised her they would help. He was tired of this... endless battle.

He heard her talking. Al answering. Dread filled his every fibre and without thinking, Steve rushed into the messy house as a pain cut through his neck.

Julia was on her knees, holding her throat. Blood. It was all he saw. She bled.

"James," she choked out but her soul was faint as Steve hurried to her. "Steve," she said, but her word was more a painful gagging.

He could hardly breathe either, the pain on his neck was so intense. "Here." Steve pulled his shirt off and wrapped it around her neck. "Hold your hand against the couch and transfer the pain there. Like you did in the tunnel with me. All the energy, all that hurting, push it into the couch. Focus on healing. I'll whisper to your body."

Before he could open his mouth an invisible fist rammed into him. What the hell? He looked up and caught sight of Al's soul flashing to his left. The prick could go invisible? Steve was surprised.

"Your evil bitch is dying, but it takes time for you god-like pricks to cash out. Betcha wish you'd killed me when you had the chance."

He had enough blood on his hands, he'd find a way to heal Al. Steve was sprawled out on the floor and scrambled to his feet, searching for Al, trying to ignore the ache in his neck.

"Kill..." Julia mouthed. Her hand snapped on his wrist, and he sensed the power he'd been avoiding throb in his wrist. It would be easy to kill him. Whisper his soul to Afterlight with one little word.

"*Soul,*" Steve focused on the blinking soul he saw.

"Do it," Al snapped. "Fucking pansy son, what more do I have to do to you? Kill me already."

"*Heal,*" Steve whispered but at the same time Julia whispered, "*Live.*"

Al's body appeared and tumbled over.

Julia cried out as her soul clouded over with pain, so Steve rushed to help her. Her soul went nasty grey as her pain crashed into him. Their souls merged. Steve took in deep breaths, transferring the hurting into the coffee table. When her body relaxed, he knew he had it all, and he stood with her in his arms.

"*Heal,*" he whispered to her neck. Tingles washed over him as the powers surged between them. Steve healed his own body many times, but this was the first time he'd ever cured someone else. "Feel it healing?"

Healing was good magic, but it was hardly enough to counter what he'd done to Bobby.

He cradled Julia and she gripped his arm with her bloody hand. "Al," she mouthed the word, tears and pain making her wince.

Steve went to Al's body. Time to deal with him.

"*Soul, return.*"

Nothing happened. Why wasn't Al coming back? He ran his fingers over the power to call on souls, but his magic was a mess. He didn't know any of the powers in his wrist.

"You have my magic?" Steve asked Julia.

She shook her head, tears hot on her cheeks. "I have mine. I gave you back yours."

If that was the case, when she'd whispered, she'd used the magic to send a soul to Afterlight since it was activated by the whisper *Live,* too.

His father's words haunted him. "*You must die to live.*"

Panic knocked him to his knees. "No. No. No. I was supposed to save him."

Julia came to him and gripped his arm. "You, I... We... we freed him from his immortal body. He's moved on. He's healed, Steve. We did save him."

"Moved on?" Steve couldn't breathe. He focused on his new magic, feeling each one in case... "We killed my dad?" He thought about the colours in her soul. She had the dark swirls Al normally did. "You did this? You used magic to kill Al? My magic?" He should have felt remorse or pain, even anger... but an incredible relief washed over him.

"It's over, Steve. We can live and whisper to help others, together. I'm sorry this magic frightens you. It's good magic. Your dad needed to move on."

Steve checked her neck, it was healing nicely. He pulled away to study her soul. It was dirty grey. The beautiful light it used to be was gone.

She was like him, now.

James moaned from the other side of the couch.

JAMES

James sat against the back of the couch. He felt wonderful inside. He watched the gash on his arm heal itself. "This is incredible. Watch how I heal. Wow. Can you do this, Steve?"

Steve knelt beside him. "Not like that. It sucks when I heal myself. Julia tells me she made you immortal with her power. I can't kill you because I used the power on Al. I didn't mean to, but I'm sorry if you wanted me to use it on you."

"Liar. No way did you kill your old man."

Steve shrugged. "He's dead. It was my magic."

"I ain't some pinhead." James looked up, this was clearly a problem for Steve. He didn't want Jules to be like him. James was quick to reassure him. "Doesn't matter. I don't need to end this life. I'll find my soulmate and we'll vanish into the heavens as an immortal god. You do the same. We'll be gods together. That power can find another poor sap to control it. No worries. This is it for me. *Comprends?*"

"Why is everything so easy for you?" Steve sat beside him so they were staring at their feet. "I feel confused inside." He sighed. "I turned Julia evil. I wish I was good inside, like you."

"It's about perspective, Steve. You see, on one side of the coin you stop someone from breathing, but on the other, you allow them the freedom to never need air again. Same action." He glanced over at Steve. "Steve, you were given these powers because the gods felt you deserved the right to wield them as you see fit. How I see it, they don't judge you."

Steve frowned. "When I was young, I believed there was no good or bad, it was all just right."

"Maybe you were right. I feel pretty good about things. Sucks that we lost Bobby in the mess of things, but who knows if we could have even saved him. Al had him pretty mucked up inside. This way he gets to come back and try again. Brand new, with no Al to mess with him. Gives me comfort that you used your powers to help him find peace."

"Say it like that and you make me come off a hero."

James got up. "A hero doesn't get to choose which actions

make him one. You made my sister smile, first time I witnessed a real smile on those lips in a long time, and that makes you my hero, doesn't matter what else you did or didn't do. Come. The world awaits. About time we do something useful with this life."

Yeah, James was eager to do something heroic, too.

JULIA

They were flying.

Julia gripped the red orb Mischief had given her. The magic in it kept her afloat at Steve's side as they soared toward the city.

She caught her breath when the first of the city lights broke the darkness; little sparkles lighting up the night. She'd never seen anything so magical.

"Am I dreaming?" Julia asked.

Steve gripped her hand. "Every moment with you feels like a dream to me. Tonight is just for us. Tomorrow is a big day."

The *Get Naked and Muddy* group were breaths from their first worldwide whisper. Steve wasn't excited to be a part of it, but Julia was. They would make a difference, tomorrow. Tonight she just wanted to watch the lights with Steve.

"A Whisperer seals their linked souls with a bond of marriage. A vow they make to each other," Steve said, pulling her from the beauty. He handed her the ring. "I made this ring for you myself. I whispered to it, to keep our bond strong and our words honest. Every night I want to dream with you. Forever."

"I can't imagine dreaming without you."

Out of nowhere, a butterfly came between them and met up with a second. They danced while Julia and Steve hovered over the city, the lights little glistening magical beacons. A familiar dreamy feeling washed over her as he pulled her closer.

Elsewhen Press

an independent publisher specialising in Speculative Fiction

THE
MIND'S
EYE

Christopher Nuttall

For centuries, men have been dreaming of telepathy, the power to read and influence the minds of others. Now, all around the world, telepaths are finally starting to appear. Men and women are developing awesome powers with the potential to dramatically change society. Governments are soon starting to become aware of them, even recruiting them, while striving to keep knowledge of their abilities hidden from the general public. Academic researchers too are discovering telepaths and it isn't long before awareness of their existence starts to spread. But non-telepaths, ordinary people, don't want to have their minds read or controlled; the telepaths soon find themselves widely regarded with fear and hatred. Inevitably, some of them want to fight back.

Christopher Nuttall has been planning sci-fi books since he learnt to read. Born and raised in Edinburgh, Chris created an alternate history website and eventually graduated to writing full-sized novels. Studying history independently allowed him to develop worlds that hung together and provided a base for storytelling. After graduating from university, Chris started writing full-time. As an indie author he has self-published a number of novels, but this is his eight novel to be published by Elsewhen Press. Chris is currently living in Scotland with his wife, muse, and critic Aisha and their new son.

ISBN: 9781908168573 (epub, kindle)
ISBN: 9781908168474 (352pp, paperback)

visit bit.ly/MindsEye-Nuttall

About the Author

Born and raised in Saskatchewan, Tanya enjoys using the tranquil prairies as a setting to her not-so-peaceful speculative fiction. She is married with two children which means among her accomplishments are the necessary magical abilities to find a lost tooth in a park of sand and whisper away monsters from under the bed. As director of a non-profit Francophone community center, Tanya offers programming and services in French for all ages to ensure the lasting imprint and growth of the Francophone community in which she was raised. What she enjoys the most about her job is teaching social media safety for teens and offering one-on-one technology classes for seniors.

Tanya was fifteen when she wrote her first column. She has a diploma in Journalism/Short Story Writing. Today, she actively submits to various newspapers, writes and publishes the local Francophone newsletter for her community, and maintains a blog at Life's Like That. In 2014 her debut novel *Ghosts on the Prairies, A Sacred Land Story* for adults, was published by Elsewhen Press, followed by *Petrified* a young adult Whispering novel, from Sunbury Press.